Outwitting Paradise

Miranda Herald

My Koala Pouch

Contents

Also By Miranda Herald

Loves Cats Series:

Prequel Chapters: Willa's Blooper Reel

- FREE at www.mirandaherald.com

Book 1: Loves Cats, Anonymous

Book 2: Swipe Right for More Cats

Book 3: Free Shipping with More Cats

Puzzling through Romance Series:

Prequel Novella: Blundering through Paradise

- FREE at www.mirandaherald.com

Book 1: Outwitting Paradise

Book 2: Misplacing Paradise

Book 3: Hiding Paradise

Smitten Scientists

Book 1: Catch and Release

Book 2: The Turtle and the Hare

Book 3: Wild Goose Chase

Chapter 1

Shipwrecked in Paradise

Brianna

I *hate paradise.*

Brianna collapsed on the beach and coughed up sea water. She lay in the sand for a few minutes facing a dense, dark green jungle, thick with vines and colorful flowers. This island looked so inviting when she was safe on the shores of the mainland. An unintended swim-for-your- life could really change one's perspective. *I should have gone for the hotel's facial instead of this do-it-yourself seashore scrub.*

In disgust, she picked seaweed out of her sandy brown hair as she sat up. She turned around to gaze into the crystal blue water but couldn't see any sign of her little boat anywhere. In fact, there were no boats in sight at all.

She took stock of what she had on herself. Her phone and purse were probably at the bottom of the sea by now. Her wet clothing clung to her slightly plump bottom and voluptuous chest. She checked her pockets: a hair tie, a soggy receipt, and a quarter she had found lying on the pier.

Great. How am I going to get back to the mainland now? She couldn't swim back to shore after a three-hour boat ride. She had barely made it from her sinking motor boat to this island.

Well, it isn't too far from land. Boats are bound to come by here frequently. Deciding on building a signal fire, Brianna walked around the beach looking for driftwood. Her clothing dried in the sun as she found a few small pieces of wood. There was enough to cook a meal or provide a little heat at night, but not enough that anyone on shore would notice.

After taking off her wet shoes to dry in the sun, she built a small teepee out of the firewood she'd found. Without a lighter, Brianna tried rubbing two sticks together beside her newly made fire pit, just like she had seen in the movies. After about twenty minutes of rubbing blisters on her hands, she gave up.

Maybe I need a change of plans. What would someone on one of those wilderness survival shows use to survive for a few days? Fresh water and food should be my first steps. Brianna looked over at the jungle and a shiver ran down her back. It looked more foreboding than inviting.

She ventured in but decided to not stray too far from her landing spot. She now considered this her campsite, even though the only thing that marked it was a few pathetic pieces of driftwood in a small pile.

I should probably figure out how to make a shelter too. Her fingers itched for her phone to look up how-to videos. She would just have to do her best on her own. Her survival depended on it.

Standing on the threshold of the jungle, she spoke aloud, "God, thank you so much for saving me from the water. Please help me get rescued and not bitten by poisonous snakes. Amen." Feeling braver, she spotted a small path in the dense undergrowth.

Don't jungles usually grow really fast? I wonder if this path is well-traveled by animals... or humans. Brianna confidently took a step forward, and immediately, her foot got stuck.

Upon closer inspection, she noticed her foot was caught in a small snare. It was a loop of metal covered in a type of soft rubber, potentially to protect the foot of whatever trapper had set it. A few monkeys chattered at her from a nearby tree.

Feeling frustrated and alone, Brianna shouted, "'You spend too much time at home,' my roommate said. 'Go enjoy your time on Florida's sunny beaches and meet people,' she said. 'Why don't you go for a relaxing boat ride and enjoy the sun?' Well, news flash, Mavis, this is not relaxing!"

She had to admit, life was feeling a little stagnant at home. After graduating from college, Brianna didn't have a direction. Her life wasn't really going anywhere. She needed a change... a goal... a challenge.

She had signed up as a vendor for a crab-themed fair, but not because she loved crabs. She used the excuse that she wanted to sell her handmade glass figurines at the small beach community festival. There was no logical reason she had to travel all the way to the beach to do so, but she wanted a change of scenery, and her best friend had encouraged her to go.

Mavis was always adventurous and getting into trouble, laughing all the way. She was moving in with her boyfriend and leaving Brianna behind. Brianna had found herself feeling jealous and abandoned. She'd wanted some adventure in her life too. This, however, was not what she had in mind.

Brianna kneeled down and examined the small noose around her foot. It was a pretty simple design. She yanked on her foot and the loop tightened. With nothing to cut it with, she fiddled with the metal mechanism behind the loop. Eventually, she realized that if she pushed up on it while holding it taut, then she could loosen the loop and release her foot.

Well, I will definitely need to keep an eye out for more animal snares. I wonder if the owner of the island is illegally trapping and shipping exotic animals for pets? She had seen a movie where they did that. It would explain why the owner of the island took extra care to make sure the trap didn't injure its target.

Brianna moved the trap out of the way and then reset it. Maybe she could catch something for dinner.

Her arms were sore from moving logs to make a giant arrow towards her camp. She pulled out some of the undergrowth and tried to make her path back to the beach very obvious. The last thing she needed was to get lost. She gingerly made her way a few more yards, scratching her face on a low-hanging branch. There, she found another snare. Brianna stepped around until she heard the beautiful babble of moving water.

The sound led her to a six-foot-deep, steep ravine with a three-foot-wide stream in the middle. Brianna looked at the water, perplexed. She needed that fresh water, but she couldn't tell how deep it was. There was no way she was going to jump down there. She wouldn't be able to get back out. One near-drowning experience was enough for one trip.

Looking around in the dense jungle behind her, she finally found a long log. Maybe if she pushed a log over the edge of the ravine, she could use it as a ladder to get down to the water and back up again. Although, the next problem would be carrying water. *Perhaps I could use a large leaf and secure the top with the hair-tie in my pocket.*

She was glad to have a plan, even if it was shaky. She searched around for a dead log that looked sturdy enough to hold her weight and found a large branch that had fallen off a tree and was maybe five feet long. It was a bit on the small side of what she was looking for, but after pushing and heaving for ten minutes, she wasn't sure she would have been able to move anything much bigger.

Heaving with all her might, she pushed the large branch up to the edge of the ravine and broke off any smaller parts of the branch that might scratch her while she climbed. She pushed it over the edge, trying to control its descent to stay close to the side of the ravine. Her goal was to get it stuck in the mud at the bottom. She hoped it would still be long enough to span most of the mud walls surrounding the stream.

It was almost perfectly in place when she laid on her stomach and leaned over the edge to get into a better position for pushing it deeper into the mud. To her horror, the strong current caught the bottom of the log and pulled it downstream. The rest of the log soon followed with a splash and disappeared.

In frustration, Brianna got up and kicked a pile of mud into the stream. The mud went flying, but it had covered a rock that hurt her big toe, despite the tennis shoes she wore. With a yelp, she examined her toe and wiggled it back and forth to make sure no bones had broken. She didn't know how long she would be there. She had to be smart and not let her emotions get the best of her.

Walking the length of the stream, she hoped she would come across an area where the gorge was shallow enough or receded gradually enough that she could reach the water. After walking for about fifteen minutes, fighting her way through an over-grown path, she found a weird bucket contraption by the side of the gully.

Someone had locked a bucket to a large timber pole that dangled over the ravine. The pole had a metal chain that extended from the top to the bucket. It looked almost like a giant fishing pole except for the golden box in front of it that was decorated with a pattern of intricate flowers.

How in the world did this get out in the jungle? Who would take the time to build such a thing when a simple bucket on a rope would have sufficed? Brianna didn't have any answers, but this contraption showed one thing. People. Maybe she wasn't alone on the island after all.

Brianna took a few moments to examine the flowers. She realized one of the ceramic tiles on top of the golden box was missing, and the other tiles could move up and down into the missing tile space.

It's a puzzle. A sliding tile puzzle. How odd.

Manipulating the tiles into different configurations showed she could combine the partial flowers to create full flowers.

She felt a little ridiculous doing the puzzle. She was alone in the middle of the jungle, fighting for her survival... but the puzzle was close to completion. When she slid the last tile into place, the golden box looked beautiful covered with sophisticated flowers. She then heard a soft popping sound, and a small drawer materialized from the bottom of the box.

Her fingers grasped the key that lay in the drawer and used it to unlock the aluminum bucket from the chain. "All right, this is odd," she said aloud. "Who does this guy think is going to steal his bucket? The parrots?"

Water dribbled down her chin as Brianna took a drink of refreshing, clean water, hoping there was nothing in it that would make her sick. She returned the key out of an organizational habit more than worrying about needing it again. After a few attempts, Brianna gave up trying to make a leaf into a water canteen. She unhooked the bucket from the chain and used it to take some fresh water back to her camp with her.

Brianna looked around and realized that the trees seemed to throw off longer shadows than before. She made her way back to her camp to make a lean-to. She didn't know how much time she would have before it got dark.

Brianna carefully retraced her steps, leaving the snares untouched. She collected wood along the path, keeping an eye out for the arrow pointing to her new 'home'.

Sadly, Brianna noted the snares were empty when she walked past them. She had seen lots of little critters scampering around the surrounding jungle. Upon reflection, the snares seemed set for a much larger animal than a capybara or lemur.

I sure hope they didn't set it for a predator like a bear or something.

As she reached her part of the beach, she saw the sun was lying heavily on the horizon. Brianna found a Y-shaped tree on the edge of the jungle and set her largest log into the crook of it. Then she leaned the rest of her sticks against the spine of her lean-to and dug the other ends into the sand to make sure they stayed put. She covered it in dirt and leaves to make sure no water could get in while she slept. It was dirty and small, and she was cramped, but for tonight, it was home.

Sitting in the sand next to her lean-to, she watched the fading light. It unfolded into a beautiful array of orange, yellow, and red on the horizon. Now that she had stopped moving, her stomach growled. She had packed a lunch to eat on this very shore. It was sitting at the bottom of the ocean now. She hoped at least the fish were enjoying it.

A few small white crabs peeked out of their holes in the sand and scampered around, looking for their dinner. Was she hungry enough to eat a crab raw? Not yet. She really wished she had a way to light the small pile of logs in front of her. It would bring her comfort, even if it wasn't the best beacon.

Eventually, Brianna succumbed to exhaustion. She crawled into her lean-to as her eyes tried adjusting to the lack of light. She couldn't help imagining bugs crawling around her in the darkness. It made her itch all over. It had to be better than sleeping out on the sand with crabs crawling over her, right? In the darkness, she wasn't too sure anymore.

Surely the owners of the boat she rented would come looking for her when she didn't return it? On second thought, those fellows didn't look like the most reliable pair. Nor, apparently, did they rent out the most reliable boats. At least when she didn't reach out to her best friend and soon-to-be ex-roommate, she would come looking for her. Mavis was the one who had encouraged her to visit the enticing island when they had talked on the phone. Eventually, she would find her, right? She just had to survive a few days.

One thing was for sure, she needed to focus on finding something to eat tomorrow so she could keep her strength until rescue came. She listened to the night calls of the jungle as her exhausted body finally gave in to slumber.

Drifting off to sleep, Brianna imagined she heard the footsteps of an enormous creature around her lean-to. She was startled awake by a deep growl that made the hair on her arms stand up. It took her a few minutes to gain the courage to peek outside. When she finally did, she saw nothing out of the ordinary, but the cloudy nighttime sky left it impossible to see more than a few feet in front of her. *Maybe it was a dream?* There was no threat... for now.

Chapter 2

Outsmarted by Canned Food

Brianna

With sand covering her mouth with grit and ants crawling on her right arm, Brianna woke with a screech. She jumped up to swipe off the insects and knocked down part of her lean-to. With a groan, she tried to fix it, but sticks kept falling over. *If only I could deal with this after a cup of coffee.*

The sun was fully up in the sky, and there were still no boats closer than specks in the distance. Her stomach now ached, not used to having to go without.

Looking at the sand around her lean-to, she noticed a watermark from the high tide stopped about a foot below. All of her footprints from yesterday had washed away. She was lucky she didn't wake up to find her little house flooded or washed away.

She walked a respectable distance down the shore, looking for some type of clam or crab, finally ready to try it raw. To her excitement, she came across a coconut tree. She could see the fruit high up, but there were three-foot-long metal spikes shaped like javelins sticking out of the sand. They were positioned sticking outward from around the base of the tree, making sure no one could get too close.

I don't have the strength to climb straight up that bare tree. The spikes make it so I can't even get close enough to touch it. Her stomach growled. *I'm so hungry even my leather tennis shoes are looking good enough to eat! I have to get one of those coconuts down.*

Brianna hungrily circled the tree like a shark that had scented its prey. After closer inspection, she realized the side of the tree facing the jungle had small indents cut into it, lined with a thin metal. Someone had spaced these metal notches about every six inches from the bottom to the top of the tree.

Carefully avoiding the sharp tip, she wrapped her hand around one of the metal spikes, and then yanked on each one until they came out of the sand, one after another. Could she use one of these to try spearfishing? Maybe she could throw one like a javelin and knock the coconuts down. After nearly stabbing herself while trying to throw the spear above her, Brianna paused and studied the sharp spike again.

The spikes clicked into the metal notches when placed horizontally against the tree. She gingerly placed her foot on it to test if it could hold her weight. When that was a success, she clicked the rest of the spears into place parallel to one another, so they formed a ladder to the top of the coconut tree. Every so often, she had to descend to grab more spikes, but eventually, she made it close to the top.

At the top of the tree, she used her last spike to knock down the three closest coconuts. Thinking of the growling she dreamed about last night, she kept the last spike with her, so she had some kind of weapon. Just in case.

Picking up the dark brown coconuts, Brianna carried them back to her camp. Happily, she softly sang, *I've Got a Lovely Bunch of Coconuts* while she tried to pry one open.

The coconuts were harder than she expected, so she used the biggest rock she could carry and dropped it on the coconut, breaking it into a dozen pieces. She picked up a fragment of the coconut and ate the flesh of the fresh fruit directly off the shell.

The fruit tasted divine, but she noticed liquid seeping into the ground under the broken fruit. She would have to be more careful on the next one and keep the coconut water to drink.

After enjoying her coconut, Brianna picked up her bucket and traveled back to the stream to get some fresh water. She was careful to avoid the snares when, out of the corner of her eye, she spotted something up in the trees. It looked like a treehouse about thirty yards to her right.

Finally. The person who owns this island! They can help me call for help, and I will sleep in a proper bed tonight!

In her excitement, Brianna stopped watching the brush for snares. Another rubber-coated snare caught her right foot, but this time, her momentum sent her flying flat on her face. Bruised and embarrassed, she hoped the person in the treehouse hadn't seen that. Then, as her ankle smarted, heat rose into her cheeks. What was this person thinking setting traps everywhere? Couldn't the animals have any peace walking around this for-saken jungle?

Carefully extricating her foot from the snare, she brushed the dirt off the new scrape running down the right side of her arm. She walked gingerly on her ankle until it felt better. At least she didn't sprain it, although she was going to be bruised and hurting tomorrow from that fall.

The base of the treehouse didn't have any ladders or obvious ways to get into it. "Hello! Hello! Is anyone in there?" she yelled at the top of her lungs. When she didn't get an answer, she continued. "Hello? I'm sorry to trespass. I really just need help to get back to the mainland."

Brianna still didn't hear a response. *Well, maybe he isn't here right now.*

She looked around the base of the tree for a way to climb up. It was high, at least twenty feet, so there had to be a ladder somewhere. She checked the tree for any odd markings, like the coconut tree, and finally found a little poem on a plaque at the base titled, Laughing at Life.

The poem read:
Love kept at bay will make a sorry man by day.
Only faithfulness can guide gentleness.
Only patience preludes peace.
Kindness is the key, wouldn't you agree?
Don't forget, integrity is more important than popularity.
Ordinary self-control shows one's goodness within.
While evil secures its hold from the inside out.
Noting joy from strife will give you the meaning of life.

Brianna stared at the poem for a long time. *What nonsense was this? Whoever owned this island must be a lunatic. What was going on? Who left poetry for the monkeys?* Brianna read through the poem again. She tried to force herself to laugh, like the title suggested. Nothing happened. *It can't get any more absurd than this, can it?*

Brianna felt ridiculous as she tried to make the tree laugh. She shouted, "You know treehouse builders really get no respect? I mean, they go out on a limb to build them!" Brianna watched patiently, but nothing happened.

She stared at the sign for a long time. Finally, she noticed that the first letter of each word spelled out the words, LOOK DOWN. Brianna looked down, and at first, saw nothing. Then she brushed away a bit of dirt and some dead leaves to see a button sticking up out of the ground. She pushed the button with her foot, poised and ready to jump out of the way if something came flying at her.

A small trap door opened up out of the ground, and a ladder ascended to the treehouse. Brianna took her foot off the button to walk to the ladder, but the ladder immediately disappeared back into the trapdoor. Brianna tried to pry open the trapdoor, to no avail, before realizing the button was pressure-activated.

Turning in circles and studying the ground, she looked for a rock big enough to hold down the button. There was nothing nearby that was heavy enough to work and not so big that she couldn't move it. Frustrated, Brianna went back to fill up the water bucket. When it was full, it held down the pressure button so she could finally climb the ladder.

Slowly, Brianna opened a small door and gently padded into the treehouse. Immediately, the smell of rotten fish assaulted her nostrils, but she ignored it as her head turned to examine her surroundings. The ten-foot by ten-foot room was mostly empty except for a small table in the center. The table had an expensive-looking knife on it, and behind that was a shelf with a single can of stew and a can opener. Excited for an actual meal, Brianna quickly took a few steps forward and reached for the can.

Immediately, a trap door on the floor dropped beneath her. Brianna didn't have time to scream as she plummeted down into a metal net. She hadn't noticed it flattened against the bottom of the treehouse when she had climbed up, but she sure noticed it now. The force of her descent caused the flattened net trap to tighten around her like a sack. Brianna tried to climb out, but it was secure at the top. She hung from the tree like an ornament from a Christmas tree, and there was nothing she could do about it.

She yelled a primal scream into the depths of the forest. She felt scared, exhausted, and unsure of how she was going to get out of this one. She had no food and no weapons. Even her bucket that was filled with crisp, cool water was sitting at the base of the treehouse.

There was nothing in her possession that would help her. She pictured the table and knife in the treehouse above her. *Maybe I should have reached for the knife instead of the food. At least with a knife, I would have a weapon to defend myself. How long will I be stuck here before someone finds me?*

Evening found her cramped in the net. Curiously, she felt more comfortable falling asleep dangling in the sky than she had when she was worried about wild animals, insects, and crabs getting her all night. *Day two on the island wasn't much better than day one.*

A gruff voice called out, waking her up with a start. A handsome, well-groomed man stood on the ground below her. He had a bit of a pooch around the middle, looked to be in his late twenties, and had wavy, dark brown hair. He wore a short-sleeved green polo shirt and was looking at her expectantly. Mr. Handsome studied her and called out again, "I said, what are you doing trespassing on my island?"

Chapter 3

Anything for a Turkey Sandwich

Brianna

T he man used a button to lower the net to the ground. Brianna tried to scramble to her feet, but her limbs had fallen asleep. She clumsily stumbled around, trying to get her bearings.

The man spoke harshly. "Get on your boat and get out of here. Didn't you see the no trespassing signs? They are there for a reason. I also don't appreciate being woken up in the middle of the night to traipse around the jungle and rescue people. Go have a party on the mainland or something. Leave. Don't come back." The man turned away.

Frustration bottled up in Brianna's chest. She was so hungry and angry that she was ready to explode. Glaring, she shouted at her disagreeable rescuer.

"Go have a party? You know, if you didn't trap people on your puzzle-infested island, then you wouldn't have to rescue them! Besides which, your arrogance didn't leave you even a moment to ask about my well-being. If you had, you would realize I'm stuck on this island, and not by choice. Just because you missed a few winks of your beauty sleep, which you obviously need, does not give you the right to speak to me in that manner."

The man took a deep breath before slowly turning back towards Brianna. His frown transformed into a charming smile with a dimple in each of his cheeks. *Hello Dr. Jekyll, goodbye Mr. Hyde. What is this man hiding?*

His eyes looked at her pleadingly. "Can we start over? I'm sorry. You're right; I shouldn't have spoken to you like that. My name is Nathan Riley, and I live on this inhospitable island that we named Riley's Paradise. Why don't you come with me back to my house? I have food, a shower, and you can have a spare bedroom for the night. You can tell me how you got here and my employee, Dugan, will return you to the mainland in the morning. Please forgive me and let me make it up to you."

Surprised by the sudden change in personality, Brianna paused, thinking it over for a bit. *I don't know this man, but he looks sincere. What choice do I have? Going with him seems like a better option than spending another night stranded in the jungle.*

She picked up the spear that still lay below the treehouse. She would stay on her guard tonight, just in case. "I'm not interested in any funny business. Can I lock my bedroom door? Can I get a warm shower?"

Nathan lifted an eyebrow and smirked at her when she went for the spear, but wisely said nothing. He simply nodded his consent. Feeling a bit more comfortable, Brianna continued. "My name is Brianna Higgins. I would love some food and somewhere to stay tonight. Thank you for rescuing me from that animal trap."

They walked down the main path where Nathan manipulated something by a bush to their right. Brianna was so tired she felt like she could hardly focus, but it piqued her interest enough to mumble, "What are you doing?"

"Just making sure you don't get caught in any more animal traps!" He laughed as if he had just shared an inside joke with himself. *This guy has spent too much time alone. I hope he isn't taking me to some jungle hut made of sticks.*

"Do you have many dangerous animals on this island? Or are the traps set to catch animals for food?" she inquired after they stopped a second time. Nathan moved a wall of vines in a swift pattern that caused them to part.

He sidestepped her answer. "Animals aren't always the most dangerous predators."

Brianna groaned in frustration and snapped at him, "Can you just give me a straightforward answer?"

"You have nothing to fear here."

At that moment, a huge square-shaped building came into view. They painted it in shades of brown with green edging, so it camouflaged well. It looked to be part of the surrounding jungle instead of standing out.

Brianna stopped and stared. *The walls remind me of a castle that's impossible to enter uninvited. I was dreading a jungle shack. I was expecting a small cottage with a few bedrooms. One thing I had not considered was a veritable fortress in the middle of the jungle.*

Nathan watched her staring at the enormous building with her mouth hanging open. He said, "This is my humble home. I call it my Little Birdhouse, or sometimes I refer to it as the compound."

Little Birdhouse? His explanation left Brianna more befuddled than before.

Nathan pointed with his head to the right side of the building. "This way is closest to the kitchen. I'll get you settled, and then I have to let my head of security, Dugan, know that you will be spending the night with us."

He led her to a door in the house that looked more like a castle gate than a normal door. Nathan typed in a security code. A small screen popped up to scan his retina, and he did some weird blinking. Concerned, Brianna inquired, "Do you have something in your eyes?"

"What? Um no." After he verified his identity, a portcullis opened upwards. The two of them entered and stopped at a second portcullis that opened upwards a few moments later. Brianna looked around and saw a hole in the stone above her as she passed between the two gates. She shivered. *What have I gotten myself into? Wasn't that called a murder hole in traditional castles?*

Nathan led them into a large courtyard with a giant statue of an angel in the middle. The angel was looking up to heaven and had water running down her hands like she was reaching into an ethereal mist. A plaque on the bottom read, "Sophia, Loving Wife and Mother". To the right of the engraving, there was a picture of a beautiful blond-haired woman smiling and a small engraved red heart. He must really love this woman to make a giant statue dedicated to her, he doesn't seem like he knows how to do anything halfway. He seemed like a man that loves with his whole heart.

Nathan led her through the courtyard and through a door on the left-hand side. "This way to your supper, milady."

Brianna tried to come up with something snarky to reply, but in her exhausted, bedraggled state, the best that came out was, "Does this mean you're learning how to take care of a guest?"

Nathan's gaze quickly moved over her body, from her head to her toes. She shivered even though it wasn't cold. "I'm truly sorry about our initial meeting. We have had trouble in the past with trespassers, and I jumped to conclusions and overreacted. Most people would say that I am normally a very courteous host, and I hope you soon see that side of me as well." She followed him down a clean but plain hallway.

The hallway ended in a large modern kitchen with dark wood-grained cabinets and a brown and white granite countertop. The right side of the room held a table large enough to sit about twenty people. To the left was a granite island with enough room to cook on and still fit six stools. Nathan pulled out one stool for Brianna and then opened the fridge. "Let's see here. I have sandwich makings, some leftover chicken parmesan, or butterfish. Or if you don't mind waiting a bit, I could throw a frozen pizza in the oven."

The mere mention and proximity of food made her mouth water. "A sandwich would be amazing!"

Nathan brought all the sandwich materials to the granite island and set out a plate so she could start making something to eat of her own preference. Nathan poured her a large cup of water and then got himself a cup and a plate too.

"I think I'll join you. A turkey sandwich sounds perfect after our nighttime excursion." He reached for the cheddar cheese at the same time as Brianna. A static shock ran through her hands. From the wide-eyed expression on his face, she could tell he felt it too. They both swiftly jerked their hands away as a shuffling sound caught their attention.

A large, good-looking man in his early thirties with dirty blond hair and a goatee shuffled through the door with a blanket wrapped around his broad shoulders. He reminded Brianna of a woodsman. His hoarse voice croaked out, "Sir, thank you again for going out tonight for me. Did everything go all right with the..." He paused as his gaze landed on Brianna. She was sitting on the island, eating her sandwich much faster than was ladylike. "Well, I'll be a fish on a hook. I see we have a guest. Would you like me to air out one of the guest rooms?"

Nathan sternly replied, "Go spend the night in your room here tonight, Dugan. You're sick and can barely stay on your feet. I told you I could handle this. Go to bed before you pass out. Brianna is on our island involuntarily. I will get her settled tonight, and if you're feeling better, you can return her to the mainland tomorrow."

Dugan nodded and studied Brianna for a moment. His large muscles made him look ridiculous huddled under the blanket. "If you have this handled, sir, then I'll go lie down." He turned and shuffled back out of the kitchen.

After Dugan left, Nathan locked his eyes on Brianna's. His right brow arched over his soft brown eyes. "Now, how did you end up on my island without a boat?"

"Well, as I'm sure you know, from shore, this island looks beautiful and deserted. The perfect private paradise, only a few hours' boat ride from civilization. I was trying to be adventurous for once and went for a ride. Unfortunately, my three-hour tour didn't go as planned. When I got near the island, I saw buoys in the water with No Trespassing, Private Property, and Trespassers Will Be Persecuted signs."

Brianna gulped down the last bit of her refreshing glass of water. "At first, I was angry with the locals who rented me the boat. They knew full well that this island was my destination, but they said nothing about it being private property. I decided to just use my phone to take a picture of myself with your island in the background. It was at that point I realized my feet were getting wet on the boat."

Brianna paused her story to take another bite of her sandwich before continuing. "I looked around and tried to figure out if there was a hole or something, but I haven't been on boats a lot and saw nothing obvious. A wave hit my boat and my phone slipped out of my hand, headed straight for the water. I didn't have time to think about the consequences. My body just automatically lunged for the phone."

Brianna had a flashback of sputtering and flopping around in the sea.

I thought I was done for.

"I came up shocked, but otherwise all right. I tried to find the boat, but all I saw was the last bit of the hull as it sank beneath the waves. That's when I swam towards the island. It was a lot closer than the mainland. I can swim, but I'm not a strong enough swimmer to make it a few hours' boat ride back."

Nathan looked deep in thought and muttered to himself, "Bilge pump, possibly?"

Brianna started on her second sandwich; she hummed the song, *Hotel California*, content now the edge of hunger and thirst was gone. She didn't want to make herself sick from stuffing herself, so she said, "Do you mind if I take another sandwich with me to the room you promised?"

Nathan nodded, so she made a third sandwich to take with her for later. She stood up. "Thank you so much. That was the best turkey sandwich I've ever eaten."

Nathan smiled. "Would you like me to show you to your room now? Do you want a fresh change of clothes?"

Brianna nodded gratefully. "Thank you so much for your hospitality. That would be wonderful. Can I also borrow a phone to call my friend? She has to be worried sick about me since I haven't called her in a couple of days. I have to let her know I'm okay."

Nodding his head with a faint smile upon his lips, he replied, "Sure. There is one in the guest room I'm taking you to. Call whomever you want."

Nathan led her upstairs. "Can you wait here a second while I get you something fresh to wear?" He went into a sparsely furnished room and rummaged around. She thought it was probably his bedroom. Shortly after, he walked back to the hallway carrying a small pile of men's clothing. He winced as he held up the clothes for her to examine. "I know these are too big, but I have nothing closer to your size. The sweatpants have a tie in the front, so at least they won't fall off. They're clean."

Gently taking the clothing from him, she held them at a distance from her current attire, attempting to keep the garments clean. "Thank you." Now that her belly was full, fresh clothing felt like the greatest gift he could have given her.

He led Brianna down the hallway. They passed a few more bedroom doors. Eventually, he stopped at one and led her inside. It was a nice-sized room with a blue and white design. There was a beautiful mahogany queen canopy bed with a small mahogany desk in the corner. To the left was a matching dresser, a bookshelf, and a door to a en suite bathroom. A love seat faced a stone fireplace.

Nathan waved his hand to show her to go in. "Make yourself comfortable." He pointed to a door. "There is your bathroom, and over there is a cozy bed for the night. Your door has a lock if you would like to lock it from the inside to make yourself more comfortable. Although, it's not something you need to worry about. No one will bother you while you're here."

Nathan spent a few minutes expertly lighting a fire in her fireplace, then turned to Brianna. "Good night until tomorrow." He walked to the door and held the handle but didn't leave immediately. He turned to her in the firelight, and she suddenly realized that she really didn't want him to leave. After so much time being frightened and alone over the last few days, she wanted to stay in his warm, reassuring presence. "Is there anything else you need?"

You. She was glad to have him around after being utterly alone for days. A part of her didn't want him to leave, but she would never invite a man she just met to stay with her for the night, even if he was standing in the firelight. His shirt was slightly unbuttoned with just enough chest muscles showing to make a woman curious. If Mavis was here, she would have probably already jumped him.

The way he was looking at her so intently gave her a warm feeling in her middle. Maybe he didn't want to leave either. Brianna gently chewed on her bottom lip, unable to think of a reason he should stay. "Umm... I should be good. Thank you... unless you have some Band-Aids handy?"

Nathan smiled at her and nodded. "That I can do. I'll bring them by in a little while after you have time to get settled." This time, he opened the door and left quickly, like a man on a mission.

Brianna locked the door behind herself before setting down her third sandwich and going into the bathroom. She looked in the mirror and saw a wild thing looking back at her. Dirt matted her normally mousy brown hair, and small sticks stuck out at odd angles. Her skin was flaking from the healing sunburn. Scratches and bruises covered her arms and legs. Her cheeks burned to think of such a handsome man as Nathan seeing her like this.

He definitely seemed gruff when she met him, but he had been only sweet and thoughtful since he brought her to his home... or his compound. With this big of a house and having an employee, he would probably have other people living here. *I just haven't seen a soul, and I've been here for two days now.*

What would make a man move out into the middle of a jungle on a deserted island and fill the place with traps and riddles? He referred to having problems with trespassers, but what could have made him so suspicious of strangers?

She'd felt so comfortable talking with him over turkey sandwiches, but why in the world would he call this place his bird cage? Was it metaphorical for keeping the Tweety Birds of this island in or keeping the Sylvester cats of the world out? *Nathan has definitely aced the whole mysterious stranger vibe. All I can do is think about him and puzzle over his story.*

She made a quick call to Mavis, who picked up immediately. Instead of letting Brianna say a simple hello, Mavis immediately launched into asking a barrage of questions, not even taking a breath to allow her friend to answer. "Where are you? Are you all right? Why haven't you answered your phone? Are you mad at me? I know I kind of pushed you to take this trip and find a bit of adventure. Maybe I shouldn't have urged you to leave your room and just left you alone to make your glass animals all day."

After listening quietly, Brianna tried to interject. "No, I'm not mad at you..."

Mavis, voice pitched at a frequency that only dogs could hear, kept going. "Unless you're still upset about the job? I know you were disappointed when you never got a call back from that office job you wanted. I was going to buy a plane ticket and come find you, but then I thought maybe you took my advice about hooking up with a hot stranger. Whatever the case, you have ghosted me for DAYS and now you call me in the middle of the night. That is soooo not cool!"

Trying to keep her voice calm and not further upset her friend, Brianna skimmed over the more dangerous parts of the past two days. She knew if she told Mavis about the boating accident and being stuck most of the night in a rope trap, her friend would fly down to rescue her. While it was true, she'd had a rough past two days, she was doing fine now. Tomorrow, she would be back in her hotel room before Mavis would even get there. It was best not to worry her. She could always fill her in on more details later.

"Well, I actually *have* been on an adventure, just like you convinced me to go on. It has been... invigorating, and I am being taken care of by a mysterious handsome stranger on Riley's Paradise Island. I just dropped my phone in the ocean and haven't been able to call until now."

Mavis let out a small gasp on the other side of the phone. "Details! Have you two been too busy to leave the bedroom or laying out on the beach drinking fruity drinks out of coconut shells?"

Unsure how to respond, Brianna paused for a few seconds. Her mind couldn't help conjuring an image of herself lying out on the beach in her swimsuit next to Nathan, his bare chest and the manly scent of sandalwood nearly overwhelming her good sense. She pictured them laughing by the shore... eating turkey sandwiches.

It's not like I've never seen a good-looking guy before. I need to get a grip!

"It's really not like that. Yes, I have been drinking out of coconuts, but I just met the man tonight. Yes, he's sexy, but I will never see him again after I leave his island tomorrow. Now, I need to take a shower. I just wanted to let you know I'm all right."

Mavis made a groan. "Why do you always have to be so responsible? The whole reason you went on this trip was to live a little. You have a sexy, handsome stranger right there in front of you, and you're acting like you don't know what to do with him." Mavis paused, and her voice became even more excited. "Unless you're freshening up for a midnight rendezvous you don't want to tell me about? Alright, I'll let you go, but I want to hear more about this sexy stranger when you get back to Ohio.

We may not be roommates for much longer, but I'm still your best friend. So that means you have to spill it all."

Brianna couldn't help but smile as she hung up the phone, Mavis may have been unconventional, but at least she cared, was always there for her, and sure kept life interesting. "Yes, we will talk soon. Bye."

Next on Brianna's to-do list was to get clean. She would not let that walk-in shower with dual shower-heads go to waste.

The water felt glorious as she used the rose-scented soaps to scrub chunks of mud off of her legs and a silky lavender shampoo and conditioner in her hair. She had to use her fingers to detangle her hair and pick twigs out. Luckily, the conditioner helped. After three rounds of shampoo, she finally felt clean again. She stepped out of the shower and washed her clothes with shampoo, and hung them up in the bathroom to dry overnight.

Nathan gently rapped on her door. When Brianna answered, she saw him standing in the hallway with a small basket containing antiseptic, scissors, bandages, and a few other miscellaneous first aid supplies. "Can I come in? I brought a bit more supplies than just Band-Aids. I saw a cut going down the back of your neck and I'm sure you don't want it to get infected." His eyes crinkled at the sides as he gave her a mischievous grin. "I can be an excellent host, you know."

Brianna nodded and moved to the side so Nathan could enter. "Yes. I was looking at my injuries in the shower. I could use a bandage on my knee and hand too. Thank you."

Nathan took out the antiseptic and nodded to her. "May I?" Brianna sat on the couch in front of the fireplace and pulled the neck of her shirt down so he had access to her freshly cleaned wound.

Nathan moved towards her with the antiseptic. She felt a sharp sting as the antiseptic touched the cut, but the bandage he expertly placed over the area immediately soothed it. "There you go. Do you mind if I put some aloe on that sunburn too?"

Brianna nodded and lowered the shoulder of the large shirt enough that it exposed her shoulder. His gentle hands placed the soothing gel onto her shoulders, giving her instant relief. She pulled down the cloth covering the other shoulder to feel the same relief, but his sure fingers seemed to take longer, lingering where they touched.

"Well, that should do it." Nathan's voice sounded deeper than it did before. "I'll leave the rest of these bandages here so you can replace them as needed. Is there anything else I can get for you?"

Brianna got up from the couch and moved away. She feared the attraction that she felt for this stranger. She softly responded, "No, I'm fine. Also, I know I didn't say it before. Thank you, Nathan. Thank you for saving me."

Nathan quickly left, and Brianna turned the latch behind him. She ate her last sandwich and slipped into the firm queen bed that was covered with a soft pillow top.

It feels so good to be in a soft bed with a full tummy. I never knew what an amazing gift being clean could be.

She prayed thanks for her survival and for Nathan finding her. Her abused body relaxed as she drifted off to a peaceful, exhausted sleep.

***

A little girl's heart-wrenching scream of terror came from the room next to her. Brianna bolted upright and out of bed. She tried to clear her head of the exhausted fuzziness of interrupted deep sleep, looking around frantically for the assailant.

Chapter 4

Brianna the Ninja

Brianna

Her mind still groggy from sleep, Brianna looked around her room for an intruder. She stopped and took a moment to come to her senses. Her door remained shut and locked. Nothing looked out of place. The screaming stopped, but Brianna could hear pitiful crying through the wall behind her bed. The crying of a small girl.

Realizing she'd left her spear in the kitchen, she picked up the metal fireplace poker and held it up, ready for action. As quietly as she could, she tiptoed to her door, unlocked it, and eased it open. She saw the empty hallway she had entered through a few hours earlier. Everything was mostly dark except for a dim night-light down the corridor.

Brianna's blood boiled as her imagination tried to figure out what would have caused such terror from a little girl.

I was so excited to not be alone on this island, but is my hero who saved me from the net and cared for my wounds not such a hero after all? Out here, on this island paradise all by himself... maybe these rooms contain his many victims. Does he use his charm and good looks to lure unsuspecting women and children here?

On second thought, when I first met him, he didn't seem overly charming. He tried to get me to leave. Maybe that was part of his plan? Scare someone and soften them up so he can rub his firm hands on their shoulders in the firelight and make them drop their defenses.

Brianna did her best impression of a ninja as she slowly inched down the hallway, keeping her ears on alert and sticking to the shadows. She held her arms stiffly; ready to protect herself with the fireplace poker. Her scared, sleep-deprived imagination played out all manners of wild scenarios.

Maybe I will unravel all of his evil plans. At the last possible second, I will trick him with my wit, and the girl and I will escape. Nathan has to have a boat out here, doesn't he? The Coast Guard will save us and they will praise me for keeping my head while in unspeakable danger.

Brianna brought herself back to reality. She had successfully slunk down the hallway, alerting no one. She was here. Slowly, she turned the doorknob. She tried to open it silently, but it creaked, and she winced. She looked around the room, ready to bash in the head of the first person she saw. Fortunately, she didn't look down until it was too late.

A small child barreled into her legs and knocked her off balance. The poker dropped at her feet, the clatter muffled by the carpet. She tried to catch herself against the wall. The little girl clung to Brianna, her little chest heaving, but barely a sound escaped her mouth any longer.

Brianna looked around the room and saw that there was no one else around.

Hmm... the little girl must have just woken up from a nightmare.

Brianna hugged the girl tightly as her breathing slowed. She felt a bit embarrassed to have let her imagination run wild. Under the influence of darkness, she had jumped to a pretty horrible conclusion about Nathan. She should have trusted her instincts about him... wherever they led.

"Hello, little one. What's your name?" Brianna quietly spoke to the little girl, trying to not frighten her further. The girl didn't respond, and Brianna realized that her slow, even breathing meant that she had fallen asleep. She tried to stand up and carry the little girl back into her bed. As soon as she moved, the girl whimpered in her sleep and clung tighter to Brianna.

"Please, God, watch over this little girl," Brianna prayed. She didn't know the child's story, but hoped that she could be of some comfort. At least for tonight. Eventually, exhaustion from the last two days caught up with Brianna. She too fell asleep, cradling the little girl.

***

"WHAT ARE YOU DOING WITH MY DAUGHTER?"

Jolted awake, shock and confusion flooded her veins, Brianna didn't know what was going on as Nathan snatched the little girl out of Brianna's arms. The poor little thing startled awake and cried. Nathan towered over Brianna. He clutched the little girl to his chest and glared at her. His warm gaze from the night before turned to ice. "What were you planning on doing to her with that fire poker? I should have known better than to let my guard down and let you into my house. Trespassers are always up to no good. Get. Out!"

"Hey, wait a minute..." She started to defend herself, but Nathan's complete attention focused on the child. She heard a gentle crooning coming from him as he cradled the little girl close to his chest. "Little Bird, are you all right? I've got you." She settled down almost immediately, letting only small huffs escape her lips.

Deciding not to upset the little girl further, Brianna quickly retreated to her room. What made this man so defensive about strangers? She was just trying to help.

Back in her room, Brianna gathered up her mostly dried clothing and wracked her brain about how she could get away from this crazy island and even crazier inhabitant. She was coming up empty and tried desperately to think how the professor from Gilligan's Island made a boat out of a coconut tree.

Roughly twenty minutes later, she heard a gentle knock on the door. Scared of what waited on the other side, Brianna opened it only the smallest crack. She stayed poised, ready to shut it and lock it at a moment's notice. Nathan stood there shame-faced with his head slightly bowed. Brianna felt like she would get whiplash from her interactions with him.

"I'm here to apologize again, Brianna. I overreacted to what I saw and didn't ask questions. She is all I have left, and I tend to be overprotective of her. I went crazy at the thought of someone hurting her, but it was totally unjustified." Nathan paused and brushed his hand through his hair. "Please, can I come in? It would be easier to talk if I wasn't trying to explain myself to a single eyeball peeking around a door."

Brianna kept the door inched open. "Are you going to be nice? You know, I only wanted to comfort her."

Nathan looked at his shoes and then looked sincerely into her eye. "You have my word. I'll be nice. Please, let me make it up to you."

Opening the door slowly, Brianna stepped out of the way as Nathan entered and handed her back her poker. "Here, I expect you'll need this. Your fire is down to embers, and you never know when you'll need to brain someone with it. Jenna explained she had another nightmare. She's had a lot of those since her mom died. Thanks for going to comfort her."

Nathan looked Brianna deeply in the eyes and it brought Brianna back to his apology. Tapping a loose finger upon his chest, he made steady eye contact and a small smile tentatively grew on his face. "You didn't know her, but you stayed with her anyway. I'm sure it wasn't comfortable spending the night on the floor, but you stayed for my Little Bird. For that, I will be forever grateful." Nathan took a deep breath, looked away, and continued his apology. "I know how loud she can get with her nightmares. I'm sorry she disturbed you. Normally, she comes to my room when she's having trouble sleeping. I'm really sorry I yelled at you this morning."

Nathan paused and Brianna jumped in. "I'm just glad she's okay. When I heard her scream, I didn't know what was going on." Brianna was unwilling to admit the terrors that her flighty night-time imagination had come up with. "The poor sweetheart. It must be so hard to lose her mom, and she's so young. How old is she?"

"She's five. Her mother has been gone for over a year now. She died from a heart condition that was pretty rare at her age. It was very sudden. Jenna is still having trouble coming to terms with it."

There was a long pause until Nathan turned away and broke the tension in the air. He poked at the fire. He didn't throw a new log on and wasn't making progress in getting it started again. Maybe he just needed to do something with his hands. "While I did want to apologize, sharing my woes isn't the reason I came to talk to you. I wanted to invite you to come down to breakfast. Our housekeeper is in today, and she made up a buffet of goodies when she heard we had a guest. Would you join me? Then, of course, we will take you back to the mainland."

Brianna's stomach growled, answering for her. She smiled at him cautiously, not as quick to forgive his outburst as he was to cool down. "I would love to join you for breakfast on one condition. Next time, please don't jump to conclusions and go straight to anger. Just ask me. I'm not hiding anything."Nathan nodded and they silently walked down to breakfast together.

Brianna took the time to notice the decorations. The walls were all rather bland. In fact, most of the walls were empty, with a randomly placed bright glass mosaic on one wall and a stoic painting of knights in battle on the next. As they neared the kitchen, Brianna smelled bacon and fresh bread. Her eyes soon beheld a plethora of danishes, eggs, waffles, breakfast meats, and breads.

A cheery older woman greeted them. "Nathan, you're here! I thought I sent you up to fetch our guest, not to chat with her until the food was cold. Come, make yourself a plate." She turned to Brianna. "Miss, it is a pleasure to meet you! My name is Debbie. I work for the Rileys. I do some cooking and light cleaning here two days a week and on the other side of the island for Mr. Riley one day a week. They really are a generous family." Debbie smiled at Brianna reassuringly. "It can be quite cheerless on this island with these bachelors moping about. Just looking at you is like a breath of fresh air. Welcome to Riley's Paradise Island. Now, help yourself to a plate. Eat!"

Brianna turned to grab a plate when a whirlwind entered the room and started hugging Debbie's legs. "It's Debbie day! Hooray!" Jenna hugged Debbie in excitement.

Debbie returned the embrace with one arm around the little girl. "Good morning! My word, little one! I believe you grew two inches since I saw you on Thursday!" Jenna giggled until she noticed Brianna out of the corner of her eye.

The little girl hid behind Debbie's legs and examined Brianna cautiously. Brianna knelt down to Jenna's height and smiled.

"Good morning, sweetie pie. I didn't have time to introduce myself last night. My name is Brianna. How are you doing this morning?" Brianna waited expectantly, but Jenna just stood there, not answering. "It's okay, sweetheart. I know you don't know me. Would you like to help me eat some of these delicious cheese strudels?' Brianna held one pastry up and Jenna's eyes lit up. She quickly made her way to the table and let Brianna help her make a breakfast plate.

Debbie winked at Brianna and said with a chuckle, "I see you know the fastest way to a child's heart, sweets!" Then she went back to cleaning up all the dishes from making breakfast.

As they ate, Brianna gently talked, teased, and joked with Jenna, trying to get the little girl to open up. "You know, I had the funniest dream last night. Would you like to hear it?"

Jenna nodded her head, so Brianna continued. "I was sitting in my seat on an airplane, eating some peanuts. I was ready to explore the whole wide world when I noticed that the pilot of my airplane was a kangaroo! At first, I didn't know what to do, so I asked the kangaroo if she knew how to fly the airplane. The kangaroo just ignored me, but then a cute little joey popped his head out of his mother's pouch. He ate a handful of nuts right out of my hands and then he landed the airplane right at our next destination. Australia."

Nathan sat beside Jenna, watching the two interacting intently. Brianna didn't know what to say to him right now. He was an enigma she hadn't quite solved yet. He really seemed to be suspicious of strangers, but she had also seen that he was a kind and thoughtful man. The way he looked at her and followed her movement with his eyes made her blush, but she didn't mind. His strong jaw and chiseled cheeks made her heart beat a little faster.

She decided to just focus on the little girl. Jenna was cute and funny. Before she knew it, Brianna would be back home, and this entire experience would feel like a strange dream.

When Nathan finished his cup of coffee, he perked up and joined in the conversation. "So, Brianna, tell me a bit more about you. Where are you from and what do you do for a living?"

Jenna got up and got out her crayons and paper. The tip of her tongue stuck out of her lips as she focused hard on her drawings. It looked like she was drawing some sort of spaceship.

Brianna looked up from Jenna and saw Nathan smiling encouragingly at her. She settled into the ease she felt with him when they were eating turkey sandwiches. He seemed like a really nice guy when he wasn't freaking out about trespassers.

"Well, I enjoy making glass animal figurines and selling them at craft fairs, but I can't say that I truly make a living off that. I thought I aced an interview for a human resources job close to my apartment, but they never called me back. I really put a lot of effort into the mock training outline and financial estimates they asked me to put together, but I guess it wasn't meant to be. When I get home, to Columbus, Ohio, I will have to hunt for a job pretty hard. Unfortunately, rent is due every month!"

Jenna held up her picture. "Look, Brianna! It's a picture of a kangaroo and her joey flying the airplane. That's you in the back of the airplane with me and my dad, enjoying the ride."

Brianna picked up the picture and scrutinized it appreciatively as the little girl bounced in her seat, obviously delighted at the attention. "You know, this is some fantastic art. I think you have some genuine talent here."

Jenna hopped out of her seat. "Can I tell you a joke? My Uncle Jackson taught it to me. He lives on the other side of the island." Brianna smiled and nodded her head. Nathan's phone buzzed. He stood up and walked a few feet away before answering. Brianna focused her attention back on Jenna. "I would love to hear it. I'm all ears."

"Knock Knock."

Brianna cheerily responded, "Who's there"

Jenna giggled as she said, "Bean."

Slightly less sure, Brianna asked. "Bean, who?"

"Bean awhile since I've seen you." Jenna started cracking up over own joke so much that Brianna couldn't help but join in. Nathan hung up his phone and walked back to join the table. He ran his hand through his hair before talking, and Brianna worried that something wasn't right.

Nathan slightly lowered his head and peered at her through wide-open eyes as he apologized. "Unfortunately, a storm is coming through that looks like it's shaping up to be a doozy and Dugan is still in pretty rough shape. Depending on when it clears up, I can take you back to the mainland tomorrow or maybe the day after that. Do you mind staying with us a little longer? I have a few things I need to finish up this morning, and then Jenna and I can give you a tour of the main living areas of the house if you like"

She looked over at Jenna and smiled before she replied. "Sure. I have no desire to swim for my life again, so I am happy to stay until the storm passes. Besides, I have this adorable little conversationalist to keep me company. "

Nathan stood and made another plate of food. "Debbie, Dugan isn't feeling great today, and looking worse than I've ever seen him, so I'm going to take him his meals and check on him throughout the day. After I take him his breakfast, I have to work for an hour or two. Do you mind entertaining our guest for a bit?"

Debbie turned from the dishes. "It would be delightful to have the company. Let me finish up these dishes and we can get to know each other, Brianna."

Nathan told Brianna, "I promise I'll be as quick as I can."

Then, in a rush, Nathan took off through the door.

As soon as he left, Jenna turned to Brianna and words seemed to tumble out of her mouth. "Your hair looked like my mommy's in the darkness, but now I can see you in the light, you don't look like her at all. Your hair is the wrong color and not as nice as my mommy's was, but you still have pretty, soft hair."

Brianna couldn't get a word in edge-wise as Jenna's motor mouth continued. Brianna decided to just listen to Jenna quietly and try to keep up with the conversation. "I don't talk about Mommy in front of Daddy a lot because it makes him sad. I miss my mommy and have bad dreams sometimes. Uncle Jack says that someday I might get a new mommy, but we will never forget my real mommy. I love Uncle Jack. He's my favorite uncle. He tells me jokes and can hug as strong as a rhino. Are you going to be my new mommy?"

Chapter 5

The Governess

Nathan

Later that day, rain pummeled the roof as lightening flashed through the windows that Nathan passed. He walked speedily down the hallway to Dugan's room, but his mind wasn't on the storm terrorizing his home, it was on Brianna.

Thinking back to their tour that afternoon, he pictured Brianna, laughing and joking with Jenna. She leaned down and listened intently to all of his Little Bird's stories while she gushed over their beautiful home. He was pleasantly surprised how well Brianna did with Jenna, she certainly had a way with children. She was comfortable to be around and fit in quite well, and Nathan realized that Jenna wasn't the only one charmed by their afternoon with her.

It made him feel guilty for allowing his suspicions to lead him to jumping to conclusions that she was there to cause trouble, twice. She was nothing like the smugglers that came before. His life experiences made him feel justified to be suspicious, but Brianna was different, and he was determined to not keep making the same mistakes. After spending most of the day with her, a plan was forming in his mind as he picked up his pace down the hallway. After dinner, he excused himself to do a few more hours of work, but his thoughts continued to center around that intriguing woman.

He pictured her last night sitting in front of the fire. She looked so tempting in his clothing that was way too big for her. He could see the gentle curves of her voluptuous chest rising with each breath as it hid beneath the fabric of his borrowed shirt. When he stood behind her, rubbing ointment on her exposed shoulders, it took all of his willpower to not kiss the delicate curve of her neck and make his way to her mouth. He hadn't wanted to take advantage of the exhausted and injured beauty and, unfortunately, that attractive, intriguing woman was only a guest for that one night. Unless, he could convince her to stay.

Nathan knocked firmly on Dugan's door. "Dugan. Are you there?"

A few moments later, the door opened. Dugan filled the doorway in his crimson red robe. There was some color in his cheeks that wasn't there last night. "How are you doing? I brought you some dinner With Brianna still here, Debbie out did herself again."

Dugan's face lit up. "Well, I'll be a blue whale looking for krill. I'm starving this evening. Thank you for bringing it by. I know when I called you earlier I said I was still too sick to be out on a boat for hours, but maybe if I get something in my stomach tonight, I can manage it tomorrow morning. The storm is receding and I am feeling a lot better from this morning."

Nathan shook his head. "Actually, there has been a change in plans. You have that family member who does background investigations, right? I need a background check run on Brianna Higgins from Columbus, Ohio, ASAP. She is fantastic with Jenna and I'm thinking of offering her a job, but I don't want to ask her without doing my due diligence. It would be irresponsible of me to hire someone without doing a background check on them first. Send me any information you find. I will be in my office doing some research." Nathan turned to leave when a thought struck him. "Oh, and you don't need to take Brianna back to shore. You rest and I'll take care of it tomorrow after this nasty storm passes."

"As you say, sir." Dugan nodded at Nathan and took his plate into his room.

Nathan headed to his office to put in a few more hours of work, but he found his thoughts drawn back to the mysterious new stranger on his island.

She's smart. The fact that she solved so many of my traps and puzzles was impressive. I've never had an idle tourist explore that much of the interior of my island before. The snares scare most people off, and they don't dare enter farther into the jungle.

Nathan went into his office and sat in his big, overstuffed swivel chair. He glanced at his desk and gave a pile of paperwork a guilty look. That was what he was originally planning to work on this morning, but he turned to his internet browser. Searching through social media networks for Brianna, he looked through picture after picture of her smiling face. Mostly, she was with a woman named Mavis and sometimes at fairs with intricately made glass animals. They further convinced him she was the kind of woman he could trust.

He came across a string of pictures of Brianna with a man that gave him an uncharacteristic ache in the pit of his stomach. He pushed the disappointment away. Since there was nothing to be concerned about regarding the welfare of his daughter, he decided it was none of his business. This could still work as a business arrangement.

She needs a job, and I need an employee. In fact, it would probably be better to keep a healthy distance between myself and an employee. All that other stuff adds too many potential complications.

His fear of strangers made him keep putting off getting Jenna a nanny since his wife passed away, but it had become a problem long ago. Jenna was usually well behaved, but it was really hard to hold a serious board meeting when a plastic pony galloped up his pant leg.Debbie helped when she was around twice a week, but his little girl needed more time and attention than he could give her while trying to work full-time. Besides, Jenna was supposed to start school next year. He definitely didn't have the bandwidth to start homeschooling her, and the closest school was a few hours boat ride away on the mainland.

He thought about bringing in a tutor like he and his brother had, but she was so young that he really needed someone to monitor her throughout the day and sometimes when he was away on business trips. He knew the term wasn't used commonly anymore, but what he really needed was a governess.

Suddenly, Jenna came running into the room and gave him a big hug. "Daddy!" she squealed and gave him a big hug. Jenna caught sight of a cover he was considering. He was in charge of the video game segment of his father's company. The cover was for one of the video games his team was producing. It was a first-person adventure game that showed a gigantic dragon flying over a Scottish castle. In large letters at the bottom, it said *Riley Games*.

Jenna picked up the cover and examined it closely. "Wow. This reminds me of a story I thought of the other night. Want to hear it?"

Nathan smiled. He loved taking time for his greatest treasure. "Sure, Little Bird. Tell me about your story."

Jenna dropped the cover back onto his desk and jumped up out of Nathan's lap. She looked around to make sure she had enough space and then acted out her story as she spoke.

My little girl really has a flair for drama.

"First, I was sitting by the fireplace when, out of the smoke, a large white dragon grew. It grew and grew and grew until it was so big that it couldn't fit out my window anymore. It broke through my window and looked at me while chomping with his big, sharp teeth."

Jenna smiled at her father and showed off her own teeth for effect. "Then the dragon said, 'Hi. My name is Harriet. Wanna go for a ride?' I told the dragon, 'Sure! I've always wanted to see the snow. Can we go to see a polar bear?' The dragon said, 'Yes, I would like that too.'"

His Little Bird hopped up, lifted her arms out to her sides, and pretended to fly around his office as she continued her story. "So, I jumped onto the dragon's back and hung on really, really tight as we flew all the way to the North Pole. At the North Pole, I jumped down from the dragon into the snow. Oh, no! My feet were cold! I had forgotten to bring shoes. I was cold, so the dragon took me home." Brianna finished her story with a flourish and then plopped back into her father's lap as she awaited his reaction.

Nathan hugged Jenna. "That was a great story, Little Bird. Thank you for sharing it with me."

Jenna hunted around his desk for the paper and crayons he kept for her. She beamed. "Thanks, Dad. Brianna liked it too. She said I'm a talented actress. Here, let me draw the dragon for you. Maybe you can use him in your game."

Nathan helped her locate her art supplies, and then gently said, "Jenna, what do you think of Brianna? Do you like her?"

Jenna's eyes popped open in surprise. "Oh, that's why I'm here. Debbie sent me to tell you that my new friend, Brianna, went to her room to go to bed." Jenna giggled. "She almost fell asleep at the table and we were having cookies for dessert!"

Nathan chuckled along with his daughter, then questioned her again. She could get distracted easily sometimes. "Jenna, you spent a lot of the morning and afternoon with Brianna. What do you think of her?"

Jenna's face lit up. "I like her! She gave me a danish, and she liked my stories. We played hide and seek in kitchen while Debbie made dessert. I want to show her my room. Can she stay and play again tomorrow?"

Nathan shook his head. "I'm sorry, Little Bird. I told her I would take her back to the shore."

"Can I come too?" Jenna asked hopefully. Nathan shook his head. "Unfortunately, not this time. I need to talk to Brianna about grownup stuff for a bit. Although, I can take you in the next few days, and maybe we can go see a movie?"

Jenna pouted while quietly working on her drawing, and Nathan settled back into his internet search. Nathan's computer pinged with an email from Dugan. He skimmed through Brianna's life history. He didn't have time to read everything in depth, because he didn't want to leave her waiting too long, but from what he saw, she was a responsible, upright citizen. Exactly the role model he wanted for his Little Bird.

Jenna interrupted him. "Look at my picture! I decided to give it to Brianna. It's a picture of her riding on the dragon's back with me. Do you see what's in her hands? Those are my shoes. She remembered them so we could stay and see the polar bears."

Nathan smiled at her. "What a wonderful picture. Would you like me to deliver it for you?" She nodded and smiled.

He took the picture and left Jenna drawing another masterpiece. Doubts swirled through his mind. *Brianna is so good with Jenna. I know why I want her to work for me, but what's in it for her? I know I'm not offering her the corporate HR job she wanted or a chance to sell her art. It's so far from her home, family, and friends. Do I even have a chance of her saying 'yes'?*

Nathan thought back to breakfast and their stroll around the common areas of his house. Everything seemed different. More alive. Instead of him and Jenna quietly eating a quick meal of eggs or cereal, they laughed and talked. Brianna charmed Jenna with her stories, and in return, Jenna acted out her own play.

I'm also pretty sure Debbie found chores to keep herself occupied in the kitchen in order to eavesdrop. It seemed she was curious to hear Brianna's answers to his many questions too. Nathan realized Brianna had only been there a handful of hours and she had already transformed his entire household.

This was the first time since Jenna's mother passed over a year ago that his Little Bird looked so well-rested. He really felt like having a female influence here all the time would be good for Jenna, besides the fact that he had failed to come up with a solution for her schooling in the fall. He had to make this work with Brianna.

He was used to hiring employees left and right for *Riley Games*, but it had never felt so personal before. Sure, if things didn't work out with Brianna, he could find someone else who was probably even more qualified to come to the island, teach and watch Jenna, but right then, he didn't want anyone else for *this* job.

Nathan finished reading through Brianna's life. She had a pretty straightforward job and college history and no police record. Perfect. He thought about the pictures he saw on the internet of her with another man. They still stirred up jealousy deep in his heart, but he reminded himself that he was making a job offer. He hadn't seen the man in any of the more recent pictures, so maybe things weren't currently working out. Regardless, it shouldn't affect her ability to be an excellent governess for Jenna. Personal things were her own business.

It's a long shot, but I hope she says yes.

Chapter 6

Should I Stay, or Should I Go Now?

Brianna

"**K**nock, knock, knock."

Brianna opened the door the next morning. She was in the room Nathan had given her the first night she was there. Nathan stood at the door with a charming smile on his face. He smelled of cologne and dressed in a well-made collared polo shirt that showed off his biceps. He held up a piece of paper in one of his hands and held it out to her. There was a picture of a dragon with the two of them riding on its back and signed with a J.

Still examining the picture, she said, "Awww. Your daughter is so sweet. I am really going to miss her. Will you tell her I will hang this on my refrigerator at home to remember her by?"

"Sure." Nathan leaned closer, searching her eyes. What he was trying to find, she wasn't sure. "If you've had enough rest, we can head out. It's a beautiful day for a boat ride, and I need to head and talk with the people who rented you that boat."

Brianna nodded. "I don't exactly have much of anything to pack, so I'm ready whenever you are. I can mail you back the clothing I borrowed after I get back to the hotel that I'm staying in. Then I can clean them."

Nathan frowned at the suggestion. "No, don't worry about it. I have plenty of other clothes. Leave them here or take them with you. Whatever you prefer. I won't miss that pair." The two of them started down the hallway. "Would you mind if I take you out to lunch when we get back to the mainland? I know a fantastic place for lobster that's right on the shore. It has delicious food and a beautiful view. Although, it is a favorite hangout for the seagulls."

Seeing the sincerity in his invitation, she replied, "Sure. I'll have to eat, anyway. It would be lovely to have some company. Thank you." After she said it, she realized it was true; she didn't want her time with this amazing man to end. Brianna looked down at her ruined clothing that she put back on after attempting to wash them out and dry them overnight. "On second thought, I'm not dressed for lunch right now."

Nathan shrugged off her clothing concerns. "If you're worried about your appearance, throw that sweatshirt I gave you over the top. It's a seaside restaurant. They have good food, but they serve people in bathing suits without shoes or shirts. You'll be fine. As for the boat rental, I'll take care of that."

Nathan led Brianna out of his compound and down a path through the jungle. "After your experiences over the last few days, I probably don't need to remind you to follow right behind me, right?"

Brianna paused for a moment to smell a large, bright bird of paradise flower near the edge of the path. Nathan pulled out a pocket knife, cut off the bloom, and handed it to her.

"These are one of my favorite flowers, even though they are quite common around here. Jenna loves how they attract butterflies and hummingbirds. That's why she got the nickname Little Bird." he told her. "She's my Little Bird of Paradise."

They continued down a path until they could see water shimmering in the distance through the trees. Brianna spotted a small perch in a tree and pointed it out to Nathan. "What's that up there?"

Nathan looked over to see what she was referring to. "Oh, good eyes. That's a surveillance perch. Someone can hide in the tree and see both Otter's Cove and the surrounding jungle fairly well." Brianna shuddered as she imagined snipers in the trees. Nathan was watching her closely and quickly added, "But you don't have to worry. Jenna and I usually use that spot for its greater purpose. It's a superb bird-watching spot."

The jungle path ended at a small cove with a dock sticking out into the middle of it. As they approached, a medium-sized, brown creature slid under the water. Maybe a sea otter? A seal? There were also several boats on the dock, and Nathan directed her to a sailboat then set up the sails.

"We call this Otter's Cove. Now, sit over there to distribute our weight on the boat and counteract the wind. I would suggest not getting up after we get out to the ocean, unless you want to get knocked in the head by the boom and swim for your life again."

Nathan untied them from the dock, started up a small trolling motor, and settled in front of a wheel that controlled the ship's rudder. They moved slowly and peacefully out of the cove, but once they hit the open water, Nathan turned off the motor, and opened the sails, then the boat really picked up speed. Brianna was too far from Nathan for conversation, but the ride was enjoyable. She relaxed and daydreamed while the wind blew into her face and a soft spray of water cooled her skin.

She saw a pod of dolphins playing in the distance.

Brianna had to admit, she was jealous of Nathan. He got to live and experience this beauty every day. She had to return to Ohio. The weather always seemed to be rainy or snowy there, while Nathan woke up surrounded by paradise every morning. *Maybe I should move south. I would miss Mavis, but I can make glass figurines anywhere. Most of my sales are online, anyway. Hmm... if I could live anywhere in the world, where would I go?*

After about two hours, Brianna spotted land. An hour after that, they could make out the details of the marina. Brianna's legs were aching, and she needed to go to the bathroom. The boat was fun for the first hour, but she was ready to reach dry land.

When they reached the marina, Nathan tied up the boat and sails and offered Brianna his hand to help her off the boat. Not trusting her legs, she carefully stepped over to the dockside. Her weight made the boat wiggle, and she quickly leapt off with a small shriek.

Nathan laughed. "Careful now! We don't want to tip it!"

They headed down the marina dock, and Brianna excused herself to use a small port-a-potty that was nearby. Walking on, Brianna pointed out the fishermen who had rented her the faulty boat. Both men looked like they had seen better days, wearing dirty, patched clothing. One even had a beard that looked like he had never cared for it a day in his life. Nathan walked over to the two fishermen and addressed them politely. "I live on the private island out there, Riley's Paradise. I heard you're telling people it's a great place to visit. It's not. Its private property and visitors are not allowed."

Much to Nathan's surprise, the two fishermen laughed. One called out, "Is that your latest crab-catching haul?" They leered as they pointed at Brianna. "Everyone knows you have the place booby-trapped. Those tourists come to me looking for an adventure and come back surprised when they almost get trapped there. It always gives us a good laugh, and it gives them stories to tell their children. They usually spend an hour or two on the beach and return. They aren't bothering anyone."

Then, as if noticing Brianna for the first time, the fisherman narrowed his eyes. "Hey, weren't you the one we rented to a few days ago that never came back? Where's my boat? You signed a contract and have to pay for a brand new one if you didn't bring it back."

Nathan's eyes narrowed at the men's arrogance. "First off, this young lady will not be paying you anything. You gave her a unseaworthy boat and put her life in danger. From what she told me; it sounds like your boat sank from a faulty bilge pump. An accident that you could have avoided easily with regular maintenance."

Nathan looked both men in the eye to make sure they were listening to his every word. "I will have my lawyer contact you about any contracts that you have with her. Second, that island is private property for a reason. I do not appreciate tourists on my island, and it can be dangerous for them to wander around where they're not welcome. You will not send any more tourists that way or I will sue your business for everything that it's worth. This is not a laughing matter. Do I make myself clear, gentlemen?"

One fisherman turned white from the chastisement. The other more outspoken fisherman turned red in anger but held his tongue. All he replied was, "You had best be on your way, sonny."

Nathan, his face blank, replied, "Have a good day, gentlemen. I'm sure we will have no further misunderstandings in the future." He turned to Brianna. "Come on. We're done here. I promised you a seaside meal, and you must be famished by now."

The two walked down the docks. They turned right and walked a few blocks until they came to a fishing pier. A fancy restaurant called McClanny's stood beside the entrance to the pier.

After they were seated and had ordered, Nathan nervously tapped his fork against his finger. Brianna listened closely as he spoke. "So, Brianna, I know we got off to a rocky start, and for that, I'm sorry. Riley's Paradise really is a nice place to live. It says so right in its name. I built my house to have all the modern conveniences, and I wanted to tell you it really impressed me how you handled my Little Bird."

Brianna finally asked what she had been dying to know since she arrived on the island. "So, what's the story behind this island? Why are there so many puzzles and traps everywhere?"

Nathan took a deep breath before starting his story. "Well, my brother and I grew up on this island with our father. He's a board game tycoon. He loves puzzles of every kind. Every birthday and Christmas present we received from him was in a locked box, cipher encoded, or at the end of an elaborate scavenger hunt. Usually, a present would take us several days of work to find."

The waitress stopped by, bringing them each an iced tea and spinach artichoke appetizer bites. After the waitress left, Nathan continued his story. "My brother and I had the run of the island. Even though we had tutors come to us, we had a lot of free time on our hands. We spent countless hours fighting monsters in the jungles and swimming with mermaids in Otter's Cove." He took a sip of his iced tea. "We set up harmless traps for each other on the island, and it became a game to see who could outsmart the other and catch them. Our father thought our traps were hilarious, and he encouraged us and helped us with our designs. It became a bonding time with my father and a challenge to outwit and get back at my brother. Once, we even had smugglers come to the island that put our traps to the test."

Nathan studied her, fully alert. "Now it's your turn. What brought you to the area all by yourself? I'm surprised you didn't bring a significant other."

Brianna blew on her hot appetizer. "Nope, just came myself. Well, I told you over breakfast how I make small, hand-blown glass animal figurines. They paid my half of the rent while I lived with my best friend, Mavis. Unfortunately, I don't make enough to cover all the rent by myself. I fear I may have to go back to being a waitress like I was in college. Last week, when I booked a table at the local crab festival near here, it was an attempt to both make some money and take a break to reevaluate my normal life. I did well enough that, after the festival was over, I took a few extra days to enjoy the beach before heading home."

Nathan nodded. He ran his hand through his hair and took a sip of his iced tea. She added, "This hasn't exactly been the vacation I imagined, but your island and your house are definitely beautiful."

Nathan gave her a genuine smile, but she noticed out of the corner of her eye that he was bouncing one leg up and down slightly. It surprised Brianna how this normally confident man started his next question, pausing slightly between each few words, as if gauging her reaction. "So, I had a proposition. A job offer, really."

Brianna's eyebrows shot up in surprise as she waited for him to spit out what the offer was. What could she offer him? Did he need someone to clean his house? Polish his boats?

You are handsome, but please don't offer me a million dollars to sleep with you.

Unaware of her thoughts, Nathan powered on, speaking a bit more rapidly. "So, I've been thinking about what to do with Jenna when she starts school in the fall, and you two seem to have hit it off."

Ah, a babysitter. That she could do, but why would he be asking her when there were a million other people that lived closer and were probably more qualified?

Nathan talked about the benefits of working for him. He didn't seem to realize that he never actually voiced what he was asking of her. "There would be a high budget for whatever supplies you might need or think would be helpful. You could just tell me what you need. You would have most evenings, Saturdays, and Sundays off. There would be a good-sized stipend on top of your room and board..."

Brianna physically held out her hand and stopped him there. She was trying to make sense of all of his incomplete thoughts. "Are you trying to ask me to take care of Jenna and teach her?"

Nathan straightened himself up. "Well, yes, I am. I know you have a whole life back home, so I completely understand if you need to head back. I just thought I would ask if you're interested. Jenna's really too old to have a nanny, but she needs more companionship than a tutor. I've put off hiring someone for too long. Would you be interested in coming back to Riley's Paradise and being Jenna's governess?"

Chapter 7

Lost Little Bird

Brianna

Two weeks later, Brianna was back at the island and settling into the guest room she had previously used. She was now officially an employee of Riley Games, as Jenna's governess. Mavis had helped her pack up her apartment and practically pushed her out the door. It felt weird leaving Ohio. She had lived there her whole life, but it was also exciting. She had a world of adventure awaiting her on a island most would call paradise with a handsome new boss and an adorable little preschooler. Maybe it ended up being for the best that she didn't get that HR job, otherwise she would have never found this opportunity.

Brianna's first day on the job started strong. After she whipped up some eggs and fruit for breakfast, both Jenna and Brianna spent a few hours coloring and playing board games in the kitchen. Eventually, Brianna could tell Jenna was getting antsy.

"Jenna, would you like to show me around today? You know, the places where you like to play and spend time." Brianna sipped a cup of hot tea as she made Jenna and herself a few sandwiches for lunch.

Immediately, Jenna's eyes lit up in her normal fashion. She spoke so fast that her sentences ran together. "OH, YES! I can show you my room, I can show you my playroom, I can show you my best friend, Theodore." Jenna lowered her voice and whispered, "I can show you my secret hideout too, but you have to promise not to tell anyone."

Brianna smiled. "As long as you're safe, your secrets are safe with me, sweetie pie. I would love to see all of your favorite things, especially your secret hideout." Brianna looked at Jenna questioningly. "Who's Theodore? Does he live on the island too?"

"Of course Theodore lives on the island! He's my best friend. We play together all the time. He is the best at hide and go seek." Jenna got up from her seat and grabbed Brianna's arm, pulling her out of her chair. "Come on, I'll introduce you. You will be best friends too."

Brianna chuckled and held her ground. "Wait. Wait. After lunch! You can show me in a few minutes after you have something in your belly. I don't want to be starving as soon as we embark upon our adventures, do you?"

Jenna shook her head solemnly and wolfed down her sandwich. She rushed her plate to the sink and stopped in front of Brianna. "Now can we go?"

Brianna smiled. "I barely took two bites of my sandwich. Why don't you sit here and draw a map of where you want to take me while I finish my lunch?"

Jenna studiously settled down with some paper and markers. She drew lines of various colors and had X's marking several spots on her map. She marked one specific spot with a W instead of an X. "That is just in case a pirate gets a hold of my map. They won't find my treasures if I mark it with a W," she explained.

Brianna quickly cleaned up from their meal, and the two hurried down the hallway. Jenna's first stop was to show off her bedroom. When they arrived, Jenna flung open her door and strode inside with her hands out to her side. She looked at Brianna expectantly, as if she was welcoming Brianna to take in all the splendor of the room.

When Brianna had previously met the sobbing Jenna in the entryway, it was dark, and when Nathan had woken her up with his temper, she had escaped as fast as she could. She never really took in her surroundings before.

Now, in the daylight, the room looked very similar to Brianna's in structure. Only, instead of the beautiful hardwood accents, everything was purple. The walls and carpet were purple. The canopy bed and dresser were purple. In fact, every shade of purple overwhelmed Brianna's senses. Pristine stuffed animals of every creature, color, and size covered almost every purple surface.

Jenna ran to a large curtain and pulled it back to allow daylight into her room. Beyond the curtain was a sliding glass door that led out to a balcony overlooking the jungle. She jumped up onto her plush purple bed and rooted around in the covers until she found a small, worn stuffed monkey. Jenna brought it over to Brianna.

"Theodore, I want you to be kind to my new friend Brianna. She is nice. She's new here and needs friends." Jenna addressed the stuffed monkey and then turned to Brianna. "He likes it if you pet his head really gently. Then he will be your friend too."

Brianna smiled and leaned down to Jenna's height. She gently petted the monkey's head. "Well, Theodore, it's so nice to meet you! Jenna has told me so much about you. It would be a genuine pleasure to have a wonderful friend like you. Would you like to join us on our adventure to see Jenna's favorite places around the house?"

Jenna giggled and then nodded the monkey's head up and down. A new thought struck Jenna, and she threw Theodore back onto the bed, forgotten. "Come on, Brianna! I'll show you where I like to play with my dolls." Jenna took off out of the room and down the hall before Brianna could stop her.

"Wait for me!" Brianna called. She laughed as she chased the little girl through a maze of corridors. They finally ended at a large mahogany door that was open only by a crack. Brianna followed a few yards behind Jenna but stopped dead when she entered the room.

Nathan sat in a large office at a giant mahogany desk that had an opening about three-feet long. The massive size and opening of the desk made it look more like a table with drawers than a normal desk. There was a giant portrait of Jenna on one wall. Another wall displayed old English swords and a Katana. Everywhere else held ceiling-high bookshelves filled to the brim. Beneath the massive desk, Jenna had a whole doll city set up. There was a collection of three-inch dolls that had houses, castles, shops, farms, limousines, and carriages.

"Come on, Brianna! You can come down here and meet everyone!" Jenna beckoned Brianna to come under the desk, oblivious to the fact that her father's legs and desk chair were the backdrop for her city.

"You know what, Jenna? I don't want to disturb your father's work. Come on. You can show me your friends another time..." Brianna stood in the doorway, looking around uneasily. The room emanated Nathan's manliness, and no matter how hard Jenna prompted, she couldn't bring herself to climb under the desk so close to Nathan's torso.

Nathan pushed back his chair. "It's fine! I admit I'm getting a lot more done with you watching her, but I always have time for my Little Bird and I miss having her around all the time." To Brianna's great surprise, Nathan lay on his stomach and picked up the doll closest to him. He made his doll pretend to get onto a horse and ride back to the castle.

Nathan looked up at Brianna. "Jenna comes and plays under here while I work sometimes. She makes sure her dolls don't get lonely because, apparently, I don't pay enough attention to them." He looked at Brianna with a goofy grin and kind eyes. "Would you like to help us save the princess from a dragon? He really likes to eat marshmallows. I'll distract the dragon with marshmallows while you guys save the princess!"

"Daddy!" Jenna chastised. "If the dragon is gone, the princess can just walk out and save herself!" Then, deep in thought, she asked, "Do you think the dragon will share his marshmallows with the princess?" She looked at her father with pleading eyes.

Nathan looked at Jenna, then Brianna, and then back to Jenna again. "Why don't you two go down to the kitchen? We asked Debbie to pick some marshmallows up for us last week. I have a few things to finish up here, and I could definitely use a break. How about I meet you two out in the courtyard in about an hour to roast marshmallows together? Does that sound good, Little Bird?"

Before Nathan said his last word, Jenna jumped up from under the desk and shrieked, "Yippee!" then ran past Brianna and down the hallway.

At least I'm getting my exercise chasing after this little one, Brianna thought.

Brianna gave Nathan a tentative smile. "Sorry we disturbed you. I didn't know she was taking me to your office. If you're too busy, you really don't need to meet us for marshmallows."

Nathan rose and walked over to Brianna. "This brief visit was a breath of fresh air. Never feel that I'm unavailable if you two need anything." He lifted Brianna's hand and stared into her eyes before dropping it. To Brianna's utter embarrassment, her cheeks flushed with heat. "Of course I will be down for marshmallows. A knight never goes back on a promise." He turned to go back to his desk.

Brianna left Nathan's office befuddled. She looked around, trying to remember which direction Jenna took her and which direction would lead to the kitchen. Maybe she needed Jenna to help her make a real map of this place.

After obtaining marshmallows and metal sticks for cooking them, the two ladies made their way to the courtyard. Brianna knew they had some time to kill, so she suggested they play hide and go seek. Jenna happily agreed.

"One, two, three..." Brianna counted loudly, then searched for Jenna. Giggling from behind a decorative bush in the courtyard directed Brianna to the little girl's location. Brianna pretended like she was looking in various other places before she reached the place Jenna had hidden.

"You found me!" Jenna laughed. "My turn! My turn! I'll count while you hide." The little girl covered her eyes.

"No peeking!" Brianna warned. Then she moved about the courtyard, looking for the perfect hiding spot.

"One, two, three, seven, eight, ten. Ready or not, here I come!" Jenna yelled at the top of her lungs. Brianna quickly crouched behind a stone near the pond. She thought she would have a few more seconds. Almost immediately, she felt a tap on her shoulder.

Jenna shouted, "You're it!" then giggled. "I could see your hair sticking out from behind the rock. You need to hide better. I know a great hiding spot. Count again!"

Brianna counted while Jenna ran off. She heard a bit of a scraping noise coming from the courtyard. Could the little girl be moving something?

"Ready or not, here I come!" Brianna opened her eyes and looked around. At first glance, she couldn't see her. Unconcerned, she went more thoroughly through the courtyard, looking in every tree and behind every bush and boulder in the garden. She walked around the fountain, but there was still no sign of her. When she was getting to the end of the garden, Brianna got an uneasy feeling in her stomach. *Where is Jenna?* She listened really hard but heard nothing.

"Jenna? Okay, it's time to come out. You're right, that was a fantastic hiding spot. I can't find you." Brianna listened for a response. When she heard nothing, she felt more and more panicked inside. "Jenna? Where are you? I need you to come out now. We're done playing."

There was no sign of Jenna anywhere. That's when Brianna noticed the door from the courtyard out to the jungle was wide open.

How could I have lost my charge on my very first day at the job?

Brianna let out a last anguished shout. "Jenna! Jenna! Where are you?"

Jenna was gone.

Chapter 8

Gross Slimy Slug

Brianna

Brianna's stomach was in knots as she exited the compound and looked around the edges of the jungle. She yelled out Jenna's name periodically.

Where is she? I should have never let her out of my sight! Jenna could be anywhere... and in any kind of trouble.

In a panic, Brianna rushed around, not worried about her surroundings anymore. She saw a movement out of the corner of her eye. Something had moved in the brush to the right of her. *Was that a person?*

"Jenna? Is that you? Please come here!" Brianna yelled.

A monkey scampered up a tree. *Is Jenna over there? Did she scare the monkey into the tree?* Brianna stepped into the brush and called again, "Jenna!"

She shrieked as a cool, thick, sticky goo poured down onto her head. There was so much of it covering every inch of her clothing before she knew it. She spat in disgust. Some had even gotten into her mouth.

From behind, Brianna heard Nathan's voice. "Brianna? What are you doing?" Brianna spun around as quickly as the thick goop would allow her. There stood Nathan, holding Jenna's hand, both looking at her with perplexed expressions on their faces.

Despite the slime dripping down her face, Brianna breathed a sigh of relief. "Jenna! There you are! Where were you hiding? I couldn't find you anywhere, sweetheart. I was worried."

Jenna looked at her feet and quietly answered. "I was hiding in my secret spot in the courtyard and you never found me, so I came out. Daddy was there starting a fire for our marshmallows. He said I shouldn't have hidden in there because the water running is so loud that I can't hear anyone. I didn't mean to scare you. I'm sorry."

Brianna's face softened as much as the hardening goo would allow. A giant glop fell from her chin. "That's okay, sweetheart. I'm just glad you're all right. When I get cleaned up, why don't you show me that super-secret hiding place of yours? That way I won't end up covered in goo next time we play hide and go seek."

Jenna nodded and smiled. "You look really funny! Kind of like a frog I caught in the mud or a gross, slimy slug."

"Just the look I was going for," Brianna replied dryly. She tried to take a step forward, and the goo suctioned her shoe off. She reached down and pulled her shoe out, then made slow, measured movements toward Nathan and Jenna. "Can you help me get this stuff off? Or am I going to spend the rest of my life as The Swamp Thing?"

Nathan pointed towards his house. "Come on back to the compound. Don't worry, my sticky solution is water soluble. Eventually, we'll get it all off. We need to hurry, though. It's hardening and will be very hard for you to move if we don't get you rinsed off soon."

An uncomfortable Brianna sarcastically mumbled to herself, "Eventually. Perfect."

They walked towards the compound as fast as Brianna could go. Unfortunately, that was only about as fast as the slug that she felt like.

Nathan slowed his pace to match hers. "When Jenna told me what happened, I figured you must have been looking for her. She knows all the tricks about this place and can be quite a challenge when she plays hide and go seek with me. I just don't understand why you would have come looking out here. The only reason we could find you so quickly was because we heard you yelling. When I heard my slime trap engage, I knew you would need some help quickly."

Brianna tried to roll her eyes at Nathan, but it lost her intended effect under all the goop. "When I couldn't find Jenna and I saw the door ajar, I just assumed that's where she had gone."

Nathan frowned at her response but said nothing more on the subject. "May I suggest a bath after we hose you off? That slime is quite pungent."

Brianna felt humiliated as Nathan hosed her down like a dog that had been playing in the mud.

This is it. He's going to fire me after the first day on the job.

Brianna went to her room and bathed with scented soaps several times and used a heavier amount of body spray than usual to mask any lingering odor. She felt clean and passed her own sniff test well enough that she made her way back out to the courtyard.

Nathan and Jenna were laughing by the campfire, eating the marshmallows they had cooked when Jenna got distracted by a tiny butterfly and tried to catch it with her hands. Jumping and frolicking about, the determined little girl ran off into the courtyard garden. To Brianna's relief, she stayed well within eyesight.

Brianna approached Nathan and spoke with regret. "I'm so sorry I let Jenna out of my sight and set off your weird goo trap. I understand if you want to find someone else to stay with her. My first impression on the job has not been stellar. I can pack up and be ready to leave by later tonight or tomorrow morning. Whenever it is more convenient for Dugan to take me back to the mainland."

Nathan looked at her with a puzzled expression on his face. "Au contraire. I was thinking about how you were fantastic with Jenna all day. I hoped this minor incident wouldn't scare you off. For Jenna's sake, I hoped you would give us another chance."

Nathan offered Brianna a perfectly golden-brown marshmallow and continued, "I think I should be the one to apologize. This island isn't like other places. Here, there is a large learning curve. I think that by leaving you ignorant of how our quirky island works, I've set you up for failure. I've had no one come to the island and help with Jenna before because I honestly didn't want to share my secrets." He gave a long, dramatic sigh. "It's time. So, I've come up with a proposal."

Nathan put down the empty marshmallow cooker and focused all of his attention on Brianna. "I was wondering if you would stay. In return, I will take a few evenings after dinner to show you around the island and help you learn to navigate safely on your own. I'm certain that by the time we're done, you'll feel confident enough to take Jenna out for walks. Hopefully without getting yourselves covered in my sticky solution or caught in a trap." He studied her face as if looking for the slightest expression. "I hope this island will eventually feel like home."

Brianna's mind whirled with the unexpected change in direction their conversation had taken. *I thought there was no coming back from the goo debacle. Apparently, I was wrong. What do I want? Was I so quick to accept being fired because this island scared and overwhelmed me, or was it the bewildering inhabitant in front of me?* Nathan waited patiently for her response.

"I'm not scared of the island, and I think that's an excellent compromise. I will stay, and you can teach me all the tricks of the island," Brianna replied.

"It's agreed then. You're staying." After they struck their deal, an evil glint overtook Nathan's eyes. "Although I never said that I would show you everything. I believe that the best way to understand and remember something is by overcoming the challenge yourself. I'll show you around and keep you from getting caught in the worst of traps, though. In the end, you will be the one figuring out how to overcome the challenges." Nathan smiled at her, then in a deadpan serious voice said, "In fact, I think you should start referring to me as your Sensei."

Brianna was still trying to get a good sense for when Nathan was kidding with her or being serious. He was a hard man to read. She smiled to herself; this man was just another puzzle of this island to unravel. *Good thing I love puzzles!*

Jenna saved her from having to reply to Nathan when she came running back over. She hugged Brianna's legs and looked up at her. "You don't look like a slimy slug anymore!" Then she made loud sniffing noises. "Although you do still smell kind of funny." Jenna let go of Brianna's legs and grabbed her hand. "Come on! I'll show you my super-secret hiding place."

Jenna dragged Brianna over to the large angel statue in the middle of the courtyard. Brianna looked on in confusion. *I looked all around this statue for Jenna earlier, and there had been no sign of her.* The water running down the angel's hands was crystal clear. The face looked almost mournful in the daylight. Jenna put her finger into the water near the bottom of the fountain and swished them around for a few moments.

When she finished playing in the water, Jenna walked over to the plaque on the front of the statue. She ran her fingers gently over the words Sophia Irene Riley, Loving Wife and Mother. Then Jenna pushed firmly on the heart shape next to the picture of her late mother.

Brianna stood back and watched as the back part of the fountain pulled out, leaving a stone stairway leading into a cellar only dimly lit by a light that ran along the side. "This is my super-secret hideout. No one can find me here if I don't want them to. Come on!"

Brianna pursed her lips as she looked into the dimly lit stairwell. "That is a pretty secret hideout, but I don't think we need to go in there right now." Jenna stuck out her lower lip but went to the front of the statue and pushed the heart two more times instead. A small drawer with a box inside popped out of the front.

Nathan frowned slightly and spoke sternly to Jenna. "Little Bird, you know you aren't supposed to play on the stairs that lead to the basement. That's for emergencies only." Jenna nodded her head as she went to open the box.

Nathan turned to Brianna, his tone more cordial. "I made this statue for Jenna to make sure she never forgets her mom. She was just so young when she passed. Jenna likes to come over here and play with some keepsakes from her mother. The problem is that she sometimes goes into the hidden stairwell and can't hear well over the white noise of the running water, especially when she shuts the doorway behind herself."

Brianna's eyebrows rose and Nathan quickly explained. "Don't worry, the stairs lead to the basement and there is a button on the inside so she's safe in there and can come out anytime she wants."

Curious, Brianna examined the statue. "Have you always lived here?"

Nathan ran his hand through his hair. "My late wife, Sophia, and I actually lived a few hours' drive from here. She thought of this island as a few thousand acres of places for insects to hide, so we only came back to visit for the holidays. After Sophia died, I needed to get away from everything. I had a preschooler to raise on my own, so that's when we moved back to the island." He ran his hand through his hair again. "My brother had his own juvenile way of helping me through my grief. Jackson built an impossible trap and caught me the first week I was here. Getting him back gave me something to throw myself into."

Nathan gave Brianna a small smile. "Jenna and I enjoyed it here, so I built my own highly secure compound on the other side of the island away from my dad and brother. That way, I could have my space and Jenna could grow up here like I did. I felt that here, at least, I could keep my Little Bird safe. My brother and I built all the traps and puzzles on the island to either trick one another or increase security."

"Not long after we moved here, I found Dugan. A security agency recommended him to me because he was fantastic at security but kept getting laid off because he had some problems from his military days and couldn't handle being around many people all the time. He ended up being the perfect man to maintain all the traps, riddles, and surveillance here. That way I can focus more on running the video game division of Riley Games while taking care of Jenna. Although, I still enjoy adding an odd puzzle or two to the island for fun." Nathan winked at her.

Brianna thought of how her mom had handled things when her father passed away a few years ago. *She didn't build me a large monument of remembrance, that's for sure.* There was his gravestone, but other than that, she had a small framed picture of the two of them. *Nathan does everything over the top, doesn't he?*

Jenna showed Brianna what was in her little keepsake box. "This is a rock that I picked up and gave to Mommy when I was little. Mommy loved it and kept it as one of her treasures. This perfume bottle is what my mommy smelled like." She unscrewed the cap, and although the bottle was mostly empty, a light, flowery fragrance emerged. "And this necklace was Mommy's. She wore it all the time."

Jenna opened up the pendant to show Brianna the picture inside. "That's me as a baby. She said that I was a gift from God." Jenna gently placed her things back into the box. "Daddy has more of Mommy's things for me when I'm older, but for now, Daddy said that I can come here and remember Mommy anytime I want."

Jenna returned her box and pushed the heart button on the plaque again. The drawer of the fountain and stairwell closed back up, and Brianna examined it. There was a hairline crack where it had opened, but she would have never guessed what secrets it held.

Jenna jumped up and started running toward the house. "Come on! Let's go to my toy room!" Brianna followed until Nathan yelled from the courtyard and the two of them stopped.

"Before you go, I wanted to give you time to get ready for our first jungle puzzles 101 class. Debbie will be here next Tuesday and can watch Jenna while I show you around. We can explore the island after dinner."

Today is Friday. I wonder if he is anticipating our adventure as much as I already am? Now I'll have all weekend to imagine what curiosities we'll come across.

In a businesslike fashion, Nathan finished his statement. "That gives you the weekend to pick up any supplies you need. Feel free to ask Dugan to take you to the mainland if you want or need to get anything. Make sure you wear long pants, long sleeves, and bug spray on our adventures."

Jenna hopped up and down impatiently. "Are you ready yet? Let's race there!"

Brianna smiled and nodded. "Let's go!"

Brianna chased after Jenna, who giggled so much that she couldn't focus on running. Whatever happened, staying at Riley's Paradise certainly would not be boring.

She was so excited to go out adventuring in a few days. Brianna wondered what kind of amazing things Nathan had hidden on this island to require such security. She hoped she didn't embarrass herself in front of him again. She liked this beautiful island but still wasn't too sure how well she would fit in. Hopefully, she wouldn't come to regret her decision to stay.

Chapter 9

Red Alert

Brianna

"Good tidings to you and all of your kings…" Jenna sang to herself softly as she and Brianna cut out pretend food and a caterpillar from felt. "… Old King Cole was a merry old soul, yes, a merry old soul was he. He called for his milk, and he called for his cookie, and he called for his fiddlers three…"

Brianna felt her pocket vibrate and pulled out her new cellphone. It was a call from Nathan. She stood up and walked a few feet away before she answered the phone. A curt voice immediately started talking. "Brianna? This is a red alert. I need you and Jenna to head to her room and prepare the escape route. Jenna knows what to do. Hopefully, this is nothing serious, but please, be careful. I'll call you back when I know more."

Caught totally off guard, Brianna's mind reeled. *Now I have to change gears from mixed-up nursery rhymes to finding out I'm in danger. What's going on?* "A red alert? What is that? An escape route? Are we in danger?"

Nathan replied, "You're in no immediate danger, but we need to follow the red alert protocols. Ask Jenna. We've practiced it hundreds of times. She knows what to do. I'll call you soon." Then he hung up the phone without a goodbye.

Brianna stared at her phone for a moment. *Usually, in times of crisis, I don't turn to a preschooler and ask what to do.* She gently placed her phone back in her pocket.

She tried to keep her voice calm and sweet as she talked to Jenna to make sure that she didn't scare her. "Jenna, honey, I'm sorry to interrupt your hard work, but we're going to have to finish the *Hungry Little Caterpillar* book later. Your daddy just called and told me you have been working really hard on learning what to do when there is a red alert. Why don't we go to your room and you can show me how much you've learned?"

Jenna jumped up and dropped the scissors from her hand straight to the floor. "Oh, yes! I'm great at red alert practice! Come on! I'll show you!" Jenna raced out of her playroom and down the hall to her bedroom, where she paused and beckoned for Brianna to hurry.

To Brianna's surprise, Jenna pulled a full-body harness out of a chest near her balcony. She handed it to Brianna. Jenna pulled out another harness that she expertly stepped into herself. "Come on, you can put one on too. Daddy always does when we practice. Do you need me to help you, Brianna?"

Brianna looked at the jumbled mess of straps in confusion. She didn't even know where to begin. Jenna sighed in exacerbation before showing Brianna where to step into the harness and where to put her arms. It was loose, so Brianna adjusted the straps until the whole thing fit snugly.

Jenna babbled excitedly as she finished securing her own harness. "It's so fun when we have red alerts! That means we get to rappel! Do you like to rappel?"

Brianna stared at the little girl, unsure what to do next. *What have I gotten myself into now?* "Um... Jenna, what is rappelling? Tell me everything you normally do during a red alert."

Jenna puffed up her chest and spoke authoritatively. "A red alert is when we practice what to do in case a bad guy ever comes here." Jenna whispered the next part conspiratorially, "But don't worry. No bad guys ever come here anymore. My daddy and Mr. Dugan are always here to scare them away."

Jenna went to the sliding glass doors and opened them up. She stepped out onto the balcony, and Brianna followed. Above the parapet there was an overhang that held two pulleys. Each pulley was on a different side of the overhang near the wall of the building and had their own climbing ropes. Someone had already tied the climbing ropes into a series of knots with a carabiner clip on the end. Jenna clipped one of the carabiner clips onto her harness and then held the other clip out to Brianna.

She continued to explain. "When we play the red alert game, we practice rappelling off my balcony. It's kind of like hopping down the wall to get to the ground. We used to practice a lot, but we haven't done it much recently." Jenna stood on a bench near the edge of her balcony and fearlessly turned her back to the outside. "Are you ready to go?" Jenna asked Brianna, only inches from the drop.

"Jenna! Come back down here! I don't want you to fall!" Brianna grabbed Jenna's hand and helped her back down before she did anything rash.

Jenna looked at Brianna, confusion swimming across her features. "Why do I have to come down? I was just going to rappel and show you what I do during a red alert."

Brianna paused for a second. "Oh, honey, I'm sure you're fantastic at rappelling, but your father just said to get ready. So, let's just listen to him and wait here. We'll be ready to rappel in case we need to."

Jenna frowned but listened to Brianna. "When Daddy and Uncle Jackson were younger, there were *real* bad guys on the island. Uncle Jackson told me a story about the one bad guy that got away. It was scary and gave me nightmares. That's when Daddy made the red alert plan. He set my room up with these harnesses and checks that all the knots are secure every night when he puts me to bed. He said that if I'm ever in trouble to rappel down my bedroom wall like we practiced and run to the docks. If I saw anyone I didn't know along the way, I was supposed to hide. Then he would meet me down at the docks as soon as he could." The first traces of fear crossed Jenna's innocent face. "Is this a *real* red alert? Is there something wrong? Where is my daddy? Is my daddy okay?"

Brianna gave Jenna a hug and looked her in the eyes as she replied. "I'm sure your daddy is fine. I just talked to him a few moments ago. I don't know a lot of information right now, but he said that everything is probably okay. We need to be prepared, just in case, while he and Dugan check it out."

Brianna spent the next few minutes distracting Jenna by teaching her a new nursery rhyme. They sang *I'm Bringing Home a Baby Bumblebee* and made-up hand movements to go along with the song. Finally, Brianna's phone rang. It was an unknown number.

"Hello?" Brianna inquired into the phone.

A gruff voice replied. "Is this Brianna? It's Dugan."

A shiver ran down Brianna's spine. *Did something happen to Nathan?* "Hello, Dugan. Yes, this is Brianna. Is there any update on the red alert? What happened?"

Dugan seemed distracted, and he paused before answering her. "Yes, ma'am. Nathan asked me to call you and let you know he's giving the all-clear. We have the marauder in custody right now, like a pig on the spit. Nathan is on the phone with the police, coordinating a transfer to their facilities. He wanted me to tell you to go back to whatever you were doing and he'll come and visit you as soon as he gets things settled here."

Brianna sighed in relief that Nathan was all right. "Thank you, Dugan. I really appreciate the update."

Brianna turned to Jenna. "Well, we will not be rappelling today, but I think it's time to get a snack. Then we can finish our felt figures and read *The Hungry Caterpillar*. Let's take these uncomfortable things off."

Jenna led the way down to the kitchen, where they had a snack of crackers shaped like goldfish and sliced apples. It was there that Nathan found them.

"Ah, my two favorite ladies!" Nathan exclaimed happily as he entered the room.

"Daddy!" Jenna barreled into his legs. He picked her up and hugged her so the two of them were looking eye to eye. "How are you doing, my Little Bird? Were you a good girl for Brianna? Did you show her how to hook up your rappelling gear?"

Jenna pouted. "Yes, Daddy. I showed her. I even helped her put her harness on, but then she changed her mind and didn't want to rappel off the balcony."

Nathan gave Brianna a crooked smile. "I guess we'll just have to teach her how to do it so she won't feel scared next time. What do you think? Can you help me teach Brianna?"

Jenna nodded her head determinedly. "Yes! I can show her how I do it, and I can teach her how to rappel all by herself. I can even play music and make her blindfolded if she's too afraid of looking down. Do you think I should teach her how to do deep breathing like you taught me the first time I did it?"

Nathan chuckled, tousled Jenna's hair, and set her down. "We'll have to ask Brianna what she wants. Why don't you finish your snack, Jenna?"

Jenna scurried back to the table. "Can I have chocolate milk and a cookie?"

Nathan thought for a moment. "Yes. We do still have a good while until dinner, and you were very brave today. Get out the cookies, and I'll help you with the milk."

After Jenna settled down and happily munched away, Nathan turned to Brianna. He used his right arm to guide her a few feet away from the table, out of immediate earshot. He never removed his arm as he detailed the exciting events of the last few hours.

"So, today's red alert turned out to be a poacher. He isn't talking much. What he is saying, I'm not sure I believe." Nathan looked over at Jenna to make sure she wasn't paying attention to what they were saying. Then he continued, "The man claims he had only just arrived, and it was for sightseeing only, but Dugan found a camp a few miles away from where we found him. It's been there for weeks at least. The man says the camp isn't his. On his boat, we found cages for some smaller critters, like monkeys or birds. He claimed the boat wasn't his either until we asked him how he arrived on the island, and then he clammed up." Nathan shrugged. "He denied everything. Whatever he was doing, he was obviously up to no good. If that camp didn't belong to him, who else could it belong to? He had an endangered gecko in a cage with him, so he'll be in trouble with the law, regardless."

Nathan's phone chimed, and he glanced at the caller ID before continuing, "We called the police to come and take him to the mainland and sort it all out. He was probably looking to export his catches illegally in the black-market pet trade. I'm not pleased that he's been on the island for so long without us knowing. I don't think he was a direct threat to us, but Dugan and I will increase the island's security."

"Well, I'm glad you're all right. How did you know he was here? What triggered the red alert?" Brianna asked as she looked up into his eyes.

"Do you remember the treehouse I found you in?"

"Of course. I don't think I'll ever forget that."

"At the top of the treehouse, there were three items. On the table was a hunting knife, under the table was a stinky piece of fish bait, and on the shelf on the wall was canned food."

Brianna looked perplexed. "I saw nothing under the table."

"It was small. I'm not surprised you missed it. Anyway, if the fish bait disappears, the treehouse sets off a small sensor that alerts us that something like a snake or a monkey got into the treehouse and we should check on it soon. That's a green alert, and Dugan usually takes care of it within a day. In your case, you were hungry and human enough to know there was food in the cans. When you went for the food, it activated the net trap under the treehouse and sent off a yellow alert to our control room. Usually, Dugan deals with yellow alerts within a few hours. On the particular night that I trapped you, Dugan wasn't feeling good. After work, *I* went to find out who was in the trap instead. I had a small handgun in my holster just in case there was trouble, but I wasn't too worried."

Nathan ran his right hand through his hair; a movement that was becoming familiar when he was feeling stressed. "Tonight, the man who invaded the island reached for the knife first. That also activated the rope net we caught you in, but instead of a yellow alert, it sent off a red alert of potential danger to the control room. The alert went to Dugan, my brother, and me. In the red alert case, two of us go to investigate what could be a potential threat. We make sure that we're armed and ready for anything."

Brianna looked at Nathan questioningly. "Do you really get a lot of threats on this island? It doesn't exactly look like a dangerous area."

Nathan replied, "The island is the perfect distance from the mainland and is empty enough looking that it attracts some pirates and smugglers. When Jackson and I were younger, there were smugglers on the island. Things didn't go so well. In fact, a man died, and Nathan and I were very close to losing our own lives. We make sure we never have a catastrophe like that again."

Jenna finished up the last of her milk and cookies as Nathan continued, "Since you were with my Little Bird, I could go with Dugan, and we didn't have to wait for Jackson to cross the island."

Nathan looked down at his arm, realizing he had held on to Brianna during their entire conversation. He quickly moved his hands away and looked at Brianna, while rubbing one of his hands across the back of his neck. Just then, Jenna barged between the two of them, a few crumbs still on her lips. "So, are you guys ready to go rappelling now?"

Chapter 10

Adventure Awaits

Brianna

The next Tuesday, Brianna read up on homeschooling while Jenna played. She and Nathan had decided that would be the best way to meet all of Jenna's academic and legal requirements.

Jenna wanted to read a few picture books together, then they played a game and ate together. Brianna was getting quite attached to the little girl. She was so full of spunk and personality. *Hopefully, this arrangement will work out and Jenna will still need me as she grows.*

After lunch, Brianna and Jenna stopped by Nathan's office. The door was closed, and Jenna knocked erratically.

"That's enough Jenna," Brianna said. "We don't want to disturb your dad if he's busy."

Brianna turned to leave when she heard Nathan yell, "Come in!"

She heard voices on Nathan's computer as she entered the room. "Oh, if you're busy, we can come back later. It's nothing that can't wait."

Nathan smiled at the two of them and held out his arms to Jenna. Jenna ran to him for a big hug. "Nonsense. I'm muted. This meeting doesn't need me anymore. What can I do for you, ladies?"

Brianna approached Nathan's desk and handed him a piece of paper. "This is the list of school supplies I need for next week and a few things I need for myself. I didn't know if I should use my day off to go into town and pick them up or how you wanted it handled."

Nathan gave the list a cursory glance. "Of course, you're welcome to go to the mainland if you wish. You can arrange for Dugan to take you anytime. This looks like some pretty standard supplies, so if you don't want to go yourself, I can just have Dugan pick these things up with the rest of our weekly supplies. It's up to you."

Brianna considered this. "I think I'll just let Dugan take care of picking them up. I could use the extra day to catch up on a few orders of glass frogs and fish that recently came in. If I can get them all boxed up for Dugan, maybe he can drop them off at the mainland's post office next time he heads to town." She reached her hand out to Jenna. "Thank you so much, Nathan. Come on, Jenna. We need to let your daddy get back to work. Do you want to learn how to use watercolor paints?"

Jenna gave her father one last squeeze and then hurried to Brianna. "Yes! I love to paint! Can I paint a glass frog?"

Holding onto Jenna's hand, Brianna walked out of the office. "Sure you can." Then she turned to Nathan. "I'm looking forward to learning about the island tonight."

Nathan gave Brianna a lopsided grin. Butterflies stirred in her chest every time he looked at her like that, and she desperately tried to squelch the feeling when he replied, "I'm looking forward to it too."

Brianna waited impatiently for the afternoon to tick by. Jenna was tired and jumped from one activity to the next like a jumping beam. It made one afternoon feel like days had passed. *I can't wait to go on my first actual island adventure. From what I've already seen, I can't imagine what other mind-boggling riddles this island holds.*

Suddenly, an idea sparked in her mind. "Jenna, do you want to tell me a story? Can you tell me about your island outside of this compound?"

"Yes! My island is full of so many wonderful things! There are monkeys and trampolines and butterflies and chickens and goats and fruit and vegetables and flowers and bridges and boats... can we go out and have an adventure? I miss the butterflies."

Brianna sighed, not sure how much information she had actually received. "I'm hoping we'll go out soon. Your daddy just needs to show me around first. I can't wait to go on adventures with you. In the meantime, let's have an adventure right here! I think I saw some dress-up clothes in that closet. Do you want to be a pirate or a detective?"

Jenna squinted one of her eyes and shaped her pointer finger into a hook. "Arrrrr!"

***

That evening, they all ate a delicious roasted chicken and vegetables for dinner. *Debbie is such a superb cook. I could get used to this. I know there are prepared meals to heat in the fridge during the week, but it's nothing like her fresh meals. I wonder if Nathan can convince her to cook more than two days a week?* Jenna stayed with Debbie as Brianna went to get ready for her evening adventures.

Nathan urged her to hurry. "We only have a little over two hours of daylight. We want to cover as much ground as possible before it gets dark."

Ignoring Nathan's advice on wearing pants and long sleeves, Brianna set out jean shorts and a tank top on her bed as she changed her clothes for her first island puzzle training session with Nathan. She didn't pack long sleeves since she was moving to a tropical climate and she couldn't see why she would need them. It was so hot and muggy out, but it would be worth it. Her body hummed with excitement. *I'm going to be alone with this handsome, puzzling man. Maybe I'll learn some of his secrets too.*

Brianna applied some lipstick, feeling ridiculous but unable to help wanting to look nice for Nathan. *The only reason I'm going out to the jungle tonight is so I can do a better job watching Jenna. I need to know the secrets of the island so I stop getting trapped in them. How many times will Nathan keep rescuing me before he decides he was better off finding someone else to be Jenna's governess?*

Her mind knew that was all that tonight was about, but her heart thumped like she was going out on her first date. *Uh-oh. I'd better reel in that overactive imagination of mine before I have us married and having a baby together.*

After Brianna dressed, she sprayed herself liberally with bug spray and went down to the courtyard to meet Nathan. Nathan waited for her, wearing jeans and a form-fitted long-sleeved shirt with a backpack slung over one shoulder. A floppy tan hat perched askew on his head. He looked like he had just auditioned for an Indiana Jones film and nailed it. When he saw her, his smile spread across his face, and his eyes twinkled like he was up to something.

"Ready? Tonight, I thought we would cover the area directly around the house so you'll feel confident to take Jenna for a walk whenever you want." Nathan held a water bottle out to her and showed her there was a carabiner hook on it she could hook to one loop on her jean shorts. "Dugan is meeting us to get you set up with our security system first. Then you'll have access to come and go from the compound as you wish. After Dugan is done with you, we'll start where I found you covered in the goo."

Nathan walked over to Dugan. He was still in the court-yard but accessing the control panel next to the gate. Brianna watched as he typed furiously into the control panel and blinked just as furiously into the eye register. "I'm as ready as a frog for a fly, sir," Dugan told Nathan. The head of security seemed to have recovered from his bout with the flu. Dugan turned to Brianna. "I'm going to give you a simple pattern that we're going to use for both your number code and the blinking pattern. It will be as easy as warm butter spreads on bread, and it will get you used to the system. We change the password randomly every few months, so get used to using it now because your next code will have more complexity. Your number and blinking patterns will not coordinate again. Believe me, unless you want to be a trapped polecat, you don't want to input the wrong code. I believe you've already learned a similar lesson from a bit of goo, if I heard correctly?" Dugan furrowed his brow. "For right now, your code is going to be five, three, one, two. So, what you're going to do is enter your code into the keypad here, put your eye up to this retinal scanner, and then blink your code. All you need is a brief two seconds between numbers and you can start blinking the next sequence. Do you know Morse code?"

Wide-eyed, Brianna shook her head. She didn't even know anyone who knew Morse code. She was already feeling a bit out of her depth and she wasn't even out of Nathan's 'birdhouse' yet.

Dugan continued. "Hmm. Learn it. It will make memorizing your blinking patterns easier. In the future, your blinking pattern will differ from your numerical pattern, but we're going to start you out easy. Oh, and if you're ever in trouble and someone is trying to make you open the door under duress, just put in your access code without blinking. That will activate the two portcullis doors to act like a trap, and it will send out a red alert to everyone on the island. Now, why don't you try your code for us while we're right here and can help you?"

Brianna activated the gates to open and close until Dugan seemed satisfied. Then, instead of returning to the house, he took off into the jungle at a jog. Brianna turned to Nathan. "Where is he off to in such a hurry?"

Chapter 11

Watch Your Step

Brianna

The two of them walked towards the goo trap as Nathan responded about Dugan's quick retreat. "Dugan? He was staying in a spare room at the birdhouse for a few days while he was sick, but normally, he stays in a small cottage in the southern part of the island." Nathan looked over at Brianna conspiratorially. "I suspect he ran off to work on a secret project. I've seen him bring in some curious supplies, but when I asked him what it was for, he told me it didn't concern the island's security. He said I shouldn't worry about his personal project interfering with his job competency. I think he compared me to a cat somewhere in that conversation." He made a face showing mock hurt. "I took that as his polite way of saying *butt out*."

They stopped where the goo trap caught Brianna. Someone had perfectly cleared everything of slime, and the plant life looked untouched, as if nothing had happened out of the ordinary just a few days before.

Nathan showed the general area of foliage with his right hand. "Now, I will not hold your hand as much as Dugan did while teaching you about the birdhouse's security. I feel that to understand and remember something, you must figure it out and master it. I lovingly call this trap my mousetrap. Can you figure out how you triggered it the other day?"

Brianna tiptoed towards the low brush. She really didn't want to be covered in goo again. It took days to get rid of that smell. Brianna cautiously looked around for a string, fake plant, or something out of place. "I can't believe there's no sign of the trap anywhere. This entire area was such a sticky mess. I would have thought it would still be everywhere!" Not seeing anything directly on the ground in front of her, Brianna looked up at the trees and tried to identify where the goo had come from.

Nathan replied, "Well, part of Dugan's job in island security is resetting any traps that accidentally get set off. This goo is water soluble, but it could still cause some animals that wander by to get stuck. I suspect Dugan hosed it down within an hour of you tripping it. Then he replanted most of this underbrush so it looked fresh and undisturbed before he reset the trap."

Brianna gently placed her foot into some of the brush and then jumped back as if afraid something was going to grab her. With a cry of triumph, Brianna found a huge pressure plate that was lightly covered with dirt. It took up almost the entire pathway leading to the courtyard. Attached to a tree, pointing towards whoever activated the pressure plate, Brianna spied a nozzle that presumably sprayed a sticky substance all over the trespasser.

Nathan smiled. "Nice work. The trick to this one is to not walk directly on the path from roughly this tree to that tree."

He pointed to two unassuming trees in the jungle that Brianna desperately tried to memorize.

"This trap is like a final warning system before someone comes to the courtyard's main gate. The goo sprays in such an arc that it's impossible to avoid it completely. Could you imagine sneaking into a house when it takes a few minutes to move a few yards?" He covered the pressure plate and waved for her to follow him farther around the compound. Nathan took a few steps into the jungle's underbrush and pointed out an unassuming snare along a small animal path. "We also have hundreds of smaller puzzles and snares and such that aren't set up on our alarm system. They're mainly to slow down and discourage trespassing. I designed all the traps and puzzles so that only humans should trigger them. The goal is to leave the intruder inconvenienced and immobilized, but unscathed."

Nathan frowned and fiddled with the trap before continuing. "Unfortunately, every once in a while, an enterprising bit of wildlife gets stuck. There are also a few of the traps that are touchy enough that a storm will set them off, so Dugan patrols the island daily and makes sure everything is in working order."

They walked around a quarter of the manor when Nathan pointed to a pile of wood that looked like pieces of a fallen tree naturally lying along a pathway after a storm. "Now, why don't you try this one?"

Brianna looked at the logs, scratching her jaw. *I would have never thought twice about this spot being more than it seems.* At first, she thought this island was enough to drive anyone crazy, but some of these puzzles had been pretty fun. If she were at home, she would probably be sitting alone in front of the television right now instead of tackling jungle puzzles. *Does enjoying this make me nutty?*

She carefully picked up and examined the logs. Someone artistically designed them to look like wood. Although slightly corroded, she suspected they were made of metal to make sure that the 'logs' didn't rot.

Brianna ran her hand down the length of one stick and felt a strange symbol. Upon closer inspection, each piece of wood had tiny, one-inch symbols of little men. The stick figures all pointed in different directions. Brianna asked Nathan incredulously, "How in the world do you keep track of all these traps and remember all of their tricks?" Then she knelt by the pathway to see if anything was out of place there.

Nathan replied, "Well, first off, I made most of these traps. I know exactly where I placed them. I know how to get past them, and I know their workarounds in case I accidentally get caught in one. Besides, I love to walk these paths, and these puzzles ensure I stay sharp and am always aware of my surroundings."

Brianna tapped the ground, and nothing happened. She slowly put her weight on the path in front of her. Cautiously, she took one step at a time in increments while trying to study the brush and trees above her at the same time.

She was going excruciatingly slow and looked over at Nathan to see if he was getting annoyed. He stood there with his arms crossed. His face was neutral, not showing a single emotion.

Brianna came to a bottleneck in the path. There was a giant tree to the right and the compound on the left. *If I made a trap, this is where I would put it.* Brianna was so focused on trying to figure out the trap that she let their conversation lapse into silence.

WOOSH!

The ground fell beneath her right foot before she put her full weight on it. In shock, she tried to move backwards but ended up falling on her rump. In front of her gaped an eight-foot deep by six-foot wide hole. Inside the hole was a smooth rubber floor and sides to ensure that no hand-holds would be found for someone who fell in.

Nathan laughed and helped her up. "Don't worry; I installed cushions at the bottom of this trap. You may have been stuck down there, but you wouldn't have gotten hurt. Jenna loves to run around these woods. She knows most of the traps, but I would never put something here that could hurt her. I call this trap the trampoline. Think you can figure out how to get across it?"

Brianna picked up the sticks and brought them to the edge of the trap. She studied the direction that the stick men were pointing and laid them out together on sturdy land to see how they snapped together. After a bit of switching around, she found she could place two sticks side by side and make a zigzagging pathway to cross the pit.

After crossing, Brianna turned to look at Nathan in triumph. To her dismay, he loped across the pathway behind her with the ease of having done it many times before. "Nice work. On this one, my brother decided he would rather just walk around the compound the long way than play with a pile of sticks. Are you ready for one more before calling it a night?"

Brianna realized the sun was much lower in the sky but dismissed it. Feeling empowered because she had just bested the last two traps, she confidently replied, "You won't stump me!"

Nathan turned to her. "All right then. Let's make a bet. If you can complete the next puzzle before the sun goes down, then I will make you dessert tonight. If you can't complete it, then you will make something for me."

"You're on!" Brianna replied and put out her hand so they could shake on it. Nathan made eye contact as his firm hand enveloped hers, and he held on slightly longer than was necessary. Brianna's hand tingled when he finally removed his. She broke eye contact first and mumbled, "Well, we'd better get moving, then. My clock is ticking."

Nathan led her to a rock outcropping close to a back entrance to the estate. Nathan pointed to the back door. "This entryway works very similarly to the gates at the front of the compound. There's a retinal scanner and keypad."

He turned towards the large rock formation. "Above this is where our center of operations is located. I'll show you around there more on another outing, but today your goal is to get inside."

Brianna looked at the normal-looking rocks and turned to Nathan. "This isn't some kind of trick, is it? Making a bet that I'm doomed to fail just so I'll make you cookies?"

Nathan laughed. "No. It is tricky, but it's not a trick. You have everything you need right in front of you." Nathan stood back out of the way, grinning from ear to ear as he watched her get to work.

Brianna approached the rock cautiously but was losing hope. Already the sky was dimming. She felt all around the rock and found nothing out of place. She searched in the brush next to the rock. On the left side, mostly covered by some high brush, she found words engraved in the stone.

The eagle, the greater wax moth, the bear, the catfish, the manatee

The greatest of all are these.

Below the phrase was a keypad to punch in letters or numbers. Brianna pondered how a moth and catfish could be that great or what they had to do with the other animals when the last bit of daylight faded to night.

Nathan frowned and pursed his lips together. "You honestly had little time to figure that one out. We can come back later and try it again. You don't have to make me cookies."

Never wanting to be the first to back down, Brianna insisted, "No. A deal is a deal. I knew how late it was when I agreed, so I'll make us the best melt-in-your-mouth cookies you have ever had."

He led her through the back door and towards the kitchen and helped Brianna find the supplies for chocolate chip cookies. She mixed up a simple cookie recipe and put them in the oven. They laughed about their adventures that day as they waited.

Nathan told Brianna about a few of the times when he had accidentally gotten stuck in his own traps. They opened a bottle of wine and enjoyed the sweet aroma of freshly baked cookies. She sat across from the handsome man thoroughly enjoying herself, and Brianna couldn't think of a more perfect ending to a perfect day.

Suddenly, the fire alarm in the kitchen went off, and they smelled smoke. Brianna rushed to the oven and pulled out her burnt cookies. She was so engrossed talking to Nathan that she had forgotten to set a timer.

Moments later, Dugan burst into the room. His sides were heaving as if he had just run halfway across the island. He was sporting his maroon robe and held a large, red fire extinguisher. "Well, I'll be a granny without a cookie. I see smoke. Where's the fire?"

Nathan looked at Brianna and the cookies. With a straight face, he said, "I guess I didn't win that bet after all."

Chapter 12

Nathan's Falling

Nathan

Nathan tried to focus but ended up putting his head in his hands. He had to approve the launches of both the new board game and video game coming out next month. There were so many details to get lined up and ready for each launch, and his secretary was on maternity leave. Hundreds of unread emails piled up in his inbox, and he felt like he had work heaped up to his eyeballs.

I wonder what Jenna and Brianna are doing right now?

He had a meeting in two hours with his brother and father about some updates that would increase productivity at Riley Games. He needed to get them on board; lately those two had been voting against his ideas, fearing change.

His brother had such a hard time taking things seriously, that he lost interest whenever Nathan tried to do a long presentation. Luckily, he was quick enough that he could pick up the idea with a few well- made visuals. Maybe he should make Jackson some graphs to show the projected increase in profitability. *I bet Brianna could get Jackson on board. She's pretty and could probably just bat her eye lashes to get Jackson to do whatever she wanted.*

Lately, it seemed like everything was bringing his mind back to Brianna. He remembered her standing against the backdrop of the jungle, completely covered in slime. She looked shocked and uncomfortable but took it as a surprisingly good sport. Nathan stood up from his desk and looked out the window.

The woman in his thoughts was walking out of the courtyard with Jenna. It looked like they were going out of the birdhouse for a walk. Nathan watched the two laughing and running around. When he saw Brianna this morning, bug bites and scratches covered her exposed skin. He tried to warn her to wear long sleeves on their island adventures, but she didn't listen. It looked like she was one of those people who needed to learn their lessons the hard way. She must have been horribly itchy and uncomfortable, but he never heard a single complaint from her.

I wonder what this island must seem like to Brianna. I've lived here almost my whole life. To me, this is the most comfortable place in the world. Is it scary and intimidating to her?

Nathan thought back to their first night exploring the puzzles around his house. She may have a stubborn streak, but that also meant that her perseverance had gotten her through all the challenges he set before her. She had beaten his puzzles, or sometimes she had found a workaround to get past a trap. Either way, it had been more of a pleasure than he had imagined showing her around the outside of the compound and watching her uncover his secrets.

She had looked amazing in her short shorts and tight tank top. There was more than one occasion where he felt the urge to take her in his arms and feel what it would be like to kiss her plump lips. She was smart and funny, and he found he couldn't wait until he saw her again. He'd been surprised by just how much he had enjoyed his time with her.

She fit into his world so seamlessly. Although, he was thinking he made a big mistake asking her to be his employee instead of asking her on a date. As an employee, she was off-limits, and he had to keep his hands off, no matter how captivating she was. Employee and boss relationships never worked because of the power imbalance, and that wouldn't be fair to her. If he hadn't asked her to stay as his employee, she would have been back in Ohio, so a relationship with her was doomed either way. He needed to accept that and stop mooning after her like a love-struck teenager.

He watched the two figures stop at the trap his daughter had named the trampoline. He watched as Jenna purposely activated it, and Brianna jumped up with her arms outstretched, trying to stop her. She missed.

When he first installed the trampoline trap, he made sure that Jenna knew how the trap worked inside and out, but he hadn't mentioned it to his brother Jackson. The trampoline was elastic enough that if someone fell into the hole—or jumped as he watched Jenna do—they bounced like a trampoline on the first jump. When Jackson was taking a walk with him and Jenna around the compound, one misstep sent him tumbling and bouncing. The look of shock on his face was priceless as Jenna jumped in squealing with laughter until each subsequent jump had less and less bounce and the hard rubber floor didn't give at all anymore. It was worth it, but he had to keep on his toes because his brother was trying to get him back by capturing him in one of his traps ever since.

Nathan pulled his binoculars off a shelf nearby so he could get a closer look at the spectacle below. Brianna had a branch extended into the pit and was yelling something at Jenna. Jenna ignored her and bounced away. When the floor no longer bounced, Jenna tapped her foot in the sequence he had taught her. The floor rose, depositing Jenna right up to a slack jawed Brianna. Nathan wondered if Brianna would be mad now that she realized he hadn't taught her all of his tricks the other night.

He wished he could hear what was being said down there. Jenna jumped back into the trampoline trap. Brianna put her hands on her head like she was ready to pull her hair out. *Poor Brianna.* He knew his daughter could be a handful, but it was a relief to see how good Brianna was with her. How much she cared. That was the main reason he had never gotten Jenna a nanny before. He hadn't found someone he trusted to leave his daughter with. Until now.

Dugan rapped on his open office door. Nathan set down the binoculars and addressed him.

"Good morning, Dugan. Thank you for coming to see me. Come and sit. I have something I want to discuss with you."

Dugan walked into the office and shut the door behind him. The burly man engulfed the seat he sat in and looked over at Nathan. "What can I do for you, sir? How is your new employee doing with Jenna?"

Nathan sat down in his own chair. "Brianna is doing well. Jenna is flourishing with her."

Nathan pulled his attention back to the man in front of him. "I'm sure it will take a while for her to get her footing here. What I called you to talk about was an incident with the gate the other day. Did you know Brianna lost track of Jenna for a bit the day she activated the sticky trap?"

Dugan bowed his head and spoke with a slight smile. "I was watching the security footage in the control center when I saw your slime hit her. Poor girl. Like a sheep walking into a lion's den. It caught her head-on. She squealed louder than a pig slapped on his hindquarters. I half-expected to be taking her home that very night, but she has more spunk than I thought."

Nathan smiled at the comparison. He would have to review that footage himself. "Yes, that's the incident I'm referring to. Well, the reason Brianna was out there in the first place was because she said the main gate to the courtyard was open. Was there some kind of malfunction that I should know about?"

Dugan looked at the floor and grimaced. "I'm sorry, sir. That's my fault. While I brought in a few loads of supplies, I programmed it to stay open. I must have forgotten to shut it again afterwards. I'll delete that program and ensure no one can leave the door open indefinitely again."

Nathan nodded. "That'll work. I understand that this is a big island with a lot of upkeep. I know Thomas, the new hire, has been helping you with the secret garden, but you still have a lot on your plate. We can hire an assistant to help you with supplies or day-to-day security. Then you can be more vigilant in keeping out unwanted trespassers, and it would give you the ability to take a few days off every once in a while."

Dugan shook his head. "No, sir. I have all the help I need with Suzie. She's my sweater on a wintry day." They'd had many similar conversations to this one in the past. Nathan strongly believed that Dugan enjoyed his solitude and was happy setting up traps to keep away as many outsiders as possible. He agreed but thought he also needed a large enough staff to take proper care of things and keep an eye out for trespassers too. Dugan was just spread too thin.

Dugan's jaw hardened as he replied with renewed determination. "Don't worry, sir. You know my gal, Suzie and I have this island under control and constant surveillance. You are my number one priority. I'll keep you and Jenna safe from anything that comes lurking around."

"... and Brianna," Nathan added. "As my employee, she deserves the same treatment as anyone else on this island."

Dugan nodded. "Of course, sir. I didn't mean to exclude her." Dugan paused for a few moments. When Nathan had nothing further to add, Dugan pressed on. "Also, sir, lately this island feels like a raccoon getting into a garbage can. There have been an unusual number of traps being sprung. At first, I thought little about it. You know how the monkeys are always triggering things and getting into trouble. It's just... while I have been resetting traps, I noticed that some of them looked like they were cut with a knife. Do you mind asking Miss Brianna not to wander around in areas you haven't shown her to navigate safely yet?"

Nathan frowned. "I'll talk to her. Although I don't believe she's been out wandering around at all since she got caught in the sticky mousetrap. It's possible that the traps were cut from the trespassing poacher, too. Is there anything else you need to discuss?" When Dugan shook his head, Nathan shuffled a few papers on his desk. "Well, thank you for coming down. I appreciate all you do for us. If you need anything, just let me know."

Dugan nodded and quietly let himself out of the room.

Nathan opened an email. From the bullet points of potential issues coming up, it looked like his Vice President was coming unhinged. The new Pirate Quest board games for their launch came in, and all of them had wooden dice imported from Brazil that were moldy. *That's what Jackson gets for trying to cut costs.*

He sat pondering if they should throw out the entire game to avoid contamination and how he could salvage this kick-off that he had already spent so much time and money on. Nathan couldn't help that everything triggered his mind back to the one thing he wanted to think about. *Brianna seemed to enjoy playing games.*

Nathan made a phone call. He desperately tried to focus on work. Putting out fires always took all of his attention. "Hey Dad, we need to talk about pushing back the game launch for Pirate Quest."

A gruff voice answered him. "We have a lot of money riding on that launch. I'm sure you will figure out how to make it work on time, you always do. I'm glad you called, I needed to talk to you anyways. Jenna told me she has a new governess that you spend a lot of time with. Son, I better not be reading too much into that relationship. I don't want to see you make the same mistakes I made with your mother. If you're feeling lonely, go find some woman in town to warm your bed. Even a fling with your employee would be a human resources nightmare. I'd fire you before I let you put the company in jeopardy."

Nathan ran his hand through his hair. Why did everything always come back to Brianna? "Dad, it's nothing like that. I needed help with Jenna and I hired a nice woman to take care of her. Yes, I am showing her around the island a bit, but that's just so she can safely take Jenna out without them getting trapped in a net. There is nothing romantic going on between us."

After hearing a hrumph on the other side of the line, his father said. "Fine. Now when do I get to see Jenna next?" No matter how tough he was on his sons, Nathan's father always seemed to have time to dote on his granddaughter. He wanted them to have a good relationship, but he had to admit it made him a bit jealous sometimes.

Nathan sighed. "We will be over later this week for dinner. Jenna has a painting she wants to show you. I'll message you the date after I get this Pirate Quest mess figured out."

"Sounds good, son. You're a smart guy, I should have known you would be wiser than to mess around with an employee. See you soon." Nathan's father hung up after as much as an apology as he ever gave.

An hour later, Nathan finished delegating tasks to curtail his company's latest mess. The company was already going to lose thousands over this debacle, but he was trying to manage things so they wouldn't lose more. Then he heard a soft, tentative tap on the door.

Nathan ran his hand through his hair to relieve some of his workday stress. He called out, "Come in. The door is un-locked."

Like a breath of fresh air, Brianna entered the room and stood before Nathan's desk. She smelled like his favorite flower, Bird of Paradise. "Is this a good time? I can come back." Her eyes darted around the room and landed on his face, looking at him inquiringly, waiting for an answer. He felt electricity shift between their eyes. He didn't want to look away. *I feel like I'm ready to offer her half of my kingdom. I need to get myself under control.*

Nathan immediately answered, "Sure, come in. Just trying to fix a few work emergencies in here. How is your day going? Is everything going well with Jenna?" He heard Jenna squeal in delight from the hallway.

Brianna looked over her shoulder. "We built an obstacle course to burn off some energy. She loves it. If you have a few moments, I wanted to talk about Jenna's toy room."

Nathan stood up and got himself a drink from a mini refrigerator hidden under one of his bookshelves. He offered Brianna a drink too, but she shook her head. "Okay, shoot. What about Jenna's toy room?"

"Well, when you hired me, you said that we could get whatever supplies we needed for schooling. I don't know the last time you were in her toy room, but it's kind of a mess. It's full of noisy electronic toys that Jenna says she doesn't play with. Half the things have dead batteries, and the other half has broken pieces."

Nathan nodded his head in agreement. "Yes, I meant it too. Let me know what you would like to do in there and we will make it happen. I want the best for Jenna."

Brianna smiled broadly, but it soon shrank to a sheepish grin as she laid a packet of papers on his desk. *What exactly did I just agree to?*

"I jotted down some ideas and they kind of snowballed. I thought maybe we could turn the toy room into more of a child-led educational playroom. It would have low shelves that Jenna could reach and put her toys away independently. The shelves would be full of toys that develop curiosity, creativity, and free play. There would be a small children's library with a reading nook and art supplies. It would become more than just a toy room, but also our schoolroom."

Brianna opened the packet of papers she had laid out and pointed to a page with graphs on it. "Here are some price estimates and diagrams of what I was thinking. I know it's expensive, so we don't have to do any of this..." Her words trailed off, waiting for his answer.

Nathan picked up the packet and flipped through the pages. *This is impressive. This proposal is more thorough than the work that some of my veteran employees turn in at Riley's Games. There are even graphs showing projected educational returns on investment. When that company didn't hire her for the Human Resources job, they really missed a gem.*

"I think this looks great. It looks like you put a lot of time and thought into this. I will look at it more in-depth and we can talk about it after dinner."

Brianna's smile brightened the room before she left. *That smile makes me want to agree to whatever is in this packet of papers, regardless of the costs. It's not like I can't afford it.* Even with the launch setback, he was still running a multi-million-dollar company.

After dinner, Brianna would probably go back to creating more of her hand-blown glass animal baubles. She said she was trying to build up her stock. He wouldn't have been surprised if she'd asked to take some time off and sell them at a fair again soon. Nathan pictured the delicate dolphin figurine she had shown him. She had a talent.

He needed to schedule their next adventure soon. He really enjoyed his time with her and wanted to go out with her again. In his free time, he had even briefly considered adding some more riddles to the island just so she would have to stay out with him longer.

He was worse than a love-addled schoolboy. He needed to get his mind off of this intriguing woman. It was a bad idea. She was his employee, and he was her boss.

She was delightful, alluring, and great with Jenna. She would be perfect... Nathan's spirits plummeted as he remembered what bothered him about Brianna's background check. *Maybe if I get her to trust me enough, she'll feel comfortable enough to explain about the man in those pictures.*

Chapter 13

Monkey Trouble

Brianna

"Argh!" Brianna screamed. A small object hurtled into her chest abruptly, awakening her from her dreams. She scooted back in her bed, trying to figure out what was going on. *Will I ever get a night of uninterrupted sleep again?*

"Good morning, Brianna! What fun things are we going to do today? I'm hungry! Do you think we could have pancakes for breakfast? I had a dream last night that Daddy built me a house out of giant pancakes and the three of us lived inside. Whenever we got hungry, we would take a bite of the wall!" Jenna bounced on Brianna's bed while her stream of consciousness exploded from her mouth. This kind of start to Brianna's day was making her head hurt.

I was having a really pleasant dream about a certain handsome somebody. I want to curl back up in my covers and sleep just a little longer.

Brianna sighed and turned to Jenna. "Good morning, sweetheart. I'm glad you slept well. Give me a few minutes to get dressed and I'll meet you in the kitchen. We can discuss our day there. Pancakes sound great!"

Brianna forced herself to smile at the little girl before she promptly raced out of the room in the same whirlwind she had entered.

Coffee. I will get a coffee machine for my room. That will make everything better.

During breakfast, Brianna and Jenna made chocolate chip pancakes together and discussed her toy room while they ate. Brianna nonchalantly threw out some ideas that had gotten approved by Nathan. "You know, Jenna, if you help me clear out the broken toys and the ones you don't like anymore, then we would have space to put some shelves in that room. We can put some new toys on them you'll want to play with."

Brianna watched Jenna intently to judge how she was feeling about the idea. The little girl didn't show too much emotion until she heard the words 'new toys'. Then she lit up. Brianna continued explaining her vision. "The shelves would be nice and low. They would be easy for you to get toys out and play with."

Jenna's little body wiggled, humming with excitement at the promise of a new playroom. "We could also make one corner a reading nook, where we could cuddle up and read together. It would have a bookshelf of your own books, just like your daddy has in his office. Then we could put a table in the middle of the room so you can color and paint, and we can do fun crafts together. What do you think about that? Would you be able to help me?"

Jenna clutched her hands together and squealed. "Really? I love to paint! And I could have my own books about princesses!

Daddy could come in and read to me, and he could borrow some of my books too!" Jenna's excitement died down a little as she considered her next question "Do I have to have swords on my bookshelf?"

Brianna laughed. "You only need swords on your shelves if you want them there. For your special room, you can help me decorate it however you want. We could paint a giant tree behind the book nook or have the room look like outer space. I know you love your princesses. We could do a castle and princesses on the wall if you wanted."

Jenna looked at her questioningly. "Purple dragon riding princesses?" When Brianna nodded, Jenna jumped up and yelled, "Yippee!" Then she took off, presumably to the toy room to begin the process of weeding through her toys.

"Wait!" Brianna yelled to Jenna, but she was too slow. She quickly put their dirty dishes into the dishwasher and chased after her. They had a full day ahead of them working in that room, and she wanted to be at her best for her upcoming night out with Nathan.

***

That night, after dinner, Brianna had a few minutes before she was supposed to meet with Nathan. She sat at the desk in her room and did a quick internet search on the riddle she had found and left unsolved a few nights ago. A generic eagle, a specific type of moth, a manatee... what in the world could these creatures have in common? She wrote as much of the riddle as she could remember. She might have to go back and write the rest of it down during one of her free evenings.

Brianna put on long pants, a long-sleeved shirt, and a bandana. She had learned her lesson about not being prepared last time. Now she was ready. She picked up a small backpack with useful things she found around the compound. She had a pen and paper, some string, a pocket knife, a towel, a water bottle, and a timer.

That evening, Nathan greeted Brianna and explained his plan for showing her around the island. "Last time we went puzzle exploring, we covered the area directly around the compound. Tonight, we will tackle the northern part of the island. My house is on the north-eastern part of the island, so we really only have a few miles to cover. That will leave us a night to travel the south-eastern part of the island, a night to explore the middle of the island, and another night to adventure slightly into the western part of the island where my dad and brother live. Ready?"

Brianna smiled. She felt much more prepared than last time. "Let's go!"

The two walked away from Nathan's birdhouse and into the jungle. It rained like a fine mist. Nathan pulled a light rain jacket out of his backpack and offered it to Brianna. "Here, put this on. There's no point in both of us getting wet."

Stubbornly, Brianna shook her head. "No, I'm fine. The rain is very refreshing after a hot day."

Nathan shrugged and put the rain jacket on himself. Within five minutes, Brianna's clothing became drenched. All the trees and rocks seemed to smell fresher and look more vibrant than normal. A different array of animals and birds hooted from the trees. A lot of the monkeys, birds, and insects were hiding from the rain, but there were more frogs jumping around than she had ever seen before.

"Eek!" Brianna squealed as an enormous snake slithered out of the path. It was so well camouflaged that it had been impossible to see until it moved. A few yards later, she yelped as she slipped on a wet rock. She bumped into a tree that dropped even more rain down upon her head.

It's not like I could get any wetter or muddier than I already am. I know I'm not the most graceful person, but this is ridiculous even by my standards. The beauty of this wet jungle is deceiving. I feel like I'm trying to walk on a slip and slide. Brianna began following Nathan where he couldn't see her. She felt it would be slightly less embarrassing when she fell in the mud again.

Nathan paused and turned around to face Brianna. Water dripped down his raincoat and from his exposed nose. "Are you doing all right back there? We can always head back to the compound and cover this area another night."

Brianna's jeans were chafing her legs. Instead of feeling that initial relief from the heat, she was now shivering. Not wanting him to think she was some weak girly girl, she held her head high. "No, I'm fine. We're already out here and I'm ready for some riddles." She stared at Nathan with a challenge in her eyes. "Are you afraid of a little rain?"

Nathan gave an exasperated sigh and then led the way again. He stopped at an odd-looking artificial tree. The tree had four golden rings with four symbols spread across each ring. Brianna looked at the symbols.

The first ring seemed to have a food theme with different fruit circling it. There was a banana, apple, pear, and strawberry. The second ring had different animals: a monkey, frog, cat, and a bear. Symbols of people circled the third ring. There was a man, woman, baby, and child. Brianna ran her fingers over the fourth ring. This ring had shapes. A diamond, circle, square, and triangle. Brianna twisted the ring. It smoothly moved independently of the other rings until it clicked into place again a quarter of the way around the tree.

The rain came down harder, so Brianna shielded her eyes with her hands while she studied the symbols. She desperately looked for a pattern. She tried a few combinations and nothing happened.

I'm not sure how long I will last out here. Maybe we should go back. She shivered again, unable to hide it from Nathan this time. Nathan unzipped his jacket. "Here, take my coat. Don't be stubborn."

Brianna set her jaw and shook her head. "No, thank you. I've got this." Nathan cocked his head and pursed his lips but zipped his jacket back up.

Nostrils flaring, she set back to work. *How dare he act like I'm the insufferable one! That settles it. I'm staying out here and solving these puzzles, no matter what it takes. I will not accept his raincoat, even if I get pneumonia out here.*

Finally, she set the first ring to apple, the second ring to bear, the third ring to child, and the fourth ring to diamond. When the last ring clicked into place, the entire tree began to rotate, slowly. The tune of the alphabet song played in Brianna's mind as the tree spun faster and faster.

Brianna stood still and looked all around herself. Her mind whirled. *I wonder what kind of magnificent thing this tree does? From the previous puzzles I've seen, it will do something im-pressive.* She watched as the tree picked up speed. She watched intently and looked for clues to tell if the tree would open, sink into the ground, or go flying off into the air.

The rings stopped spinning and ended in a random order. The tree stood still. Nothing happened. Frowning, Brianna turned to Nathan with one eyebrow raised.

"It's a two-parter," Nathan answered before she could voice her question. "Think of this part as the key or lock that allows you to solve the next part."

Brianna rolled her eyes, the effect lost in the rain. Shivering, she sharply said, "Really, all of that for nothing? Where to next, Nathan?" The two of them continued down the path until they came to a large tree that had fallen across their way.

Nathan put up his hand, presumably to run it through his hair. Touching his wet hood, he lowered it again. "I'm going to have to send Dugan over here to fix this one." Nathan kneeled down and examined where a few ropes were attached to a log. "Looks like the rope broke. I think Dugan must be overworked. He knows how quickly things can rot out here. Although, something could have chewed through it too. It's hard to tell in these conditions." Nathan stood up and turned to Brianna. "Well, between the weather and this trap being out of order, I suggest we call it a night. You're outright shivering now. You won't be much good to Jenna if I let you get sick."

Brianna saw a movement out of the corner of her eye and only half-heard Nathan's last words. *It's a tiny monkey. The poor thing.* Instead of hopping into the trees to get away from her, it thrashed on the ground, trying to use a leg that wouldn't work.

"Oh, you poor injured baby. It looks like you broke your leg. Did you fall when the rope broke?" The monkey unsuccessfully tried to hide under a large leaf. Nathan came over to see what had caught Brianna's attention.

He looked down at the small creature. "How unfortunate for that little fella. I'm sorry he got the brunt of a faulty trap. We try to minimize this kind of thing, but accidents happen. Brianna, why don't you head back? I'll take care of this."

Brianna narrowed her eyes as she looked at him. "Take care of this like an act of mercy or take care of this like help that poor little monkey?"

Nathan didn't answer.

Without a word, Brianna unzipped her backpack and took out a towel. It was wet from rain soaking into her backpack, but it was the best she had. She went over to the monkey and used the towel to scoop him up gently and hold him against her chest. She did her best to leave his injured foot untouched, but the monkey cried piteously and struggled in her arms.

Nathan came up behind her and handed her his raincoat. "Here, this will at least keep the rain off him. If you have any chance of saving him, we need to get him warm and dry right away. In my workshop, I have some small wooden scraps that you could use as a brace. We have some medical tape in the first aid kit that you could use to wrap it too."

Brianna covered the monkey with Nathan's coat, making sure he had an air hole through the fabric. Out of the rain and getting warm, the monkey finally settled down.

Brianna looked over at Nathan. "Thank you for the raincoat. I appreciate you offering it." Brianna had to admit she felt a bit of satisfaction watching the vexation cross Nathan's face as the rain quickly drenched his clothing too.

Brianna held her package protectively close and looked at Nathan. "Any idea what to feed a baby monkey?"

Chapter 14

Dr. Doolittle in Training

Brianna

"Please! Please! Please! I promise I will be really careful when I hold him," Jenna begged.

Brianna shook her head. "I'm sorry, Jenna. This monkey is hurt. We have to give him lots of space and rest. He might not survive even if he had professional care, and we've never healed a monkey before. We just need to do the best we can to care for him and leave him in God's hands."

After drying and splinting the monkey's broken leg, Brianna spent all night researching the habits and diet of her new friend. Her research had allowed her to determine that he wasn't exactly a baby anymore, but probably still young. This was a good thing because he was old enough to eat solid foods.

Brianna read how baby monkeys needed their mother's milk and cow's milk could cause him digestive issues. *I can only imagine how odd I would look trying to catch and express milk from a wild monkey mother. I'll be thankful to just look for grubs.*

Brianna found a large tote that she made into a temporary monkey hospital. She made him a soft bed, made sure that he had water, and put a bowl of various fruits, leaves, seeds, nuts, and vegetables inside for him to eat at will. Finally, she put air holes in the tub's top, then Jenna promised to help her hunt for insects to feed him that afternoon.

After getting their new friend settled, Brianna told Jenna that it was time to let the little monkey rest. They went to the toy room to pack up stuff she was too old for, didn't play with, or didn't like.

"Can we keep the monkey?" Jenna's eyes were open wide as she batted her eyelashes. "He's so cute! I love him."

Brianna looked over at Jenna. She didn't want to break the little girl's heart, but she didn't want to give her false hope, either. "Jenna, sweetie. The monkey is a wild creature and will need to be returned to the wild once his leg is better. That's where he belongs and that is where he will be happiest, with his family." Brianna took a deep breath and tried to prepare her in case the worst happened. "Also, we are trying our best to take care of the monkey, but he might not make it. He was freezing and wet when we brought him home. I can't be sure that he doesn't have more injuries on the inside that might be hurting him. We will just have to pray and wait."

After a moment's thought, Brianna added, "If you want, I can make you a tiny glass monkey. I can make it look just like him, and you can keep that forever and ever to remember the little monkey. Would that help?"

With little enthusiasm, Jenna mumbled, "Okay" and glumly went back to work.

They worked for over an hour when Jenna needed a break. They had a little snack and then she picked up the picture book, *Dr. Doolittle.* "Can we read now?"

Brianna agreed. "That sounds like a great idea. We've worked so hard packing up boxes. Doesn't this room look so much better already?" Jenna nodded, and the two of them cuddled up on Jenna's play couch and enjoyed the story.

After they finished reading, Jenna turned to Brianna. "Can we name the monkey you found Chee Chee? Like in the book?"

Brianna smiled. She loved when Jenna connected with their stories. "I think that's a wonderful idea. He looks like a Chee Chee to me. We're trying to make him all better, like Dr. Doolittle did with the monkeys in the book. Want to go check on Chee Chee?"

"Yes!" Jenna squealed as she darted off of the couch.

Brianna called after her. "Wait, Jenna! We have to be calm and quiet when we go to check on him. We don't want to scare him. Can you pretend like you're a little mouse with me? We'll tiptoe into my room and check on Chee Chee without making a sound."

Jenna and Brianna were tiptoeing down the hallway as Nathan came around the bend. He raised his eyebrows and broke out into a half grin. With a playfully suspicious tone, he asked, "What sort of mischief are you two getting into?"

Brianna smiled as Jenna held her finger up to her mouth and whispered. "Shhhh. We're going to check on Chee Chee, and we have to be quiet as mice. If you can be a mouse, you can come too."

Nathan whispered back conspiratorially, "I'm kind of big to be a mouse, but I can try my best. Who is Chee Chee? Is that one of your stuffed animals we're looking for?"

A little too loudly, Jenna replied, "No, silly!" Remembering herself, she continued to whisper. "Chee Chee is the tiny hurt monkey Brianna found. We're going to check on him and then go outside to catch some bugs for him to eat."

Nathan rubbed his belly and replied softly, "Yum. Bugs sound delicious for a monkey meal. Do you mind if I tag along, Brianna? I promise to be quiet as a mouse, too."

The three compadres snuck the rest of the way down the hallway. Brianna quietly opened the door and didn't even turn on the lights. They tiptoed as quietly as they could up to the tote containing Chee Chee. Brianna had never heard Jenna this quiet since she first got to the island.

Jenna gasped. The lid was slightly askew, and there was a deep red liquid oozing down one side of the tote. Chee Chee was gone. Jenna puckered up as Nathan pulled her aside until they figured out what was going on.

Brianna went to investigate and chuckled. "Don't worry; the red stuff on the side of the bin is just strawberry juice. My window and door have been closed since we left him in here. The little guy has to be hiding somewhere."

The trio moved around the room carefully. Jenna climbed under the bed to check, and Nathan went to look in the bathroom. Brianna groaned as she neared her dresser. There were about a dozen of her glass animal figurines knocked on the ground, broken.

She picked up the glass. "Ugh. I should have monkey-proofed my room. I didn't think the little guy would be up and about so soon." After cleaning up the mess, Brianna investigated the top of her dresser. The arrangement of the rest of the figurines appeared undisturbed. She had an entire collection of animals up there. She liked to display and enjoy her work while she built up enough inventory to sell at a fair. It looked like she would have to box them up for the time being.

Amidst the remaining glass figurines on Brianna's dresser was a soft blue shirt. A few days ago, when she and Nathan had gone on their last island adventure, she had snagged it on a thorn. She sat the shirt up on the dresser in a pile to mend whenever she had some free time. Lying in the center of the shirt, the little monkey lay fast asleep with part of the fabric pulled over him like a blanket.

Brianna whispered loud enough for Nathan and Jenna to hear her and beckoned them toward her. "I found him. Come and look quietly. Remember, be like a mouse." Nathan and Jenna made exaggerated tiptoe movements as they made their way towards the monkey.

Jenna sighed and whispered, "Aww, he's so cute!" Then she chirped and chattered in a way that reminded Brianna vaguely of the monkeys speaking to one another in the jungle. Brianna cocked her head as she looked over at Jenna.

"Don't worry," she assured them. "I speak monkey now. I told him to have sweet dreams. He can stay with us as long as he wants."

Chapter 15

Spelunking

Brianna

Brianna patted Chee Chee's head. She made sure he had plenty of food and water before she left for the next few hours. She gave him a few extra strawberries too. Even though he made a mess while eating them, they seemed to be his favorite. She secured the lid of the tote with a large, heavy tabletop book about the Earth. She didn't want to find him climbing on her dresser again.

It excited Brianna to go back and try out the puzzle on the cave door that led to the control room. After the burnt cookie incident, she had researched eagles, the greater wax moth, bears, catfish, and manatees. After many notes, she finally found a commonality. She was eager to find out if she was right.

The little ball of energy that was Jenna was busy playing with Nathan and telling him about her day. *It's my time now.* Brianna sighed in relief. *I'm done for the day, and I have the whole evening ahead of me, all by myself.* Brianna quickly dressed for jungle adventures, filled her water bottle, and threw her backpack over her back. She was ready to go.

Outside the cave door, Brianna moved to the left side of the rock and ran her fingers over the words she had found engraved there.

The eagle, the greater wax moth, the bear, the catfish, the manatee

The greatest of all are these

Then she looked at the keypad below the words and punched in the letters to spell the word 'senses'. These animals all had incredible senses. The keypad flashed green, and the stone door slid to the right.

Brianna entered the cavern, looking around suspiciously for trip wires or alarm lasers. She saw a stalactite reaching from the ceiling that nearly reached a small pool of crystal-clear water. There were crevices aplenty, but it was hard to see the farther corners of the cavern where the natural light didn't reach.

Brianna walked over to the pool and saw there was an object sitting at the bottom. It looked like a statue of a cat with large teeth. Maybe a saber-tooth tiger? Brianna reached her hand into the water, and the hairs on her back stuck up as she felt how cold it was. She realized it was a lot deeper than it looked, so she pulled her arm back out and wandered around to investigate further.

In the back of the cave, a stone door covered the entrance to the rest of the cave system. Paint depicted stick figures of people hunting animals, like old cave paintings. The only difference was, these people were using more technologically advanced equipment than one usually saw in cave paintings. At the top of the picture was a large, very detailed saber-tooth tiger. He stood on a cliff overlooking all the less detailed people and animal figures. Brianna looked up, and sure enough, there was a ledge above where she stood. She stood on her tiptoes and saw four small indents on the ledge. Someone had purposely chiseled them.

Brianna went back to the saber-tooth tiger and tried to think of a way to get the statue out without jumping in for a swim. That water was icy, and she really didn't want to walk through the cave soaking wet. She went outside and got a stick. She tried to nudge the statue up the wall, but it was too heavy.

Brianna got out a piece of rope from her backpack and tied one end into a loop. She tried to loop it around the cat's neck, but the weight of the statue and slight current in the water made it impossible. A few small fish nibbled at her rope, and she noticed an almost completely white crayfish moved along the bottom of the pool when her rope touched it.

She really didn't want to go in there, but it looked like she was out of options. Brianna huffed as she looked around again. She noticed that, on the door, one of the stick figures had an exaggerated enormous foot that seemed to step on a small mound of dirt on the ground. At first, Brianna had assumed it was an anthill. *It does kind of look like the surrounding stalagmites. Could one of these stalagmites be a button in disguise?*

Brianna examined all the stalagmites. She remembered a cave tour she took a few years ago where the guide told everyone how the oils on their skin could damage the cave's formations, so she was very careful not to touch anything.

After careful inspection, she noticed that one stalagmite looked less solid than the others. She experimentally poked it with her finger, and it moved like some sort of gelatin. Brianna stomped on it like the cave dweller in the cave painting. Immediately, a hatch in the pool opened, draining all the water and fish out of the pool. She lifted her foot. The hatch shut, and the pool filled again, slowly but steadily.

Brianna walked over to the pool and saw there were foot grooves carved into the inside of the rock on the pool, sort of like a ladder. By the time she had finished examining how to get down into the pool, there was already a foot or more of water covering the bottom. Swiftly, Brianna stomped on the fake stalagmite again, and then climbed down into the pool as fast as she could.

It was slippery, but she got down without falling. Brianna stepped around the crayfish, who displayed its claws in self-defense. Brianna could feel cold water seep into her shoes as the pool filled up again. She picked up the statue—it had more heft to it than she had expected—and shoved it into her backpack and quickly climbed back out.

Surely Nathan and Dugan don't go through all of this trouble every time they want to go to their control center?

Brianna glanced down at her wet shoes and socks, then she shrugged. She had already made it this far and didn't want to give up now.

She noticed the door's frame was cemented directly into the rock wall. It was odd to see the mixture of an old, natural cave wall beside modern technology.

She gently placed the feet of the saber-tooth tiger statue into the four indents on the shelf by the door. The door clicked, and she slowly opened it, expecting to see computers on the other side. Nothing was in front of her except inky blackness.

Brianna stuck her hand through the door and a motion-activated light turned on. She stepped through the door and another light illuminated. Brianna cautiously started down the cave's corridor with only a few feet of light showing directly around her. *This is really creepy. Maybe I should have waited to do this with Nathan. Should I head back?*

At that thought, Brianna's stubborn nature asserted itself. She gave herself a little pep talk as she proceeded farther into the cold, silent, dark cave. She was doing well on this island before Nathan came along. *I can do this, I don't need him to show me everything.*

Suddenly, Brianna slipped on a wet piece of ground and stubbed her toe on a bit of rock that was sticking up out of the uneven earth. She went flying and tumbled until she stopped in a mostly flat area. Her shoulder hit the wall especially hard, and her knee hurt. *There will probably be a large bruise on that tomorrow.*

Brianna sat there in the almost darkness for a few minutes, trying to reorient herself. She took stock of herself, making sure all of her body parts still worked properly. All of her limbs had survived the fall, but she knew she'd be sore tomorrow.

She groaned as she stood and placed her hand against a medium-sized stone on the wall to help herself up. The stone moved, and she fell back down in surprise. To her amazement, she hadn't just knocked the rock out of the wall, but it had swiveled down, revealing a three-inch diameter hole with something inside.

All fear vanished as she imagined what was in the hole and who had put it there. She pulled a long, hard leather tube out of the rock wall and placed the stone back over the hole. It looked to be covered in a thick, waxy substance and was mostly in decent shape except for the leather strap that looked rotted away from age. Carefully, she pulled a wax stopper off of one end of the tube and pulled out an old leather parchment. A map!

Brianna tried to look at it in the dim light but couldn't make out many of the details. The map showed a subsection of a larger piece of land near a shoreline. A sea serpent was springing out of the water near a pirate ship. Forest and rivers covered the land with a castle close to the shore. Weird creatures, both frightening and harmless, were drawn over the entire map. One looked like a man with a wolf's face, and another looked like a tiny homeless man with a broom. A few sections contained lettering that she didn't recognize and couldn't decipher.

I recognize nothing on that map. It definitely isn't Riley's Paradise Island. I'll have to take it home and research it. Why in the world would Nathan have put that map down here? Who was he hiding it from? Where does it lead?

Brianna placed the parchment carefully back into its waxed leather tube and placed it into her backpack. She continued down the corridor a few more yards until it ended at a ladder. Climbing the ladder, she found a circular door at the top, directly above her head. She twisted the door's lock and pushed, poking her head up to see a perfectly modern kitchenette. Her brain registered shock at the abrupt change in the environment. It was like stepping into a different world.

Brianna climbed out of the cave system and gave her eyes a few minutes to adjust to the open windows and the modern architecture surrounding her. A refrigerator hummed softly, and the smell of fresh coffee wafted through the air. The cupboards all looked new and clean, and a small two-person table stood against the wall with a few napkins resting on it haphazardly.

Brianna looked out the windows. She could see the lush jungle below her and the ocean in the distance. The top of Nathan's compound sat nestled among the trees, and another building that was harder to discern was far across the other side of the island.

The kitchenette had two doors. First, Brianna opened the door on the right. It opened to a stairway that led unimpeded to the jungle floor. The last two hours flooded back to Brianna as her cheeks turned pink. *Why didn't Nathan show me that way to get up here? He must really love torturing me.*

Then she tried the other door. They locked it with a passcode and a retinal scanner like Nathan's compound.

Brianna tried the same pattern that got her into Nathan's birdhouse. The door buzzed, showing it was unlocked, and she turned the knob and stumbled into a well-lit, cool computer room.

Now that she was back in civilization, she was suddenly aware of her unappealing appearance. Her hair was in disarray and mud covered her clothing and face. The knee of her pants had a large hole in it, and her shoes squelched with each step she took.

She saw a row of three computers and a collection of about half a dozen screens on the wall. Some showed images of the front and back of Nathan's compound and others showed key landmarks she recognized, like the dock.

Nathan swiveled around in a large, cozy computer chair. He faced Brianna, comfortably sipping a soda. Computers hummed all around him. "What took you so long?"

Chapter 16

Root Beer Memories

Brianna

Brianna's jaw dropped. She stared dumbfounded at Nathan's smug face. "How did you get here?"

Nathan's smile vanished as he looked straight into her eyes. He put his palms up in defense. She wanted to trust him, but he had some explaining to do first. "Dugan called and let me know you made it into the control room's back door. I'm very impressed, by the way. That's a hard one to figure out. I asked Dugan to come and watch Jenna so I could show you around up here, but by the time I got here, you were already in the caves underneath. Instead of chasing after you, I used the front door of the control room and met you here. Would you like a soda?"

Brianna glared at him and ignored his drink offer until she got a few more answers. "Why did you show me the back door when we could have gone through the front door weeks ago?"

Running his hand through his hair, Nathan seemed to study her shoes. He scrunched his lips for a moment before answering; he reminded her of a little boy who just got caught getting into trouble. "Honestly, I wanted to show you the cave. I had a lot of fun designing it, and I wanted to share it with you."

Share it with me? Should I read anything into that statement? Maybe her feelings weren't one-sided and he was enjoying being around her too. She hoped so. He could be infuriating sometimes, insisting she solve all the puzzles herself, but she had to admit, his mysteries also intrigued her. An accidental touch from him made her skin tingle, and a smoldering look made her insides turn somersaults. She enjoyed working for him, but she really wanted this to be something more.

Looking around at the screens, she asked, "What are all these screens, and what exactly is this control room for?"

Turning to one corner, Nathan pointed to a large, loud machine. "This control room has a power generator that supplies the entire island with electricity. If anything isn't working, Dugan or I start here and work our way through the system to find out where there is a misconnection."

Nathan swiveled his computer and pointed to a few specific monitors as he spoke. "I don't have cameras all over the island because I don't enjoy thinking that someone could watch me at any time, even Dugan. The idea just raises the hair on the back of my neck, but I believe it is helpful to have a few well-placed security cameras. These monitors are for the cameras that point to my compound, my dad and brother's house, and a few other key areas around the island, like the back entrance to the control room where Dugan caught sight of you."

Satisfied with his answers, she sat in a second swivel chair near Nathan. "I'll have that soda now. I'm really thirsty. What types do you have?"

Ticking off his fingers, he said, "We have root beer, Mountain Dew, Sprite, and some bottled water. Dugan and I don't spend a lot of time up here. There are always too many other things to do than to sit up here watching screens all day. We try to keep it stocked because it is nice to have some snacks and drinks when we need to be here longer than expected."

"I'll have a root beer. I used to love it when I was a kid, and it's been ages since I've had one."

Nathan smiled at her as he set down his own drink and got up. He left the room for a moment and returned with a root beer in hand. "Here you go, one root beer complete with many childhood memories."

Nathan peered out a window overlooking the jungle. "Every time I look out onto this island, I can't help but picture my brother and me getting into all sorts of mischief. We would try swinging from wild grape vines pretending we were Tarzan. Often, we would camp out in the treehouse I originally found you in, telling each other ghost stories all night long."

He took a drink of his soda. "We made traps to catch each other in, and once, while I was sleeping, Jackson took all of my shoes, tied the shoelaces together, and hung them in trees throughout the jungle. He made me a map that I had to use to find them, barefoot. I was furious with him." Looking back at Brianna, he lifted one finger to his lips. "As long as you keep it between us, I'll let you in on some confidential information. We may try to get the best of each other, but I truly enjoy trying to master his puzzles and solving his riddles. I think he secretly feels the same."

Her eyebrows rose at Nathan's unprompted sharing, but she was glad. She wanted to know everything about this man. Brianna took the can of root beer and enjoyed the crisp click of the can tab opening. She took a sip of her drink, and the dark bubbly liquid brought her back to the summer days when her parents and sister would rent out a cabin for a week every year at a state park about an hour from their house in Ohio.

She was pleased Nathan was opening up to her, so she shared a bit about herself to reciprocate. "As a kid, root beer was not a drink we normally had around. It was a special treat my mom would buy when we went away to stay at a cabin in a nearby state park for the week. It was always a pleasant time and something I would like to do with my own kids someday. My family didn't make goo traps or treehouse riddles or shoe-finding scavenger hunts. Staying in a cabin for the week was about as adventurous as my family got."

Nathan watched her with his full focus as she told her story. At first it was unnerving having this handsome man stare at her so intently, but she was pleased he was interested and such a good listener.

"We would go tubing down the nearby river and hiking in the forests around the cabin. I would curl up with a blanket in front of the fireplace and read a good book, or we would make s'mores. The lack of television, schoolwork, and activities left me plenty of time to think. I used to dream of my future and what I wanted to do when I grew up. I can tell you, I never imagined anything as wild as where I actually ended up!"

Nathan cocked his head slightly as he looked at her and smiled. "I'm really glad you ended up here. I'm sure a sinking boat wasn't your preferred mode of transportation, but you have been a real blessing in our lives."

Chapter 17

Sunset Boat Ride

Nathan

Nathan waited patiently in the courtyard of his compound. They had all just finished a delicious dinner of shrimp creole and rice with strawberry tarts for dessert. His stomach was contentedly full. Debbie always outdid herself when cooking for them.

Thankfully, Debbie agreed to watch Jenna for him so he could show Brianna around the island some more. Later, when they got back, Dugan would see Debbie safely home, albeit a few hours later than normal.

If only his father could bring himself to express a single feeling, then maybe Debbie would stay here all the time instead of making that ridiculous commute back to the mainland. He was always talking about her and needing to be around her as his father was obviously in love with the woman. From the wistful looks he saw coming from Debbie, he believed she felt the same. She cooked and did some light cleaning for Nathan two days a week and for his dad and brother one day a week, but each of those days meant a long commute each way. It just seemed excessive. *Although, if he made a move with that relationship, then*

I guess we would need to be in the market for a new housekeeper and cook.

Butterflies filled his stomach as he thought back to his meeting with Brianna in the control room. He felt like he had really connected with her and shared more about himself than he ever did with anyone else. He wanted to ask her out on a date, but fear held him back. Relationships always brought complications, and he didn't want to lose her for Jenna. He huffed out loud as he laughed to himself nervously. *Like father, like son. I guess I have no room to scoff at him when I can't tell my feelings to the woman I'm falling in love with either. Why are things always so complicated?*

Nathan's thoughts jerked back to the present as Brianna stepped outside and joined him. She wore a trim, long-sleeved t-shirt and jeans that hugged her body. She had a small backpack and looked ready to tackle whatever they came across. Thankfully, she wasn't carrying that monkey she saved. It always seemed to be with her and would have made tonights plans more difficult. He smiled at her. *This woman has a lot of determination. The island didn't scare her off like it would most people.*

Sophia had hated the island. They had lived their entire married lives inland for that very reason. Nathan had loved her dearly and wouldn't have traded his time with her, but Riley's Paradise Island was a part of him. Nowhere else ever felt like home.

Brianna seemed to like the island, though. She was curious and intrigued instead of frustrated by the puzzles. But why would he compare the two? A wife and an employee were totally different. *I need to stop thinking about Brianna so much. Besides, Sophia gave me the greatest gift. Jenna. I would give up my entire world in a heartbeat for my Little Bird.*

"Ready? We're heading to the southeast quadrant of the island tonight." Nathan handed Brianna a large bone.

"Do you have a dog? Are we playing pin the bone on the skeleton? Or are you planning on having me pummel someone with this like a cave-woman? This isn't human, is it?" Brianna looked at the large bone quizzically and slung her backpack around so she could put it inside.

"No. I don't have a dog. My late wife was allergic." Without further comment on the femur bone, Nathan headed out of the compound and into the jungle. *I like to keep Brianna guessing. She furrows her brow in that cute little way that shows her annoyance with the lack of clear-cut answers.*

The two walked in companionable silence for about ten minutes. Every once in a while, he would point out a colorful parrot or brazen monkey. They even saw a sloth that blended into the canopy. It was just by chance that they spotted him at all. Brianna lingered behind him, cautiously watching her feet and the surrounding brush. *Probably looking for some traps that caught her when she was first trapped on the island.* They came to a small clearing near the shore, and a peaceful, charming white cottage stood at the edge of the jungle with a small deck that extended into the sand. Nathan held out his arm to stop her.

There was a small fenced-off yard to one side with obstacles spread throughout.

"This is Dugan's cottage." Nathan reached down, picked up a rock, and threw it onto the land near the cottage. The ground immediately swallowed the rock up. "It may look like a charming cottage on the beach, but don't let that fool you. I talked with Dugan and he agreed you should learn how to reach his cottage in case of an emergency. So, what do you think? Can you make it to the cottage without getting sucked into the underground holding chamber?"

Brianna looked at the cottage, then back at Nathan incredulously. She picked up a stick and meticulously started poking different parts of the ground to see which ones were hard and stable. After determining her first step, she gently placed her foot into the clearing but still didn't put all of her weight onto the foot until the last moment. She poked the stick all around her for the next four steps until she seemed like she found the pattern and was just poking the stable land before stepping on it.

Brianna turned to Nathan. "You have to picture an arrow pointing to the right to find the solid steps, don't you?"

Nathan heard a slight humming sound, but Brianna was so focused on her task that she didn't seem to notice it.

He nodded. "Dugan and I think of it as more of a pyramid, but yes. I guess they amount to the same thing."

Brianna stopped stock-still. The humming sound was growing louder and fiercer the closer they got to the cottage. She looked nervously into the surrounding brush and the trees.

"Umm, Nathan... what is that growling noise? Are there predators like panthers or something on this island? Did you bring a gun? Should we turn back?"

She tried to take a step back and retreat into the jungle, but on such a small unseen pathway, it was impossible to get around Nathan safely.

Nathan didn't budge, he just smiled at her. "Don't worry, it's just Suzie Q."

Brianna held onto Nathan's arm and slid her body around him on the solid step, so Nathan was now standing in front. He liked how she clung to him.

"Exactly who or what is Suzie Q? I'm not in the mood to be eaten by a velociraptor today."

Nathan gripped her hand and took the last two steps onto the sand around the cottage. The stable pathway had taken them in an arc, and they now stood near the front of the cottage. Suddenly a humongous muscular tan dog with a black muzzle leapt out of the shade underneath the cottage's porch. Her stomach bulged and hung low to the ground. The dog braced her legs and growled fiercely at Brianna, completely ignoring Nathan.

Brianna stood frozen, clinging to Nathan's hand, seemingly unsure if she should try to escape back down the hidden pathway into the jungle or stay completely still. She stayed still by default of indecision until Nathan nudged her. "It's time to make friends. She really is a sweetheart once I assure her you're a part of her pack." When Brianna still didn't make a move, Nathan continued, "She is also easily bribed. That's her biggest downfall as a watchdog, but don't tell Dugan that. He won't hear any complaint about his sweet Suzie Q."

Nathan walked up to Suzie and patted her head. She whined and leaned into his hand without taking her eyes off Brianna.

"In fact, she's due to have puppies in another few weeks. Dugan has been working on a kennel and training ground of sorts so he can train a few pups to station around the island." Nathan seemed to ponder that for a moment. "Suzie patrols at night while we sleep. Maybe if we got a reputation as an island with fierce wild dogs running around, the locals won't think it's so funny to send unsuspecting tourists over here to bother us."

Nathan continued to talk calmly about Dugan and island security to keep Brianna calm. Finally, Brianna seemed to remember the large bone she was carrying in her backpack. She swung the backpack around swiftly, but the dog curled her lip, and spittle escaped around her sharp canines. Brianna moved much more slowly after that.

Nathan talked soothingly to Suzie as Brianna unzipped her backpack. "It's okay, girl. You know me. This is a friend of mine. Her name is Brianna, and she brought a treat for you. You don't need to worry. We aren't here to disturb Dugan's things. You're all right. We're friends."

Brianna seemed to take a painstakingly long time retrieving the bone. She tossed it in front of Suzie. The dog sniffed the bone suspiciously. After deciding it was an appropriate payment for crossing into her territory, Suzie picked it up and dropped it under the porch, then sprawled out behind it. She gnawed happily as her tail wagged.

Nathan could feel Brianna's tension ease, and they both continued past Dugan's house and down the beach.

"So, in the event of an emergency, what if I have to get to the cottage and I don't have time to hunt down a bone first?" Brianna asked.

"Oh, don't worry. Now that she's met you and accepted you, she won't react like that when you come into her territory again. We'll go back without a bone to make sure the two of you are the best of friends."

Brianna rolled her eyes. "Gee, I can't wait."

Nathan shot her a grin. He took off his shoes and socks and rolled up his pants. Then he walked down to the water to let the incoming tide wash over his bare feet. He looked back and saw Brianna was following suit.

"So, you brought me out here to get scared by a dog and then get my feet wet?" she asked.

"No. We'll head to our next destination soon. I just couldn't pass up the opportunity to enjoy the cool water on my feet after a long, crazy day at work. It seemed like everyone needed something from me today." He reached out into the water and picked up a bumpy red starfish. Its arms moved about in his hand, the cilia underneath tickling him as he handed it over to Brianna. She studied it and then placed the small mollusk gently back into the water. She looked so beautiful, outlined by the dropping sun behind her.

Brianna wiggled her feet in the wet sand. "So, I was thinking about the glass animals I make. Do you mind if I take a week off at the beginning of November to sell at another festival? I found one that's just a few hours' drive inland. It's an okra festival. I could get a stand and try my hand at making glass okra pods besides my regular animals. If it's all right with you. I really enjoy working here and don't want to mess that up."

Hope grew in Nathan's chest. He wanted her to be comfortable staying with him, but he didn't want her to feel like she couldn't live her own life, too. "Sure, that should work out. Let me know the exact dates and I'll block it off of my work schedule. " Nathan watched her beautiful smile form back at him, and he wanted to offer her the world. He blurted out. "You know, you can take that time off as paid leave. I really should have given you a vacation policy when you started. I'll type something up."

Clasping her hands together, Brianna looked up at him, batting her eyelashes. "Really? That is so generous! Thank you so much." To his surprise, she stood on her tiptoes and planted a small kiss on Nathan's cheek. She turned away to pick up her socks and shoes.

He stood there, stunned. It may have been a small, innocent peck, but his cheek still tingled where her lips touched. Why in the world did he keep cementing her into the role of his staff member when what he really wanted was her? He was just trying to be a good man, but it felt like he was just putting more obstacles in his way.

They walked together through the water after he picked up his socks and shoes. He picked up a beautiful shell to take home and show Jenna. Unfortunately, the sea snail inside was still alive, so he threw it back into the ocean. He gave a jellyfish that had washed up on shore a wide berth and made sure Brianna did the same.

Soon they came to Otter's Cove. He had taken her there before, but last time they approached the dock from the jungle. It currently had several boats tied up to it, all different sizes. There was a walk-around motorboat, a sailboat, a small fishing boat with a cabin underneath, and a decent-sized trawler with a living compartment.

Brianna studied the boats they were approaching and grimaced. "Before the accident, I used to get excited about boats."

Nathan turned to her and furrowed his brow. He sometimes forgot what it must have been like for her when she had first gotten stranded on his island. To him, this quirky paradise was home. To her, it must have seemed like a dangerous prison.

"Well then, we should fix that. You don't seem like the sort of woman who would let fear rule her. Let's go for a ride."

Brianna looked at him and bit her bottom lip. "Shouldn't we be getting back soon? I don't want to be out having a leisurely boat ride when Debbie is waiting to go home."

Nathan smiled at her and gently dismissed her concern. "You don't have to worry about Debbie. She loves to be with Jenna and always says she's lonely when she goes home. In fact, she would probably live here on the island with us right now if my father wasn't so emotionally inept."

Brianna cocked her head and asked, "What do you mean by 'emotionally inept'?"

With a large sigh, Nathan said, "My father has been mooning over Debbie for the last year and a half since Jenna and I moved back here. I believe she feels the same; he just needs to make a move."

With his eyes downcast, Nathan frowned as he expanded on his thought. "Maybe he's afraid since my mother left when Jackson and I were only boys. She worked for my dad. They fell in love and moved to this island that my father had grown up on. The isolation proved to be too much for her, though. One day she took a boat out and we never heard from her again, just found the boat docked on the mainland. Maybe he's afraid if he brings Debbie to live here with him, she will leave him too."

Brianna moved closer to Nathan, took his hand in hers, and looked up into his eyes. "I'm sorry that happened to you. It must have been devastating."

Unwilling to look her in the eye, Nathan sadly said, "It is what it is. Jackson wants to go look for her, but I can't help feeling that if she wanted to be a part of our life, she would be here. She doesn't even know she's a grandmother."

The conversation must have been getting too emotionally intense for Nathan because he quickly changed the subject. "Anyway, When Dugan takes Debbie home; they will take the trawler so Debbie can curl up with a good book and chamomile tea while he drives her home. She says there's nothing more peaceful than losing herself in a romance novel amidst the rocking of the waves."

Brianna finally conceded, still not looking too sure. "Okay. A short ride, wouldn't hurt I guess."

Nathan led her to the trawler. They placed their shoes by the door, still in their bare feet. Nathan started up the boat and left to untie it from the dock.

Nathan looked over at Brianna, who seemed fascinated with the interior of the ship. There was a large common room with a kitchenette that sported quartz countertops, white cupboards, and a mini-fridge. There was a cozy couch with a welcoming throw blanket and a small fake fireplace on the other end of the room.

"Check it all out. Let me get The Little Bird out in the water and I'll be right with you. That door in the back leads to a small sleeping quarters. The other glass door leads out onto a porch. I'll meet you out there whenever you finish looking around."

Nathan saw Brianna catch herself when he pushed them off the dock. It took her a few minutes to get her sea legs under her as he sat down in the captain's chair and maneuvered the boat out of the cove. He only took them a short way out into the ocean.

Nathan turned the boat so the back porch would face the setting sun and then put down an anchor. He activated the boat's night lights in case any other vessels were out. After grabbing two glasses and a bottle of wine from the mini-fridge, he went to find Brianna.

Brianna had taken a blanket and nestled in a chair on the back of the boat. She was watching the water lap against the hull. Nathan pulled over a chair directly next to her as the sun began to set. God painted red, pink, and orange strokes across the sky as it dropped lower and lower.

He poured them both a glass of wine as they relaxed and watched the last bit of daylight disappear. Their eyes adjusted to the dark. Luckily, the moon shone bright enough to see. The cabin lights from the boat would have ruined the mood.

Nathan looked over at Brianna. He really was in trouble. She looked so peaceful next to him that his lips burned to kiss her. Brianna must have noticed him staring at her. She turned towards Nathan, and he felt himself getting lost in the depths of those trusting eyes.

How would it feel to kiss her? Would it feel as right as I think it would to hold her in my arms? Brianna slightly angled her head up towards him, lips slightly parted, as if mirroring his thoughts.

She's not mine, though. I can't let this go any further. I simply must know the truth before I get in any deeper.

Instead of a kiss, he stared deeply into her eyes and softly asked, "Are you still married?"

Chapter 18

Married with a Sword

Brianna

Brianna pulled away from Nathan in shock and narrowed her eyes. "What are you talking about? Why would I be married?" She thought he was finally going to kiss her. Her whole body had tingled at the thought, eagerly awaiting his touch and anticipating what his lips would feel like on her own. Instead, a cold frustration now rushed through her, washing away the sensual feelings and ruining the romantic mood.

She watched Nathan carefully. He let out a deep breath of what looked like relief when she said she wasn't married. Then he grimaced and wouldn't look her in the eye.

A business-like persona took over Nathan as his expressions leveled out and he answered her without conveying much emotion. "Well, I do a thorough background check on all employees before offering them a job, and I came across wedding pictures on your social media accounts. You had rings and a marriage certificate..."

Brianna thought back to the mock wedding she had with her ex-boyfriend, Tom, from Halloween last year. They had known each other over a year and dressed up as a bride and groom from a movie that they both loved. It was a comedy where the bride and groom had swords and fought their way through zombies to marry each other.

Cozy atmosphere broken, Brianna stood up, placed her hands on her hips, and asked him in clipped words, "Why didn't you ask me before running a background check on me?" On one hand, she had to admit she would have done the same before entrusting her little girl to a stranger, but it would have only cost him a handful of words to ask her first.

Nathan set down his glass and stood up as well. He looked down slightly, so they were eye to eye. He winced at her question, placed his hands gently on her shoulders, and spoke with his head tucked down. "I'm sorry. I didn't think it through. You needed a job, and I needed an employee, so I thought it was a perfect match, but you're right. I should have talked to you first."

Brianna's anger evaporated at his apology. She relaxed her muscles; he was only trying to look after Jenna's best interests. She couldn't blame him for being a protective father. "Why in the world would you think that was a real wedding? Did you really think I would move out to this island and leave my husband behind? We were wielding swords in the pictures for crying out loud!"

Nathan broke eye contact and ran his hand through his hair. "I don't know. I guess I thought maybe you guys were separated or something. Your background check was contradictory. It said you weren't married, but there was also no judicial record of a divorce. In the pictures I saw you had a marriage certificate and, believe me, I've had one before. It was real-looking." He gave her a forced, one-sided smile. "Regarding the swords; themed weddings are a big thing right now."

Brianna breathed audibly at him as she tried to read his expression to see if he was serious, and it looked like he was. Yes, they posed like they were doing a proper ceremony with rings and everything, but the pictures were still ridiculous. Did Nathan really think she would wear a tacky wedding dress with giant pink tulle flowers around the bottom? Would she be sporting a sword when she had a real wedding?

She imagined her real wedding being an elegant affair on the beach of a beautiful tropical island. A handsome man with dark hair would wait for her next to the priest as the sun set behind them. He would smile at her in delight at the thought of spending the rest of his life with her. That would be her fairy tale wedding, not holding a heavy sword in one hand as a ring was slid on the other.

She slouched back down in her chair and picked up her glass of wine. "Tom had a friend that was fantastic at altering things on his computer. He made us a fake marriage certificate for a mock wedding. It was just a joke."

She hadn't thought about that night for a long time. They broke up a few weeks after they took those pictures. Nathan must have been very thorough in his investigations to find them at all. *How could Nathan have thought they were real?* Then she took a deep breath. *Maybe that isn't the real question I need to ask myself. Why am I so upset that Nathan thought I was married?*

"Why didn't you ask me about it earlier? We could have cleared this up a long time ago."

Nathan shrugged. "Well, you're my employee, and I didn't think it was really any of my business, so I decided not to pry about the details."

Brianna placed her hand over her face. "So, let me get this straight. You thought it was perfectly okay to do a background check on me without asking, but talking to me about possibly being married was not your business."

Nathan nodded his head slowly, frowning. "Yes. I followed the same procedures with you as I do when I hire any additional worker. I do my due diligence to make sure they aren't a security threat but try not to pry into anyone's personal life beyond that."

Staring at him with her mouth hanging open, Brianna didn't know what to say next. Just moments ago, she had felt so close to him. She had wanted him to hold her and kiss her and tell her he thought about her all the time, like she thought about him. His body language made her think he was on the same page; the way he hung onto her every word and seemed to make excuses to be close to her. She really thought he was leaning in for that yearned for kiss...

Now, he'd made it clear. She was his daughter's governess, and not a thing more. He didn't care about her in any other way than her ability to do her job. While she enjoyed watching over and teaching Jenna, now she had to figure out how to cut her emotions off from Nathan. She didn't want to embarrass herself and overreach this boundary he'd put between them.

Employer and employee. Her hope of having found love died and her heart felt like it was breaking into a hundred sharp, painful pieces.

Chapter 19

The Woman of his Dreams

Nathan

The day after the disastrous boat ride, all Nathan could think about was Brianna. He tried to write an email to his staff about their new vacation policy, but his heart wasn't in it. He ran the scene on the boat through his head repeatedly. There were so many things he could have done differently and said better.

All he'd really wanted to do was kiss the woman. Why did he let his big mouth get in the way? In fact, now that he had asked her about it, he felt ridiculous thinking the wedding was real. He had seen a lot of outrageous themed weddings lately on the internet from *Star Wars* to *The Little Mermaid*, but he should have known Brianna was different.

The fact that she wasn't married was a tremendous relief. It may not have been something he needed to worry about with a regular employee, but his feelings for Brianna were far from normal. No matter how hard he tried to forget and ignore those wedding pictures, he couldn't help it when they continued to nag at the back of his mind. He tried to push his thoughts and feelings for Brianna away, but it seemed they were never further than right below the surface. Besides, it would have been a real travesty for such a lovely woman to be married in that ugly dress. Although, he wouldn't have minded seeing her wield a sword again. That image made his skin flush.

He tried to finish up his workday, but eventually just shut down his computer regardless of his workload. He ran his hand through his hair again. It probably stood straight up because he'd done that so many times. *What should I do about Brianna?* His father's voice boomed in his head when he said something along the lines of, 'I'd rather fire you than let you create a human resources disaster from messing around with one of your employees.' Nathan considered officially firing her and paying her under the table to watch Jenna so he could ask her out, but he thought that idea would probably end up biting him in the butt. He didn't want her to ever feel a romantic relationship with him was transactional.

He didn't want to mess things up at work and did didn't want to ruin things with Brianna and lose her as Jenna's governess. His little girl was thriving under her care. His Little Bird needed Brianna just as much as he wanted her, but Jenna's needs came first.

She occupied all of his thoughts while awake and asleep. He wanted to hold her and kiss her and make her laugh and smile. He wanted to tell her how much he cared about her and have her tell him the same. Shaking his head, he realized he was too far gone to back out now. He had tried to keep his distance, but that captivating woman stole his heart anyway.

What he needed now was for her to choose to be with him, with no complications or strings attached. Nathan groaned as he held his head in his hands. Getting there was an impossible mess that he didn't think he could ever untangle. When he wanted to kiss Brianna and make her his, he had solidified their employment relationship, saying that he didn't need to know anything in her personal life beyond her ability to do her job. He was such a dolt sometimes. He had created a chasm of professionalism between them he didn't know how to cross.

Nathan heard a gentle knocking at his office door. "Come in!" he called.

The woman he had dreamed of all night tentatively stepped through the door. In his dreams, she had thrown herself at him, declaring that she couldn't live without him and had refused to work for him so that they could be together. He had covered her in passionate kisses and whispered the sacred words, 'I love you' into her ear. In dreams, things were so easy.

In real life, she stayed all the way across the room from him. He didn't blame her for not knowing exactly where they stood. Every fiber of his being desired to kiss her, but he then told her their relationship went no further than work. He was confused too.

Jenna came running into the room and gave him a big bear hug. Things were simple with his Little Bird. He loved her with his whole being, and she loved him. Why couldn't all relationships be that straightforward?

Brianna cleared her throat. "I was just stopping by to drop off Jenna for the evening. You two have a good night." Brianna moved to leave.

"Wait!" Nathan called. Brianna stopped still a foot from the doorway and slowly turned around.

Nathan set Jenna down and smiled at his daughter. "Can you play with your dolls under my desk for a few minutes while I talk to Brianna? Then we will leave to have dinner at Grandpa and Uncle Jackson's house. Debbie mentioned she made a special dessert that's waiting for us over there."

Jenna got a huge smile on her face and yelled, "Hooray!" before dropping to the ground and picking up a small horse to gallop across the floor.

He felt Brianna was much more than his daughter's nanny and teacher now. She wasn't "just a governess", but had become an integral part of his family. One he didn't want to lose.

Nathan reached out and took her hand in his own. He stared into her eyes, wishing he could read her mind. Did she care for him deeply too? What if he expressed his feelings, and she shot him down and sued for harassment? Or worse, what if she said she cared for him too, but only meant it because he was her boss?

He pulled his hand away but didn't break eye contact. "Listen, I'm sorry things got weird last night on the boat. Can I make it up to you on our next island adventure next week?"

She grinned at him cheekily. "Sure thing, boss."

Chapter 20

Romantic Dinner

Brianna

A week later, Nathan took her out on another island exploration. Debbie stayed late to watch Jenna again. Since she wanted to get home slightly earlier, they started out in the early afternoon before having dinner themselves.

Brianna's stomach growled as she climbed over a fallen log. She tried to stay alert, but she was so hungry that she couldn't think of anything that wasn't related to food. She yelled up to Nathan, who was a few feet ahead of her on the trail. "When you told me not to eat dinner, you had a plan for feeding me, right?"

Nathan didn't answer, so Brianna continued. "You know, I'm not much for hunting or trapping or whatever you have planned. If you have fruit trees, I can help with that. What are we looking for? Papayas?"

Brianna looked down at the handmade pouch she had slung across her chest. Chee Chee looked up at her and excitedly chattered. At least Chee Chee listened to her. She brought the little monkey along on their adventure for the evening. Chee Chee's leg was getting much better after a few weeks, but he seemed like he was getting antsy and depressed staying in her bedroom all day.

Brianna used her meager sewing skills to make him a small pouch to carry him in. Then she sewed him a tiny harness. She gently wrestled him in and attached it to a leash right before it was time to leave. She figured that way he could see and enjoy a day outside in the jungle without the fear of him running off before being fully healed.

Finally, Nathan looked back at her with a twinkle in his eye. "You have to work for your dinner tonight, but don't worry, you'll recognize it when you see it." Then he veered off the path into some overgrown brush. Getting hangrier by the moment, Brianna made a low growling noise and followed.

"It's in another one of your damn puzzles, isn't it? You've probably hung my dinner in some trap so I can see it and smell it but won't be able to get to it until I solve your stupid riddle." Brianna glared at him. "Well, let me tell you something. I'm ready to beat your little tricks. I brought a big sharp knife and matchsticks so I can just cut or burn my way through whatever you throw at me. Sure, maybe my dinner will taste a bit charred, but that's better than letting it get cold while I mess with your riddles. I'll be eating it before you can wipe that smirk off your face!" Chee Chee, excited by Brianna's strong words, chattered his own warning to Nathan.

Nathan smiled wider as he listened to her monologue. "My, my. You get feisty when you're hungry, don't you? Once we get there, you're free to burn and cut your way straight through to your plate. I'll even help you if you want."

Brianna looked at him suspiciously. "So, it's a trap that requires both cutting and fire at the same time? At least I came prepared."

They came to a small drawbridge with a box on the front. Brianna groaned. Chee Chee tried to climb out of his pouch to investigate, but Brianna kept him firmly in place. Brianna was swiftly becoming more frustrated than intrigued by the puzzles. *Maybe I should have waited to bring Chee Chee out to the jungle when I'm not doing a puzzle night with Nathan. I would be more pleasant company.*

Brianna pointed to the puzzle with one hand while she placed the other on her hip. "Really, I don't see any food here. Why couldn't I have eaten dinner before coming out into the jungle? The chicken Alfredo Debbie was making smelled delicious. Or I could have eaten a little for dinner, then come out for our puzzle walk and had your coconuts as a snack or dessert this evening."

Nathan seemed amused by Brianna's discomfort, which only wound her up more. "You know, Brianna, if you really are that hungry, we can always eat your monkey." He gave her a wicked smile and glanced over at Chee Chee. He had wiggled his way out of the pouch and found a perch on Brianna's shoulder.

Brianna looked at Nathan in total outrage but stopped complaining. *I'm pretty sure he's kidding, but I wouldn't put anything past that man. I never know what to expect with him.*

She steeled her resolve. *The sooner I finish these puzzles, the sooner I can eat.* Brianna buckled down and looked at the box in front of the drawbridge.

The wooden box had a diagram of the drawbridge on the front of it, but the pieces were all mixed up. She looked at the drawbridge and put the puzzle pieces in order to reflect on what she could see. Then she filled in what she couldn't see with what would make sense. The last piece she moved looked like a water turbine in the stream's current. She waited.

Nothing happened. She went to look at the drawbridge closer to see if she had put anything out of place and kept her eyes out for any ropes that looked out of the ordinary. On the shore, she found a water turbine that looked just like the one on the diagram. She threw it into the water and returned to the diagram to figure out what she had missed.

After a few seconds, the bridge lowered on its own. Nathan looked over at her apologetically. "It takes a few moments for the water turbine to power the bridge." Then he crossed without looking back to see if she was following. Grumbling under her breath, she did.

After they walked for a few yards more, the path opened up to a large clearing. To Brianna's surprise and delight, there was the most beautiful waterfall cascading down a rock feature. Giant wildflowers bloomed all around the waterfall, and twinkling lanterns hung from the canopy of the forest's branches. It looked magical, like she had entered the land of the Fae.

Set near the waterfall was a fancy linen-covered table set for two. The silverware and crystal goblets sparkled from the lights. Brianna stood still, never expecting this bit of beauty and refinery to hide in the middle of a jungle.

Nathan, pleased with her reaction, lifted her hand and kissed it while staring deeply into her eyes. "Dinner, milady. I wanted to do something special to thank you for staying with us and for being so good for... Jenna. She has really bloomed, and you're becoming so important to her."

Nathan held out Brianna's chair for her to sit in and pushed it in behind her. Dugan appeared out of nowhere with a covered dish. He set a dish in front of each of them. "You two look as hungry as a bobcat eying a fowl." Then he disappeared into the forest without another word.

"Wow, this is beautiful! I did not know this island could be even more beautiful. This is so sweet," Brianna gushed. Her cheeks flushed, remembering her earlier outbursts.

I should have kept my lips zipped and walked along silently.

Nathan chuckled and lifted the lid on his meal. A fancy version of the chicken Alfredo sat on their plates. The pasta looked like a bed that a parmesan-crusted chicken 'flower' with green pesto leaves sat upon.

Nathan pointed to Brianna's meal. "Go ahead, dig in. I kind of got the impression you were hungry on our way over here. Oh, and don't forget to leave room for dessert!"

Chee Chee chattered excitedly on Brianna's shoulder until he received his morsel of her dinner. Then she tied him to a small nearby tree where he explored until he finally curled up and fell asleep on a branch..

"Brianna," Nathan began, choosing his words carefully. "Thank you for trusting me. I know not just anyone would stay on a mostly deserted island with people they don't know to watch a little girl."

Nathan ran his hand through his hair, stood up, and walked over to her. He gently pulled her to her feet and stared into her eyes, their faces only inches apart. Brianna's heart fluttered at his gentle, intimate touch. *What's going on? I'm sure this isn't how he treats all his employees.* An image of one of his other hirelings, the large and muscular Dugan having a romantic dinner with Nathan by the waterfall, made a smile flicker across her lips, but she kept that thought to herself. She was dying to know what Nathan would do next.

Taking a deep breath, Nathan spoke more softly. "The truth is, you're becoming important to more than just Jenna. You're becoming important to me too." Joy burst through her heart and warmth spread from the center of her being. Her breathing quickened to match Nathan's. *Did he just say what I think he said?*

She moved her head slightly upwards and Nathan let out a needy groan as his lips descended and covered hers. Brianna's whole body burned with fire as Nathan kissed her passionately, awakening a need deep down in her core. Everything was forgotten but the eager lips of the man she wanted more than anything in the world.

His heart thudded against her chest and she moved her arms around his neck so she could feel his full body pressed against hers. When he had embraced her, she couldn't even recall. She had never felt so alive and consumed with desire before. While she moved her mouth to the side for a breath of air, he began to ardently place kisses down her neck in a trail of tingling yearning as his hands began to fervently but gently stroke her sides. She wanted more. *Could this be something real?*

She pulled back, breaking the kiss. "Nathan..." she whispered, at a loss to describe her feelings. The rush of desire and longing had both exhilarated and frightened her. Using all of her willpower, she extracted her arms and moved away from the sexiest man alive. Her body ached where they had touched, and she was screaming on the inside for more of him. Nathan stood there, open-mouthed and panting. He didn't move, just stood still with his brow furrowed in confusion.

She needed to know where they stood. There was too much back and forth, and she didn't want to have any regrets. She already wasn't sure if she could go back to being 'just' his employee, not after this. Brianna's memory went back to the sensation of their lips meeting. She wanted nothing more than to dive right back into his arms and the pleasure he provided. She felt as if she were under a waterfall of feelings, sensations, and emotions.

Nathan got himself under control first. He looked up at the sky as he slowed his breathing and wouldn't make eye contact again as he blurted out. "I'm sorry. I shouldn't have done that.

You're my employee. I shouldn't have muddled things, and I really don't want to mess things up for Jenna. It was the atmosphere. You don't have to worry about me doing that again."

Cocking her head and biting her bottom lip, Brianna stared at him, more dumbfounded than she was moments before. " I'm so confused. Just a few days ago you were telling me how you only saw me as your daughter's caregiver. Today you're kissing me, and then the next moment you are pushing me away. I just want to know where we stand."

She wanted to reach for him, but Nathan moved to clean up after dinner. From her limited experience, he seemed to do better with tough conversations when he had something for his hands to do, so she left him to it while waiting for his answer.

Finally, he turned around with his fingers lightly touching his lips, and the agony she saw below his furrowed brow surprised her. "Brianna, I'm sorry. I have some inappropriate feelings for you, and I'm having a hard time keeping them under control. I really don't want my actions to cause you to leave. From what I've seen, romantic relationships between a boss and employee never work, and you are far too valuable to Jenna for me to let that happen. We should head back to the compound before I make an even bigger fool of myself."

"You know you weren't the only one in that kiss, right?" Brianna walked over to the tree and scooped the sleeping Chee Chee up, but even holding him didn't fill the emptiness that Nathan's body had left behind.

"I know, but I don't want you to feel you have to do something because I'm your boss. I'm sorry I complicated things." Nathan picked up the untouched dessert, waved at the rest of the clearing, and started walking away down the path. "I'll come back tomorrow and clean the rest of this up. We should head back now; Debbie wants to get home at a decent time tonight."

Looking around, Brianna picked up her pack, swung it onto her back, and tried to keep up with the man speed-walking away. She was a bit frustrated he didn't ask how she felt about what happened that night, but she also felt hopeful. In his own awkward way, he admitted to having feelings for her.

I didn't stop kissing him because I don't have feelings for him. Instead, I think I'm falling in love with the most contrary yet alluring man on Earth.

Chapter 21

A Day in the Life of a Homeschooler

Brianna

"Good job singing your alphabet! Are you ready to practice writing your name again?" Brianna sat next to Jenna at a low table. She carefully wrote her name in pencil on a blank piece of paper. "Trace over your name and then you can try it yourself in the space below."

Jenna slightly stuck out her tongue, and she concentrated on slowly forming each letter. When she finished, she looked up at Brianna, eyes shining. "I did it! Can I show it to Daddy?"

Brianna patted the little girl's back encouragingly. "You did a great job. You're catching on quickly! Yes, we will definitely show your father, but I believe I promised you a dance party and reading time first."

"Hooray! Best day ever!" Jenna got up and started dancing around the room, not caring that the music hadn't started yet.

Smiling at the little girl's enthusiasm, Brianna turned on the preschool music Nathan had approved for their homeschool preschool. She joined the little girl as they waddled around and quacked like ducks and galloped while neighing like horses.

Afterwards, they both collapsed, giggling, onto the large comfy play couch that was in the reading nook. Jenna climbed into her lap as Brianna opened a picture book about farms to read to her. She couldn't help but give Jenna a little squeeze; this was the best job in the world. She thought she would be happy the rest of her life if things could stay just like this.

After reading a few different books, Brianna helped Jenna pick out a container of little plastic animal figures and the large plastic jungle play structure that went along with it. Jenna eagerly dumped the animals on the ground, picked up a few and started an elaborate drama where the animals were trying to convince an elephant not to sneeze.

Brianna took a deep breath. The two of them had a wonderful morning, and she felt Jenna was picking up her schooling well. However, she needed some adult conversation. She picked up her phone and speed-dialed Mavis.

A cheery voice greeted her. "Hello, chicky! How is my island princess doing?"

Laughing, Brianna responded, "Mavis, I miss you so much. I think this island would be perfect if you were here. Everything is going well for the most part..."

Brianna walked out into the hallway and gently closed the door while Jenna played independently. She leaned against the wall as she murmured, "Honestly, I could really use your advice. I think I'm falling in love with my boss, Nathan."

Mavis gasped. "I knew it! I thought a hot, mysterious guy showing you around the island would only lead to one thing."

A little too loudly, Brianna said, "Mavis! Nothing happened. All we did was kiss. We just left things so confusing, and I don't know what to do."

Mavis fired out a few quick questions. "Did you kiss him, or did he kiss you? Was it a simple, chaste kiss or a sexy tongue-tangling kind of kiss? Most importantly, how does he make you feel?"

"Oh, that was definitely a spicy, heart-stopping type of kiss. The kind you never forget. He started it, but I broke it off because he keeps making me feel like the most important woman in his life, but then puts up this wall between us saying 'stay back, you're my employee.'"

Mavis chuckled. "It sounds like this guy of yours is just as confused as you are. Did you confront him and make him spell out what he is feeling?"

Less sure of herself, Brianna slowly said, "I tried. He apologized for having feelings for me, explained how toxic boss and employee relationships can be, and then changed the subject and hurried away. I'm pretty sure I'm doomed to spend my life yearning after a man I can't have."

Laughing out loud, Mavis said, "Let me get this straight. Your kisses were so intoxicating that, when you broke it off, he admitted his feelings for you and ran away because he's your boss and afraid he can't keep his hands off you?"

Brianna nodded, even though there was no one to see. "That pretty much sums it up. I like him. He likes me, but we can't be together because he's my boss."

Mavis chuckled to herself. "Oh, man. Nathan has the hots for you and he's just too clueless to know what to do about it. Men!"

Knowing Mavis could talk about her nonexistent relationship with Nathan for hours, Brianna changed the subject. "So, how are you doing? Are you enjoying your new job in labor and delivery at the hospital? How are you and Joey doing? Should I start planning for maid of honor duty?"

Mavis paused slightly before answering in a much slower pace than moment before. "I don't know. Things aren't going great at work because I just got in trouble for treating a patient without insurance. I mean, it's amazing seeing life brought into the world, but I'm not sure this hospital is the right place for me. I'm considering quitting and getting my midwife certification and possibly working in a smaller clinic. Unfortunately, things aren't going so well with Joey either. We keep fighting over every little thing. I'm sure we will work through it, but I think I moved in with him way too fast."

Full of concern, Brianna pursed her lips before responding. "I'm so sorry to hear that. Do you want to tell me more about it?"

At that moment, Jenna was out the door with a tiger in her hand. She made growling noises as she talked in a fake, deep voice. "I'm Mr. Stripes and I'm getting hungry. Can I have cookies for lunch?"

Brianna held up one finger to Jenna and spoke into her phone. "Mavis, I have to get back to Jenna right now. This little tiger is hungry. Can you hold on until later this afternoon to talk?"

Mavis picked back up her upbeat tone from a few moments before. "Yeah, of course. Nothing is urgent over here. It's just not going as well as I would like. We'll talk later. Besides, I didn't get to ask nearly enough questions about Mr. Bossman of Paradise Island. Talk to you soon!"

Brianna always felt better after talking with her best friend. "Definitely. Tonight, I'm all yours. Bye." Brianna hung up and followed Jenna down to the kitchen to convince Mr. Stripes to eat something other than cookies for lunch.

Chapter 22

The Red Door

Brianna

Nathan looked over at Brianna as they headed through the jungle. "Today, I'm taking you into my brother Jackson's part of the island. He's constantly changing the answers and the placement of his traps and puzzles, so be careful. Follow me. I have a pretty good idea of where to look out for things. I've been disrupting his traps since we were boys."

Brianna's curiosity got the best of her. "Do you see your brother often? I know you and Jenna go over to your dad's and Jackson's house for dinner sometimes, but I've been here for a handful of months. I haven't met him yet, and he lives less than two miles away."

Chee Chee was sitting on Brianna's shoulder, using her ear as a handhold. His leg was completely healed, and she knew she would soon have to release the little fellow.

Nathan smiled at them both. "Normally, he stops over for dinner every once in a while, and I see him for work matters a few times a month, either in person or virtually. Jenna and I usually go over to the main house once or twice a month to have dinner with him and my dad, but the two of them have spent the last two months on the road dropping in on our manufacturing plants, hosting in-person employee trainings, and making sales calls at a few big toy retailers They recently came home and last Wednesday, Jenna and I went over for a brief visit and dessert while you were working on your glass animals."

Nathan glanced over at her. "Also, just so you have a heads up, I got out of this trip because I didn't want to disappear for so long from Jenna and I needed to get you ettled into our island, but there will be some future trips that I will probably have to go on.

Brianna nodded her head and then cocked it. "Sure, I understand that and we will be fine when then comes up, but what exactly is the main house? Your house is so large that we usually refer to it as a compound."

"It's the house my brother and father live in. They usually refer to it as the main house because it has been on the island for over a hundred years. Occasionally, a storm will mess it up pretty badly. That forces us to do some intensive remodeling, but the roots have been there for generations. My house is only a little less than two years old. I built it for Jenna and me after my wife passed."

Brianna stumbled over a root, and Nathan reached out his hand to steady her. Even after Brianna stood up, he didn't immediately let go. Brianna stared into his eyes, wishing she could read his thoughts. It was getting frustrating being his employee because everything between them was so hazy, but what choice did she have? She didn't want to quit and leave everything she was beginning to treasure on this island.

Was he falling in love with her like she was with him? Sometimes she thought so, especially after that epic kiss by the waterfall where he kissed her with a hunger she had never felt before. Since then, he seemed to keep his distance. How could she break through from "Nathan the boss" to the man she caught glimpses of who hung onto her every word and kissed with such unfettered passion?

He slowly dropped her hands and turned to walk farther down the path. "We aren't too far away now. We should be able to get there and get back home before dark if we keep up this pace."

They continued walking until they got to a part of the jungle that looked the same as the last two miles to Brianna, but Nathan pointed to unseen landmarks. "This is the start of my brother's land. Now, his style of puzzles and traps has a bit more 'teeth' than mine. I promised you that none of my traps would hurt you. With my brother, I can't make the same promise. All of his work is non-lethal, but I can't guarantee they won't give you some bumps and bruises. Once, when we were boys, I got caught in one of his traps that broke my arm. Another time, I got a black eye."

Nathan paused and looked directly into Brianna's eyes for effect. "I would recommend that you don't come over into his territory on your own." Then he changed his tone to one that was more playful as he smiled cheekily at her. "Besides, I can always make time to go on a walk with you if you feel the need to stretch your legs beyond my part of the island. Just ask."

Brianna was enjoying their banter but changed the subject when she noticed a bit of bright red hidden behind the giant leaves of a tree. "What is that red up there? Is there some sort of structure out here?"

Nathan shrugged. "There wasn't anything here the last time I came through this path, but that was a month or two ago. I normally take a more northern route with Jenna. Jackson could have built something since then. I guess we will have to find out what's out there together."

Wrinkling up her nose, she asked, "Why are you taking me a different way than you normally take Jenna?"

A relaxed grin slowly grew across Nathan's face. "Jackson and I agreed to keep the northern path clear of any kinds of traps or obstructions so we could navigate across the island quickly and safely when we needed to. Being that I never know what to expect over here, Jenna and I usually use that protected path." With a wink, he added, "I'm using this path with you because it's more fun." His smile grew larger as Brianna rolled her eyes at him.

They continued until they reached a large, fancy, bright red door. The door had golden trim and cherubs engraved on the large knocker. *Nope. Definitely would not have guessed a random door leading to nowhere.*

Chapter 23

Look Under the Welcome Mat

Brianna

The door is almost like a piece of art in the middle of the jungle. It looks like it belongs in a fancy mansion instead of out here. In front of the door was a simple welcome mat. On closer inspection, Brianna confirmed the door didn't appear to lead to any kind of structure. Only trees and greenery surrounded the door on all sides.

Nathan saw the door and sighed. "This door is a lot like my brother, loud and obnoxious." He lifted the mat and picked up a key, then pushed the key into the lock and jerked back his hand in surprise. "Ouch! That lock shocked me." He shook his hand out and took a pair of rubber gloves out of his backpack. Properly protected, he turned the key the rest of the way. When the door finally opened, a small bell jingled.

Nathan grumbled. "I wonder if I used the knocker before trying the key, it wouldn't have shocked me. Jackson would think it was hilarious to punish someone for not being polite."

Do I really want to meet Jackson? Do I really want to find out what cuckoo's nest Nathan flew out of?

"Why didn't we just go around the door?" Brianna asked. After watching him hop around from getting shocked, she was happy to let Nathan take the lead this time.

"Once you get to know Jackson, you'll learn to ignore the obvious answer. In his case, the most difficult scenario is usually the right one. If you can figure it out, that is."

Nathan picked up a heavy stick and threw it a few feet to the right side of the door. After the stick landed, the leaves rustled and a sharp metal snap sounded where it had landed. He picked up another stick and poked the ground to the left of the door. Another sharp snap sounded. Nathan attempted to pull the stick back out, but to no avail. "Want to try it?" he asked Brianna.

Hesitantly, Brianna answered, "Nope, I'm good."

Nathan walked through the door. Brianna waited a minute or two before following him.

"So what was your childhood like? From what I understand, you and your brother grew up alone on an island trying to catch each other in hunting traps." Then she rolled her eyes and added sarcastically, "Sounds like a totally normal childhood."

Nathan chuckled. "Well, it was something like that. We had tutors that taught us to read, write, and do arithmetic. We also had a lot of free time for ourselves and the run of this entire island. Our father worked a lot to grow his board game company into an empire, and we really looked up to him. He would praise us for anything we did that was clever or out of the box."

Nathan pointed to the ground where a snare stood. "Why don't you follow in my footsteps?" Then he continued with his story, "When we were somewhere around seven and nine, we tried to catch each other in simple net traps or hole traps. To amuse ourselves, we began planning elaborate puzzles that led to each other's Christmas gifts." Nathan made an exaggerated sigh as he remembered. "One time, Jackson made me riddles to find all of my underwear that he hid around the island. In revenge, I made him a scavenger hunt across the island to find his small green G.I. Joe action figures that were all hidden amongst the green leaves. It took him weeks to find them all."

Nathan found another snare that he disarmed. "By the time we were teenagers, our puzzles and traps had become inventions in and of themselves, with electronic components, mechanics, and engineering all in play. Our father called it hands-on learning. He encouraged us and laughed whenever we could catch each other unaware."

Brianna looked over at him. "So, basically, your childhood was just as odd as I had imagined it. No wonder this island is so full of traps and puzzles. You guys have been working on them for over twenty years!"

Nathan smiled to himself, as if recalling a memory. "It's not like we ever wanted to hurt each other. We never let it go too far. It was just such a challenge to catch my brother or try to outsmart him." A regretful look flashed across Nathan's face. "Although, when I was home from college for one summer, we had an accident with some smugglers. One man died, and we never found the body of his brother. It became a lot less of a fun game after that. That's when I thought of the traps in terms of security."

Brianna grimaced as she looked over at Nathan. "You mentioned that accident after the red alert that went off not long after I started here. What happened?"

Running his hand through his hair, Nathan continued to walk leisurely as he talked. "Jackson and I weren't always the matured gentleman you see today. When we were younger, we thought we could take on the world without consequence. One summer, we found a smuggler ship parked in our very own little Otter's Cove. We thought we were so clever with all the traps we made around the island and we thought we would be heroes if we caught the smugglers ourselves before turning them in to the authorities." Nathan stopped, turned to her, and put his hand to his face while he spoke with regret. "We were so young and stupid. I don't know what we were thinking. We didn't even take into consideration the fact that they had guns. I ended up running for my life from two brothers, Alaric and Amos." His gaze became unfocused and he grimaced as if he was reliving a nightmare. "I'll never be able to forget them; they were doing the job to get Amos's son and Alaric's nephew out of trouble. They couldn't risk letting me live when I could identify them, and all of my clever traps couldn't save me. Jackson ended up risking his own life to save mine. I thought I had lost him, but a faulty trap caused Alaric to lose his brother instead."

Pointing into the jungle, Nathan asked. "Do you remember that fast stream with the drawbridge on it and the bucket puzzle?" A simple nod from Brianna was all Nathan needed to continue. "Alaric disappeared into that stream, and the police never found him or his body. I don't know whatever happened to him. If we had just called the police in the beginning, that man, Amos, would still be alive. I don't think I will ever forgive myself for that."

Brianna walked up behind him and placed her hand on his back, and Nathan leaned into her touch. "I'm so sorry that happened to you, but you guys were young and up against criminals. You can't blame yourself. I'm glad you made it out alive."

They walked along in silence again for a while. Chee Chee chattered every once in a while, excited to be back in the jungle. Intermittently, they would hear an animal startle and crash through the underbrush or a bird take flight. Otherwise, there were no other sounds but the wild singing of the jungle.

At one point, Chee Chee climbed down Brianna's body and ran off the path before she could stop him. "Chee Chee! Come back! I wanted to turn you loose closer to where we found you, not here!"

Brianna ran off the path after the monkey. Hidden behind a few trees, she spotted a a fire pit with a few remaining charred logs laid upon the ashes and a wisp of smoke escaping. Someone had pulled bushes to create a small man-made clearing around the fire. The grasses were flattened where someone had recently slept.

Chee Chee sat contentedly eating something beside the fireplace. He let Brianna scoop him up and place him back on her shoulder. Nathan came up behind her. "Looks like Jackson must have been having a camp-out. I didn't know he did that since we were boys, but there's no one else who could have been sleeping out here. I can't imagine my dad or Dugan sleeping out here if they didn't have to."

They continued walking. Eventually, a massive tower emerged from the forest, surrounded by thick, bubbling mud. From the ground, it looked like a wire ran from the tower to a tree a few yards beyond the mud pit.

Nathan picked up a large stick, pushed it into the mud, and pulled it out again. He examined the mud that remained on the stick. "It looks to be a minimum of three feet deep here. We could try to wade across, but I suggest we give the tower a shot. Jackson made quicksand in the past. I also don't like the fact that we wouldn't be able to see what was in the mud with us if we went in." He looked over at Brianna to get her opinion.

She took a step backwards and crossed her arms. She looked at Nathan in disbelief that he seemed to think going through the mud was a plausible option. "Yeah, I'll start checking out the tower. There's a wire up there. Do you think maybe it's a zip-line?"

Nathan shrugged and pursed his lips in suspicion. "It could be. Just be careful. It could have a cut in it so that once you're over the mud; it breaks and drops you in." He threw a few rocks and sticks into the mud in different spots and observed them getting sucked under one by one.

Brianna looked at him with her eyebrows scrunched up. "Geez, when did you get so jaded? Why do you guys need so many traps to keep you protected?"

Nathan grinned at her. He may have complained about his brother a lot, but apparently, he enjoyed the challenges. "Yes, some traps on this island are for protection, but this one is meant as a challenge to me. It reminds me of an obstacle course he once made with his pet alligator, Betsy."

Staring at him intently, Brianna couldn't tell if he was kidding or not. "Betsy? You call having pet alligators around Jenna safe?"

Shaking his head without looking in her direction, Nathan said, "No, there aren't any alligators here anymore. The local freshwater ones won't cross the ocean, and I made Jackson find a pleasant home for Betsy at a zoo." Then he was off, examining the base of the tower.

Brianna looked for any wires that would show electrocution or traps. Chee Chee looked around the tower excitedly, practically begging to explore every nook and cranny of this new structure. Brianna set him down and he happily scampered up the tower. Brianna followed slowly as she placed her foot on the ladder and climbed. She made her way to the top and was about seven feet in the air when Nathan caught up to her.

They both looked around the landing for anything suspicious. There was a zip-line handle attached to a support beam with a small hand-painted sign under it. It read, 'A gift for you, dear brother.'

Aww. How nice. Maybe Jackson isn't so bad after all. Brianna reached for the zip line handle. The platform under their feet fell out from under them, and they plummeted.

Chapter 24

Charmed to Meet Jackson

Brianna

Brianna and Nathan were firmly trapped in the net. After she had pulled the zip-line cord, the floorboards gave out under them. They fell, and the net had caught them. Luckily, Chee Chee was fine, but he was calling at them angrily from the tower.

Brianna could smell Nathan's manly sandalwood essence wash over her and was all too aware of every part of her body that touched his. She tried to squirm over into her side of the net, but the cramped quarters made it impossible.

Breathing in through her teeth, she looked over at him. "Sorry!"

She heard a growl escape Nathan's chest as he studied the trap. "It's not your fault; this is all Jackson's doing. I just hope he has this one set up with some kind of sensor to know we're trapped here."

Intently watching Nathan's face, Brianna looked at him from the corner of her eyes. "You know, it's kind of nice to have company in here, unlike the last time when I was in one of these for a few hours by my lonesome."

Running his hand through his hair, Nathan quietly answered, "Sorry about that. I wasn't thinking about your feelings when I took my time going out to check the yellow alert. I'll have a quicker response in the future."

Brianna sat silently, aware of Nathan's every movement. She ran scenarios through her mind where she asked him about his feelings for her but couldn't find the right words. What if she expressed her feelings for him and he turned her down? She couldn't handle that; especially not while being trapped in this small net together.

Less than ten minutes later, she heard whistling come through the woods. It started as a soft melody and gained speed and intensity until the whistler sounded like he was trying to direct a full orchestra.

Brianna craned her neck, trying to see who was coming, but she couldn't get a good line of view, no matter which way she turned. She realized the more she twisted, the further she found her way onto Nathan's lap. Cheeks turning red, she stayed still.

The whistling stopped and turned into a throaty chuckle. Brianna heard a smooth, deep voice shout, "Gotcha, Nate! You're going soft. It's been a long time since I've been able to trick you."

Suddenly Brianna's stomach felt like it was in her chest as they were airborne again. She fell another four or five feet until she landed softly... in the wet, sticky mud. Her limbs were tangled with Nathan's, and she flopped around and sputtered like a fish out of water before she got her feet under her.

Nathan grabbed her hand to steady her, then they both trudged towards dry land. He glowered under all the mud. The squelching of mud in every imaginable place left Brianna too distracted to notice much else.

Chee Chee climbed up into the leafy canopy and disappeared. Presumably, he found a easy way across the mud.

A handsome, clean-shaven man stood on the banks with dark shoulder-length hair. He wore a vibrant blue and green jacket and a mischievous grin a mile long. As Nathan closed in on his brother, his glower became darker. "Jackson," he growled through clenched teeth. "Was dropping us in a mud pit really necessary?"

As Nathan's mood darkened, Jackson's mood seemed to brighten more. "Nate, when Jenna mentioned a new teacher, I didn't realize you'd brought a beauty to our humble little island. Why didn't you warn me? Mud bath spa treatments can always be arranged, but I would have made sure that your visit was much more hospitable! I could have brought cucumber-infused water at the very least."

Jackson dramatically bowed before Brianna. "My apologies. I never meant to mix you up in our boyish squabbles." Ignoring the mud, Jackson stood up and held his arm out to Brianna. He helped her out of the mud and escorted her along the path. Nathan grumbled something unintelligible behind them as he struggled through the last bit of mud by himself.

Chee Chee climbed back up onto his perch on Brianna's shoulder. Avoiding the mud that covered her, he scolded her in angry squeaks. Finally, he found a mostly clean spot to settle down and watch their travels.

Placing one hand under his chin, Jackson raised one of his eyebrows and gave her a closed-mouth half smile. It reminded Brianna of a male model's smoldering look from a magazine she once saw, and she wondered how long he had practiced it. "If you want, we could leave my boor of a brother behind. As you can see, he may have promised you paradise, but he only delivered mud. I, on the other hand, know how to entertain a lady."

This man seemed nice but was very confident in himself. He was handsome, but also had a bit of a flamboyant side. She almost felt like he was trying really hard to be noticed and make an impression. Unsure how to maneuver around this cheerful man who was hitting on her while covered in mud, Brianna decided to ignore most of what he said until she got to know him better. "As you guessed, I'm Jenna's new governess. I recently moved to the island, so Nathan was nice enough to show me around and help me get situated before I start schooling Jenna in the fall."

Jackson's eyebrows rose. "Jenna has talked a lot about her new governess, but when I originally heard the term, I was expecting someone... older."

Brianna flung some of the mud off her hand and took the other hand off Jackson's jacket. It was now quite muddy from proximity. She looked down at her mud-covered clothing. "I hoped that soon I could navigate around this crazy island unhindered, but it doesn't look like I'm there yet."

Jackson stopped and looked at her, full of concern. He used his clean hand to lift her chin so they made eye contact. "You poor thing, my brother really doesn't know how to take care of a lady. If you would prefer, I'm sure I could find a place for you at my house."

Nathan came stomping up behind them with mud falling off him in large globs. "Since we're almost at the main house, we might as well get cleaned up before heading home. I don't want Debbie mad at *me* for a mess *you* caused."

Nathan stopped beside Jackson, placing his body between Brianna and his brother. He swung a friendly, glopping muddy arm over Jackson's shoulder. "Besides, you should get a bath too before fraternizing with my daughter's governess. I thought you had more game than to flirt while covered in mud." With that, Nathan withdrew his muddy arm from his brother's shoulder, but not before gently patting his cheek and leaving globs of mud on Jackson's face.

The trio walked a few more yards through the jungle until the path opened up into a wide clearing. In the center of the clearing stood a large Victorian-style mansion with intricate architectural designs. The bright colors allowed the detailed craftsmanship to pop out. The differences between the two houses were so drastic that Brianna stopped in surprise.

Nathan's house aimed to look like it was part of the jungle and built to resemble a fortified hacienda. Jackson's house stood apart from the jungle and was so at odds with its surroundings. It looked like a peacock at a dinner party.

Nathan stopped beside Brianna. "Welcome to my childhood home. Despite all of Jackson's promises, we should probably clean the worst of the mud off of us outside in the barn before going inside. My father's staff has chewed us out too many times over the years for tracking it into the house."

Jackson led them to an outbuilding behind the mansion. Inside was horse tack, but no sign of horses. There was a giant basket in a corner of the room and a racing boat that looked like it had giant monster truck wheels. There was also a disorganized workbench with tools and odds and ends scattered all around it.

Nathan walked over to an extra-large stall and hosed himself off. Globs of mud fell from his body and went down the drain. Jackson went over to his desk and fiddled with something that caught his attention.

Brianna looked around wide-eyed. "What is this place?"

Jackson's eyes glimmered and his smile widened as if asked what he had been dying to answer. "This is my workshop and the horse barn. My happy place where my only limitations are physics." Jackson winked at her. "But don't worry, I'm working on fixing that. Soon, I won't have to worry about those pesky physics laws."

After Nathan finished rinsing himself off, he shook himself to get the extra water off and shivered from the cold water. "Hurry, Brianna. It's chilly, but there is a hot bath waiting for each of us inside."

Jackson took the hose from Nathan and attached a small mechanical device that he was just working on at his workbench. Then he handed the hose to Brianna. "The least I could do is provide you with some warm water for your rinse off. My brother really takes you to the nicest places. First for a mud bath and then for a wash in the horses' stalls. If I were you, I would be careful about any plans he has next."

Brianna ran the water for a few moments until it turned warm. She rinsed the worst of the mud off her clothes and then Jackson handed her a dry, clean towel. "The hot shower is right this way. Come in and I'll run you a nice, hot bath. Do you enjoy lavender Epsom salts or rose oils?"

Nathan rolled his eyes at Jackson and grabbed a towel for himself from where he had seen his brother grab one moments before. "I'm sure Brianna is more than capable of drawing her own bath. I hired her to care for and teach Jenna. She's not one of your brainless floozies." Nathan growled under his breath as he led Brianna to the house.

They entered through the back entrance, but the inside was just as flamboyant as the outside. Every space was covered in a cacophony of furniture and decorations. There was antique furniture painted in bright colors with bright, soft cushions that didn't match. Small end tables held two or three lamps of different styles. Pictures hung on the walls in every style, from modern abstract splashes of color to old-looking portraits and landscapes.

Brianna followed Nathan through the house. Although she had gotten the worst of the mud rinsed off, she tiptoed along, attempting to leave as few muddy footprints as possible.

This is not how I usually visit someone's home. I feel like a child sneaking inside after playing in the mud.

The doors each had pictures, symbols, or writings on them. The carpeting in the entryway was a plush red and black pattern that gave the optical illusion that the floor had depth where it was flat. There was an odd number of mirrors hanging on every wall in patterns, shapes, and designs of every type. Brianna thought maybe she preferred the mud.

They reached a door with a picture of a mermaid on it. "This is the mermaid bathroom." He pointed down the hallway. "I'm going to get a quick shower down the hall. I'll make us some hot tea, and we'll meet you in the blue cat sitting room. Go down the hallway to the right and there's a bright blue cat pictured on the door. You don't have to ask why there are pictures on all the doors; they are my fun-loving brother's way to name each room. I think all the pictures were a minor act of rebellion after one of his tutors made him memorize parts of the dictionary. Once you feel all rested and cleaned up, we can head back to my birdhouse. Do you need anything?"

Raising a sopping sleeve, Brianna asked, "Do you think I could borrow some fresh clothing?"

Nathan stared at Brianna as if he only now realized that every inch of her figure was visible under her wet clothing. He looked like he had to force himself to look away before answering. "Of course! I'll see what Jackson has and leave it here outside the bathroom door."

Brianna nodded and then moved her sopping wet self into the bathroom. Mermaids decorated the entire bathroom. The tiles on the floor had mermaids and shells alternating in a diamond pattern. The walls were covered with an enormous statue of a mermaid and the sink was a statue of a mermaid pouring water out of two jars into a sink.

Brianna gently set Chee Chee on the ground. He explored the room. *He can't get into too much trouble locked in here with me.* She dropped the soggy clothing from her body and left them in a wet puddle on the ground. She didn't know what to do with her clothes, so she would deal with them after she cleaned herself up. *Next time I'm packing a change of clothes in my backpack.*

Brianna saw a porcelain tub but really wanted a shower. She spotted a shower curtain against the right-hand wall that was blue and decorated with lifelike fish. Brianna pulled the curtain back and her mouth dropped open as she stared. There wasn't a wall behind the shower curtain, but a large fish tank that expanded far beyond the walls of the bathroom. There were colorful fish, coral, sea stars... and a mermaid.

Chapter 25

A Most Peculiar Home

Brianna

Brianna stared at the mermaid. It was a mixture of intriguing and creepy at the same time. At that point, nothing on the island should have surprised her anymore. After she got over her initial shock, she realized she was naked in front of a giant see-through tank. She wrapped the edge of the shower curtain around herself while she determined if she needed to worry or not.

Upon closer inspection, the mermaid looked to be some kind of machine. There were gears that moved a tail up and down, but they were all arranged into a human-shaped configuration. There was long hair of floating from the top of the machine and two appendages coming from the side.

Brianna studied the tank. While the full tank extended past the bathroom, large rock formations were strategically placed so no one could see into the bathroom, nor could she see anything but the section of the tank directly in front of her.

Why wouldn't Nathan have mentioned this? This isn't a normal thing most people have in their bathrooms. A warning would have been nice.

Still feeling uneasy, Brianna's need to get clean won out against her modesty. She walked over to the shower and turned a shell knob. A mermaid that matched the one on the sink poured water from a jug down on her head. Dirt from her day's adventures turned the water brown at her feet.

The robotic mermaid swam closer to the shower and danced in the tank. Brianna absentmindedly let the water fall on her, while the mermaid flitting up and down and twirling in the water mesmerized her. Fish darted around the dancer, trying to keep out of the way, but mostly ignored her. After a while, the mermaid went back to its standard circuit and Brianna realized the water had already pruned her hands. It must have been running clear for quite a while now.

On the shower walls, she saw a collection of conch shell-shaped dispensers with gold lettering on them. Shampoo, conditioner, soap, and a facial scrub. After scrubbing herself, rinsing, and drying off, Brianna walked back into the main section of the bathroom.

Chee Chee sat next to a bowl of nuts and fruit, happily munching away. Sitting in a pile on a little table was clothing that was not hers but perfectly her size. Brianna felt creeped out but was unwilling to put on the old muddy clothing. As she looked around, she realized she didn't even have that option if she wanted it. Her clothing had disappeared.

Brianna quickly dressed and tried to remember Nathan's in-structions.

Nathan said something about taking a right and then seeing a blue room with a cat on it. That didn't sound too hard to find. *I must have been in the shower for a long time. Who snuck into the bathroom while I was taking a shower, and how did they know my size?*

Brianna scooped up Chee Chee and stepped out of the bathroom. She immediately took a right. The hallway twisted and turned different ways and passed a multitude of rooms. All the doors were different colors and designs, as she had seen before.

She passed a blue room that didn't have a cat on it, and a door with a cat on it that wasn't blue. Finally, the hallway ended at a stairwell.

Did I go the wrong way? Or did Nathan forget to mention the stairs?

Brianna saw what was at the top of the stairs. If that didn't look promising, she would retrace her steps. The stairs spiraled upwards for about two floors and then ended at a ceiling. There was no door on the ceiling. The stairwell apparently led to nowhere.

Brianna went back down the stairs. *I'm afraid if I don't find Nathan soon, I will be stuck in this house forever. Nathan will search for me, right?*

On her way back to the mermaid bathroom, Brianna knocked on the blue door and the cat door. No one answered. When she got back to the mermaid bathroom, Jackson was standing there waiting for her.

"Darling! You look as stunning as I had imagined under all of that mud. How was your bath? Did you use the bath salt? The only place they can find that type is from a salt mine in India."

Brianna looked at him suspiciously. "I got a shower. Thank you." Then she abruptly added, "Whose clothes are these?"

Jackson looked the clothing over appraisingly. "I keep a range of clothing sizes in case any of my honored guests should find themselves in need. There are a lot of things that can make you messy on this island, you know. I'm glad they fit. I usually have a good eye for size." Jackson paused and held out his arm. "May I escort you to tea?"

Hungry beyond reason, Brianna took his arm. As they moved straight down the hallway and turned right, Jackson asked her, "Did you like my fish tank? Did my mermaid robot keep you entertained?"

"The fish tank was beautiful. I've never seen such an extensive tank except at a city aquarium. I can't imagine how much it must cost to feed, clean, and filter that size of a tank, and just for a bathroom!"

Jackson chuckled. "Growing up here with only my brother for company, we both developed a lot of hobbies. One of mine was caring for aquatic animals. Besides, it isn't just for the bathroom. On the other side of the tank, beyond the coral reef that gives the bathroom privacy, there is an entertainment room that also enjoys a stunning fish tank view. This tank also doubles as my swimming pool when I'm in the mood to go snorkeling."

They reached a blue room with a cat on it, but the door was already open with Nathan pacing inside. "You found her? Oh, good. I was wondering if she had fallen into the pit of the room with no floor."

Brianna chuckled nervously, unsure if he was joking or not. "No, I just took a wrong turn and ended up at a spiral staircase." Brianna looked at the spread on the coffee table in front of her. There were mini finger sandwiches, croissants, fruit, cookies, tea, and coffee.

Jackson gestured towards the table. "I didn't know what you would like. So, I brought you an assortment. Please sit. Rest yourself and enjoy a bite to eat before you head back with my brother, unless, of course, you want to stay."

Giving him a small smile, she said, "I should probably get back with Nathan soon, but thank you for the food in the meantime. It looks delicious."

Brianna made herself comfortable and was picking up a croissant when an older gentleman burst into the room. He looked around. While ignoring them all, he asked, "Where's Debbie? I heard a woman's voice. Did she come over on her day off?"

Nathan laughed and clapped his father on the shoulder. "Hey, Dad. Good to see you too. I keep telling you. Offer Debbie more than just a servant's room and more work hours if you want her around more. Debbie isn't here. Who you heard was Jenna's new governess." Nathan gestured his hand towards Brianna. "Dad, I would like you to meet Brianna. Brianna, this is my dad and Jenna's grandfather."

The older gentleman looked forlorn. "So, Debbie's not here? Fine, then I will be in my office. Don't let your and your brother's tomfoolery disturb me, you hear?" The older man turned away when he seemed to remember that Brianna was there. "Nice to meet you, young lady. You can call me Walter. It's about time someone started teaching that girl. She's sweet as pie but will be grown before we know it!" With that, he left the room without giving Brianna a chance to respond.

Jackson looked over at Brianna apologetically. "Darling, now you see why my brother is the way he is. That jolly man who just left raised us. Can't imagine why Mom would have left that kind of charm behind! The only one who can get Dad to be civil is Debbie. Around her, he is a ray of sunshine compared to his normal self. If only he wasn't such a stubborn old man and took the time to sweep her off her feet."

They finished their snack with mostly good-humored conversation and headed outside as the sun was setting. Jackson turned to Brianna. "Why don't you take my horse? If you two stick to the north path, it's free of traps. Besides, I would be a horrible host if I let you struggle through the jungle at night."

Before waiting for Brianna to answer, Jackson got out a small dog whistle. He placed it between his lips and waited. Brianna didn't see or hear anything and looked over at Nathan to see what she should do. *Is this another trick?*

Suddenly, a large white horse with black spots ran out of the woods and came straight to Jackson. Jackson patted his head and murmured words of encouragement. He led the horse to the barn and workshop, where Brianna had rinsed the worst of the mud off earlier.

Brianna leaned close to Nathan and whispered. "We really should have taken the northern path to get here."

Nathan grinned widely. "Yes, that would have been faster, but I wanted you to get a true feel for Jackson's part of the island. You will have time to see it when we ride back on horseback."

Jackson expertly brushed down the horse and saddled her with a tandem saddle. He turned to Brianna. "This here is my girl, Perdita, or Perdi for short." Jackson laced his fingers together and put them a few feet in the air next to the horse. "Here, give me your foot and I'll boost you up. You'll need to go in the back saddle because you're lighter."

Jackson boosted her up onto the horse, and Nathan helped Brianna to get the stirrups at the right height. Jackson winked at her. "Make sure you have a solid grip on the pommel in front of you." When she looked comfortable in the saddle, Nathan moved to the front and placed his foot into the stirrup to prepare for heaving himself over the horse.

At the last moment, before Nathan swung his leg over, Jackson swiftly launched into the saddle. Making sure not to disturb Brianna, he landed a solid kick into Nathan's stomach, sending him flying backwards. Nathan landed, making an 'oof' sound, his eyes and mouth open in shock.

Jackson grabbed the reins and yelled back to Brianna. "Hold on, darling!" He urged the horse to rush out of the building and galloped off down a trail into the jungle. Chee Chee chattered angrily from her shoulder into her ear as his little fingers clung on tightly. All Brianna could do was hang on for dear life and pray.

Chapter 26

The Great Release

Brianna

Jackson stopped the horse at Nathan's compound. His flushed face also held a huge grin. He exclaimed, "Wowee! Nathan is sure going to be angry with me after that one." He smiled devilishly as he helped Brianna down from the horse. Before releasing her, he gave her another one of his smoldering looks. "A kiss after a romantic horse ride in the moonlight?"

Brianna gently pushed him back to release herself and headed for the main entrance to the compound. "I think that was closer to a kidnapping than a romantic ride. You might want to work on your courtship skills."

Jackson hung his head in play chastisement. "Anything for you, darling." There was a glint in his eye as he got back onto his horse and took off back into the dark jungle. She hoped he hadn't taken her comment as a challenge.

***

Wiping the tears from her eyes, Jenna gave Chee Chee a last gentle hug. The small monkey escaped the embrace and climbed onto her shoulder, using his tiny hands to look through her hair. Jenna sadly giggled. "I'm going to miss you so much, Chee Chee." She looked up at Brianna. "Do we really have to let him go back to the wild?"

Giving the little girl a big hug, Brianna pulled a small glass monkey out of her pocket. "Yes, sweetie. Chee Chee is all healed up now, so he deserves a chance to live wild with his own family."

Placing the glass figurine into Jenna's hands, Brianna said, "I made you something. It's a little glass monkey that looks like Chee Chee, so you can remember him always."

Sniffling, Jenna turned the small animal in her hands, examining every angle. "Thank you. I'll keep it always. Do you think Chee Chee will come back to visit?"

"Maybe. We will have to wait and see." Chee Chee chattered and jumped from Jenna's to Brianna's shoulder. "Why don't you look at some books in your bed? Your father said he would be up shortly to spend some time with you this evening."

Jenna nodded and Brianna scooped up Chee Chee and found her way out of the birdhouse and into the jungle. The soothing sounds of the parrots and monkeys were relaxing and refreshing. She took several deep breaths and let the stress of the day fade away.

The little monkey climbed excitedly over Brianna's shoulders until he found the perfect perch. He sat upon her right shoulder and used his tiny left hand to hold on to her like the pommel of a horse's saddle. Chee Chee chattered happily to Brianna, finally getting out of the compound and back into his natural territory. Brianna smiled and lifted her arm to pet him gently.

She would really miss this little guy who was so sweet and such a fun companion. She never knew what he would do next, and poor little Jenna had become so attached to him. Brianna had tried to warn her. Even though she'd explained it was finally time to return him to his natural habitat, her tiny heart broke anyway. Brianna knew she would probably shed a few tears herself. She chided herself. *I should have kept us at more of a distance from Chee Chee. We shouldn't have even given the little monkey a name.*

Brianna needed to find her way to where she and Nathan had originally found Chee Chee. Dugan had long since fixed the trap that misfired. She just had to find where it was. She wanted to return Chee Chee as near to his home as she could, and she wasn't in the mood to ask for help.

As she continued her walk, she enjoyed the peace and quiet. She had gotten used to the canopy's background noise. Where once it felt foreign and threatening, now it relaxed her, and the anxiety in her stomach melted away. She couldn't believe that after such a short time, this place felt like home.

She came to the section of the path where she was pretty sure they had found Chee Chee, and she looked around for the trap that had misfired. After about twenty minutes of searching, she finally found a sign with a series of dots and lines on it a little farther down the path. It alerted her to the trap's presence. She hadn't seen this sign before. Hmm... maybe it was Morse code?

Brianna snapped a picture of the sign with her phone to research it when she got back to her room.

She took a few minutes to examine the trap's mechanisms. She couldn't figure out how a small monkey would have been able to set off the trap. Nathan assured her they did it often, all over the island. There was a rope and some steel cords attached to a log. She wanted to believe him, but no matter how she looked at it, she couldn't figure out how a monkey had disabled the whole thing. The only way she could visualize the log out in the pathway was if someone purposely cut it. She was sad that Chee Chee became hurt, but if Nathan, Dugan, or Jenna had walked by, the trap could have seriously injured or killed them.

Finally, Brianna decided she would talk to Dugan and have him explain how the trap had misfired. That helped her to feel like she could protect the little guy from it happening again.

She turned her head to look at the tiny monkey. She nuzzled him gently with her cheek.

"All right, boy. Time to go home." She picked the little monkey off of her shoulder. He chattered happily and clung to her thumbs as she lowered him to the ground. Brianna let him go and then removed her hands. Chee Chee looked back at her as if to ask if it was okay to leave. Brianna smiled. "Chee Chee, find your family. Go have a happy life. Thank you for being a bright little star in my day."

Chee Chee was so excited to be back in the jungle that he jumped from branch to branch as fast as he could. Soon, Brianna could see him no more. A single tear ran down her cheek as she turned back towards Nathan's compound. She went only a few yards when Chee Chee came bounding out of a tree. Chattering angrily, he climbed up her leg and settled himself on her shoulder. He held onto her ear again, as if ready to continue their adventure.

"No, boy. You're supposed to stay here." Brianna picked up the monkey and set him down again. The monkey looked at her quizzically, not quite understanding what she wanted from him. Brianna walked away but was soon overtaken.

When she tried to take him from her shoulder a third time, his little hand clung tightly to her ear and the other one fisted into her hair. "All right, Chee Chee. I get the point. You liked it with us. I knew we shouldn't have socialized with you so much. You were just so cute, and Jenna was so excited."

Brianna continued to apologize to Chee Chee, knowing she should have let him stay wild. "We really didn't know if you would make it or not, so I didn't take any precautions to keep you wild. What do you think, buddy? Are you afraid of missing your bed? Did you enjoy having your gourmet meals delivered straight to you instead of hunting for your grubs?"

Brianna headed back to the compound. Chee Chee remained on her shoulder. Eventually, the little monkey relaxed and chattered happily like he normally did. He swung his long tail under the neck of her shirt and tickled her back.

When they arrived back at the compound, Brianna went to see Jenna. She wanted to talk to her about Chee Chee and how the release didn't go as planned.

When she entered Jenna's room, she found her sobbing in her bed. Brianna approached gently.

"Jenna, honey. Are you okay?"

Jenna sobbed back her reply. "It's gone! I broke the glass monkey you made me. Now he's gone and I have nothing to remember Chee Chee by. I miss him so much."

Chee Chee climbed down from Brianna's shoulder. He headed over to pat Jenna's head and looked at her quizzically. Jenna looked up at the tiny monkey. The sobbing suddenly stopped, but the little girl's voice still quivered as she asked, "Chee Chee, is that really you?"

Jenna settled down and petted the small monkey. He loved the attention and laid back on the bed for a belly rub.

Brianna gathered the small diapers that she had sewn for Chee Chee to wear around the house. She had dumped them in the garbage can when she left to release him. *I guess we're still going to need these.* Carefully, she buttoned the diaper onto Chee Chee, who was quite used to them at this point. Then Chee Chee climbed onto one of Jenna's bookshelves and snuggled in between a few stuffed animals to take a nap.

Jenna turned to Brianna. "What made you decide to bring Chee Chee back? Did you know how much I would miss him?"

"I would have missed him very much too. But I thought it would be best for him to live in his natural environment and go back to his family. Unfortunately, he's gotten too used to us and didn't want to be returned to the jungle, no matter how many times I tried to put him down and release him. He just kept climbing up onto my shoulder and wanting a ride back home. We're going to let him stay for now, but he will be free to leave anytime he wants to."

Chapter 27

Secret Garden

Brianna

Nathan reached out his hand and helped Brianna over a tree that had fallen across the path. "I'll have to send Dugan over here to clean this up," he said.

"What, are you afraid of someone tripping and falling before they stumble into one of your traps?" Brianna quipped cheekily.

Nathan looked at her innocently. "I don't want anyone to get hurt." The two of them walked along in companionable silence for a while. "Don't you tire of wearing monkey jewelry all the time? He barely leaves your side anymore."

Chee Chee peered at Nathan from Brianna's shoulder as if he knew he was being discussed. As they walked, he would occasionally chatter or switch shoulders to get a better view of something. "He seems to think I'm his new mode of transportation. I fed him and made him feel better when he was sick, so I think he's decided that he wants to keep me. I find his presence reassuring. He's cute and funny and he likes to see if he can find bugs in my hair."

"Does he find many?" Nathan teased.

Brianna gently swatted his shoulder. "I will have you know that Chee Chee is probably the cleanest monkey on this entire island. He likes to climb in the tub with me when I take a bath. Although, I think that's mainly because he likes the warmth of my blow dryer afterwards." Nathan stared at Brianna, slack-jawed. Unable to figure out what he was thinking but embarrassed by his focused attention, she blushed and changed the subject. "So, how much farther until we reach today's challenge?"

Nathan's eyes were still so focused on Brianna that he tripped. After he pulled himself together, he seemed to shake off a daydream and said, "You'll see it when we get to the valley below this hill. We're heading to the northern tip of the island. This is Jenna's and my favorite spot. I hope you like it too."

Nathan stopped suddenly and put a finger up to his lips, showing that Brianna should be quiet. She looked around, confused, while Nathan continued to stand still, listening. After a minute or two, Nathan relaxed his muscles. "Sorry about that. I got this weird feeling of being watched. I thought I heard something big walking through the brush over to the left there, but I see nothing out of the ordinary. Some critter was just making a racket, I suppose."

Nathan led her through a pass where two points of the hill dipped down and met. As soon as she emerged from the path, Brianna saw an enormous stone wall about ten feet tall, covered in thick green vines with purple flowers. The fortification stretched the distance of a football field in both directions. From her current perspective, it looked like it formed a large rectangle. *Whatever is behind those walls is really large and well protected. What in the world could be in there?*

Bees and butterflies flitted around the flowers. Directly around the base of the wall was a moat about five feet wide. Someone had taken the time to carefully trim back the trees and shrubbery around the moat to make sure no tree limbs or brush could ascend the wall.

Nathan smiled at Brianna. "This is called the Secret Garden. I think you'll enjoy what you find inside." His eyes narrowed, as if issuing a dare. "Do you think you can figure out how to get in?"

Brianna looked over at Nathan, accepting the challenge. "Of course I'll figure it out, given enough time. Nothing on your island has stumped me yet. I even found that silly little treasure map. Why in the world did you hide it in the caves you use as a back door to your control room?"

Nathan looked at her quizzically. "Map? What are you... stop! Don't go through the moat! I'm sure you would eventually get out, but then you would be too uncomfortable to enjoy the garden."

Nathan broke a stick off a nearby sapling and approached the moat. A few frogs jumped into the water as he approached, and he stabbed the stick down into the water. There was a disturbance in the water under the stick, and it stuck straight out. "Here, give it a pull. You won't budge this stick anytime soon." Then he added, "I really want you to see inside before it gets dark. How about I at least steer you towards the entrance?"

Curious, Brianna walked over and gave the stick a yank. It didn't budge, just as Nathan had told her. She tried peering under the water, but it was too muddy and murky to see anything. She saw a few frogs trying to stay perfectly still in the shallow water.

I think whatever is down there is mechanical. If it was a chemical compound of some type, it would poison the frogs, and an animal would scare them away.

She turned around to ask Nathan more about the moat. Unfortunately, she saw he was walking around a corner of the wall, so she abandoned her investigations for later and jogged to catch up with him.

Around the corner, Brianna found a small bridge that led to a massive stone door. On the door were blue etchings and a dozen tiny bottles that looked like they would hold about three ounces of liquid each. They were hanging upside down with a line drawn on each. Nathan stood a few feet from the bridge, crossed his arms, and watched her intently to see what she would do.

Brianna came up to the bridge and gingerly tapped her foot on the different boards. The two middle boards turned sideways, so that an unsuspecting trespasser would set their foot on them and fall through into the moat. The thick boards on the edges of the bridge seemed solid, so Brianna cautiously moved down the bridge.

When she got to the door, she lifted one bottle and examined it. She held it up to the etching on the door. The door carving showed an etching of a bottle with a line on it and curly lines that reminded her of wind moving over the top. The bottle she picked up first didn't line up with the door etching, but it was close. She took down two more bottles until she found one that matched the etchings on the door.

She stared at the small bottle for a while, filled it up to the line with water from her water bottle, then she blew across the top of the bottle to make a note. When she finished, a small sub-door opened on the giant door. *Just the right size for a person.*

Brianna looked back at Nathan, who had a big grin on his face. "Are you coming?" she asked. Then she carefully stepped through the door and into another world.

Chapter 28

Birds and Butterflies and Flowers, Oh My!

Brianna

The wall encompassed an acre or two of perfectly cultivated and cared for farmland. The right corner had a series of a few dozen fruit trees. A handful of goats and a llama meandered underneath, eating their fill.

A small stream trickled from one edge of the wall through the orchard to the other end. A large plot of grain and vegetable plants took up the middle part of the garden. Chickens, at least a few dozen, pecked eagerly at the ground.

The left part of the garden held a small fence with more fresh vegetables and a large greenhouse. Flowers grew through the entire garden. Peppered throughout the vegetables were bright yellow flowers, and ringing the base of the rock wall were large red and white blossoms.

The difference in plant life, scents, and sounds was so drastic from the outside jungle that it was jarring. It took a few minutes of gaping to take it all in, and there were still more details that she continued to pick up upon further inspection. Along the wall was a chicken coop with several laying boxes. A chicken-sized wire tunnel led to a feeder.

After Nathan and Brianna entered the garden, the llama hurriedly made his way over to them, followed closely by the goats. Their noses investigated each fold in their clothing, and square pupils inquired after a treat. Chee Chee climbed up onto Brianna's head and chattered angrily at the unknown, fearless beasts.

Nathan laughed and pulled some treats out of his pocket. "The llama's name is Bingo. He watches over the animals here. Jenna has named all the goats too, but she forgets and renames them every time we come up here and visit."

He laid out his palm and the goats eagerly gulped up the snacks. The goats' square pupils never left his hands as he gave a handful to Brianna. She squealed and laughed as the goats clambered around her, pushing past each other to be the first to get a treat. Brianna went wide-eyed, not knowing what to do when Bingo put his head in her hair, investigating her and Chee Chee a little too closely.

Nathan threw a few more treats out of the way for the llama and goats to go after, giving Brianna a bit of space to breathe. "So, what do you think? Worth the challenge of getting in?"

"Yes. I'm pretty impressed." Brianna smiled. "It truly is a secret garden here. I can see why Jenna would love it."

Nathan sat down on a bench that overlooked the garden oasis. Brianna followed suit. "This area is kind of a group effort to care for. Dugan looks after the structural maintenance and

Debbie enjoys coming out here to collect eggs and pick fresh vegetables. We tried to automate as much of the work out here as we could, but I recently hired a man named Thomas to come out here a few days a week. He tops off feed, cleans out the animals' housing, plants the vegetables, and takes care of the general well-being of this area. I'm thinking of hiring the man to come out full-time, but I haven't figured out what I want to do about housing him on the island yet."

Nathan pointed to different points in the garden. "Over there, by the chicken coop, is an automatic feeder designed to keep the goats out but provides high protein grain for the chickens. Over there by the goat lean-to is grains and hay to supplement the goat's feed. Mostly, Bingo does a good job of keeping the animals protected from predators." Then Nathan frowned. "Although, our chicken flock looks a lot smaller than normal. I will have to have Dugan install something to scare off hawks."

Brianna looked around, still in shock. "What made you decide to build this place?"

Nathan shrugged. "Depending on weather or circumstances, I didn't want to rely on our survival being based fully on getting supplies from the mainland. This garden area is my solution. The eggs and vegetables have provided us with a nice supplement of tasty fresh food right here on the island. The plan is to have fresh goat's milk too once I have Thomas here to milk the nannies twice a day."

Nathan stood up and walked over to the fenced-in garden. The vegetables looked sparse, and something had carelessly stepped on some plants.

Nathan frowned again. "Maybe I should just install some more cameras out here. Looks like the goats have gotten into my vegetable garden. I tried planting them some goodies of their own, but the greedy critters always think the food is better on the other side of the fence."

Nathan moved on and nodded his head towards the western side of the garden. His eyes twinkled, excited to show off more. "Want to check out the greenhouse? Think you can get in?"

Brianna warily approached the greenhouse. *I think I'm developing some kind of psychological complex where every step could lead me into a trap. How am I going to explain this island to my future therapist?*

The large greenhouse had a plexiglass type of wall that you could peer through to see rows of shelves with plants on them. At the top of the greenhouse was a series of open vents. The door to the greenhouse had a picture of a fluffy white chicken with six chicks of various colorations crowding underneath her. There was a small hole in the chicken's beak and a small poem below her on the door.

A bright new day brings clouds to play
  With food abounded plenty.
  A stormy day brings clouds of gray
  Where food becomes the currency

Brianna looked back at Nathan, annoyed. "Really? These are all the clues that you give to enter the greenhouse?" She read the poem through a few times. "Do I need a chicken? Does a chicken need to peck the hole in the chicken's beak or something?"

Nathan didn't answer like usual when she tried to ask him about a puzzle, so she went into the chicken's vegetable patch.

There were over a dozen smaller fluffy-looking chickens, whose feathers stuck out all over instead of lying flat like normal farm chickens. Some of them had such large plumes on their heads that they could barely see, and they came in a range of colors from white, black, tan, and a mixture of both.

Brianna crept up on the chickens, intent on catching one. They ignored her mostly until she got only an arm's length away. She reached out, attempting to grab the fluffy chicken that was focused on scratching and pecking at the ground in front of her. Instantly, a larger white chicken with a thick black comb came flying at her, flapping his wings and squawking. Brianna was so surprised that she fell backward right on top of a half-rotten squash.

Standing up, she wiped the debris off her pants and tried again. This time, she darted forward for a small black chicken that had great dexterity. He half-ran, half-flew across the garden. Chee Chee scolded her from her shoulder for the jarring ride. A black chicken with a splash of white was at her right, watching her wearily. She took off as soon as Brianna's eyes focused on her.

Brianna saw a white chicken with a large plume on its head rolling around in some dust, oblivious to her. She snuck up on the bird, who jumped up when she grew nearer. It looked around as if determining where an unheard sound came from. Finally spotting her, the chicken tried to take off, but Brianna intercepted her and scooped her up. *Got you!*

The chicken felt fluffy like fur instead of smooth like normal bird feathers. Were they growing mutant birds on this island? What crazy Franken-animals would be in the greenhouse? *Maybe I should start referring to Nathan as Dr. Moreau. Although, I have to admit, these chickens are wonderfully soft and cute. Like a puppy mixed with a chicken or something.*

The chicken squawked and tried to wiggle free until Brianna held the bird close to her chest. Then she settled down and rested quietly. Triumphantly, Brianna returned to the greenhouse with the chicken in hand. Nathan was grinning from ear to ear, trying to hold back laughter. Brianna marched right past him, choosing to ignore him.

She held the chicken up to the door, but it wouldn't peck. She gently tapped the bird's beak against the door until it protested. The door didn't open. Brianna read the poem and walked around the rather large greenhouse with the chicken still in hand. She didn't want to have to catch it again if needed.

When she got back to the door, Nathan stood close by with a huge smile on his face. "Need some help? We only have a little time before it gets dark. You spent most of our time playing in the garden with the chickens."

Brianna narrowed her eyes at him. "I got into your secret garden and caught one of your mutant puppy-chickens. Isn't that enough?"

Without saying a word, Nathan reached up to the top of the door, unhooked a simple eye hook, and simply pushed open the door. "After you. Although, I would put down the chicken before you enter. It's a Silkie chicken, by the way. It's a type of show bird. Nothing mutant about it. Jenna loves them, so that's the breed we have." He gave her a mischievous smile. "Although, if you're hungry, we can bring that one back for dinner tomorrow. Silkie chickens actually have black meat, a real delicacy in some places. Hungry?"

Brianna set down the chicken, which hopped away and immediately started pecking at the ground again; its interaction with Brianna forgotten. "Black chicken meat? I feel validated calling it a mutant." She entered the first of a set of double doors in the greenhouse. After they secured the first door behind them, Brianna pushed open the inner door.

The scents of fresh dirt and mint filled her nose. Her eyes first focused on a large tree growing right in the middle of the greenhouse, and a small water feature beside it. Then she noticed a plethora of plants and flowers, not native to the nearby jungles, planted on the ground, and orchids hanging on the wall. There were shelves of small plants and pots that were tiered like a ladder to ensure that they all received lots of sunlight.

With all the beauty and scents, the most beautiful part was the hundreds of butterflies landing on one flower and fluttering off to the next. Some were bright blue, and others were orange and black. Some were small, and some were as large as her palm. Brianna took a step towards a bench under the tree when a brown and white bird flushed from right under where she was about to step. Startled, Brianna jerked backward into Nathan.

Nathan caught her arm as a trilling bird sound went off somewhere in the garden. "Don't step on my quail! Their camouflage is amazing. I find they balance out the butterflies nicely."

He pointed out features as they walked upon a small gravel path. "This is my butterfly garden/aviary/ greenhouse. That's a mouthful, so I usually just refer to it as my greenhouse. Up at the top up there are vents that open in the hottest part of the day with a thick wire over them so that nothing can escape. We made the walls of a very exclusive plexiglass that's so thick that a large tree limb can fall on it without breaking it. The greenhouse mists whenever the water meters in the dirt show that the ground is dry."

After walking through the entire greenhouse, they stopped at the bench under the large tree. "When Jenna was little, we lived near the conservatory that we visited often with my late wife. She used to love seeing all the beautiful flowers and giggled at any birds or butterflies that she spotted. Even though we don't live near it anymore, I wanted to give Jenna that same quiet appreciation of cultivated natural beauty. My Little Bird likes to come here and draw the butterflies and leave mealworm snacks for the quail. She calls this her happy place, so it makes me happy too."

Unable to resist the handsome man with a heart of gold. Brianna stood on her tippy toes and gave him a lingering peck on the cheek. "Thank you for showing me this beautiful garden. Jenna is really lucky to have such a special place to visit."

Her lips tingled with the memory of their kiss beside the falls, but she didn't think the dedicated space to his late wife was the place for anything more. *Besides, I'm not sure where we stand anymore. She liked him a lot, but he hasn't mentioned the kiss since calling it a mistake.*

Nathan stood frozen, as if unsure of what to say or do. Feeling slightly embarrassed, Brianna quickly moved away from him and changed the subject. "What flowers are these yellow ones?"

***

That evening, when the two of them returned to the compound, Dugan passed them in the hall and gave them a nod in greeting. "Nathan, I was hoping to talk to you. I spent most of the day in the control room, and I have a few puzzling security concerns I want to discuss with you."

Then, with a perfectly straight face, he quietly told Brianna, "Don't worry, ma'am. We will have chicken for dinner tomorrow."

Brianna's face turned bright red as Nathan laughed.

Chapter 29

To Woo or Not to Woo?

Brianna

"There you are, Brianna!" Nathan greeted her as he walked into a room that was set up with cushy couches and a television, like a living room. "I'm sorry to throw this at you on such short notice, but I need to go out of town for the next two weeks for business. I thought my Vice President could handle it, but there are a lot of changes we're implementing at Riley Games and a big video game launch that I really should be there for. Would that be all right?"

Brianna blinked in surprise for a few moments, then smiled reassuringly. It was last moment, but he had warned her he would occasionally need to take these business trips. "Don't worry, we'll be fine. Have fun on your trip."

With a loud sigh of relief, Nathan smiled back. "I know you have my cell phone number, and I will make sure that you have my itinerary and the contact numbers for the hotels I will stay at in case of an emergency with Jenna. I'll get things cleared with my father and Debbie to make sure you can have a few evenings off while I'm gone. Do you need anything else?"

Shaking her head, she said, "No, that should be fine. By the way you talked when I first started, I'm surprised you haven't had to take a trip before now." Pursing her lips, she added, "You know, I do need one thing. A clue. I've tried researching everything I can think of and I'm not making heads or tails of this map I found. It doesn't seem to relate to this island at all. You don't have to tell me the secret of the map, but can you at least give me a starting point to work from?"

Jenna looked up from the train set she was playing with. They were having some quiet tea and snack time before Nathan came in. "A map! Can I see it? I want to find diamonds and pirate gold!"

Nathan looked at Brianna quizzically. "What map are you referring to? I never made a map."

This island was filled with puzzles and traps that he built. How could he not know about the map? Raising an eyebrow, Brianna asked, "So, I should ask Jackson, then? Is this some kind of map from your childhood? Maybe I can't figure it out because it isn't relevant anymore."

"Well, I wouldn't put anything past Jackson, but he isn't one to leave something he worked on undiscovered for years. He likes the attention that his creations and inventions bring. Can I see the map?"

Brianna had brought the map with her, hoping he would give her some clues about it. She pulled the tube out of her bag and carefully unraveled it. Jenna's curiosity had gotten the better of her and she crowded right in front of Brianna. "Please don't touch, sweetheart. This map is very fragile. I haven't made a copy of it yet."

Nathan came over and peered at the map over Brianna's shoulder. He was silent as he studied it for a few moments. Then he asked, "Where did you find this?"

"When I was attempting to get to your super-secret man cave, I found a rock on the wall that pivoted. Behind the rock was a hole that held this tube. I just stuck it in my bag and have been trying to figure out how it correlates to the island. I assumed it was another one of your elaborate puzzles."

"When we were young, my father used to tell us stories about pirates that used to hide out on this very island. One of our ancestors was once a privateer. I wonder..."

"Hello! Anyone home?" A loud shout from the hallway sent Jenna darting out the door, the map completely forgotten. Nathan didn't seem to notice. He quietly stared at the map, so Brianna left it on the table and followed Jenna to see what the commotion was.

"Uncle Jack! Uncle Jack! You came to see me!" Jenna squealed as she ran towards Jackson. He picked up the little girl with a huge smile on his face and twirled her around in the air. "Weee!" Jenna laughed as Jackson gently set her down and kneeled in front of her.

Conspiratorially, he whispered to the little girl. "Sweet Pea, I have a surprise that I brought all the way from the mainland just for you!"

Jenna gasped. "For me? Really? Thank you! Thank you! THANK YOU!" She threw her arms around her uncle's neck and squeezed him without even knowing what the surprise was. When she calmed down and backed up a bit, she quietly asked, "What did you get me? Is it a pet cheetah? You know I love cheetahs."

Jackson chuckled. "Almost as good as a cheetah." He pulled a bag of caramel creams from his pocket and handed them to her.

"Yummy! You remembered my favorite candy! *You're* my favorite uncle! I can't wait to show Daddy!" Jenna ran off, but then turned back to Jackson. "Oh, I almost forgot. I've been practicing, just like you told me to. What has two legs and runs?"

Jackson put his hand under his chin and tapped his cheek in deep concentration. "Is it me? I have two legs and I can run!"

Jenna laughed. "No silly! It's a clock!"

Jackson chuckled in appreciation. "Yes, your riddles are definitely getting better. Although, I think you meant to ask what has two hands instead of two legs. I have one for you, too. Let's see if you can figure this one out. What do you call a cow with no legs?"

Jenna looks at Jackson suspiciously. "Is this a trick? I would call the cow chocolate because it would be a brown cow and make me chocolate milk."

Jackson winked at Jenna. "You can call the cow anything you like, but it can't come!" Jackson tousled Jenna's hair as she puzzled over his response. He turned to Brianna, who had watched the entire exchange intently. He moved toward her, took her hand in his, and stared deeply into her eyes.

"Darling, I was hoping to run into you. I was wondering if you would indulge me for a few hours. I was hoping you would accompany me to the mainland and grab some dinner?" Jackson waggled his eyebrows at her. "I know a place that makes superb lobster right along the beach… that's if my brother can manage here without you."

Brianna extricated her hand from Jackson's. "Well, that is a very tempting offer, but I was just in the kitchen and Debbie is in there making the most delicious smelling steak and chicken dinner. She's expecting me, and my mouth is watering just thinking about it."

Jackson's face brightened from serious to excited. "Perfect! Then I will join you for dinner here. What more could a man ask for than a chance to dine between his two favorite ladies?" Jackson winked at Jenna. "Sweet Pea, why don't you run and tell Debbie to set out another place at the table for me for dinner tonight? It looks like I've just been invited."

Nathan came out of his office and shook Jackson's hand. With a neutral expression on his face, he asked, "What brings you over for a visit, dear brother?"

Jackson smiled brightly. "Brianna invited me to join her for dinner tonight. You know I could never disappoint such an enchanting lady. Would you like to join us too?"

Nathan looked back and forth between Jackson and Brianna. "Join you for dinner at my table? In my house? My, how kind of you to extend the invitation. I wouldn't miss it." Nathan swiftly turned his back on Jackson and Brianna. His normal light-footed gait held more of a stomp as he headed down the hallway toward the kitchen.

Jackson followed Nathan, heckling him the whole way, "You know, Natey boy, if you want to take a walk on my side of the mountain, I'm happy to escort you. I just redesigned a few puzzles, and I would hate to see you run into any trouble again." Nathan audibly ground his teeth as he proceeded down the hall.

Brianna stood there, puzzled. She went over her words in her head, trying to figure out when she had invited Jackson to join them for dinner. *What have I gotten myself into tonight?*

***

Squished between Nathan and Jackson, Brianna tried to eat her dinner, but was constantly interrupted by one of her table companions. Jenna sat across from her pretending like the peas on her plate lived in the volcano she made out of her mashed potatoes. Brianna's cheeks burned as she noticed Debbie eyeing her with a smile on her lips while she did dishes.

Jackson nudged her. "So, Brianna, how much of this area did you get to explore before you got stranded here with my brother? If you want, I could take you to see all of the local sights on the mainland."

Before she could answer, Nathan interrupted. "Unfortunately, Brianna won't be able to take any trips while I'm away on business because she needs to be with Jenna. If there is some-where you would like to go, Brianna, I can take you when I get back."

Jenna pipped up. "I would like to go! Daddy and Uncle Jackson, can you take me to see the sights? What are the sights?"

Brianna chuckled as both men's eyes grew large and finally fell silent. Brianna said "Sweetie Pie, I'm sure your daddy and uncle would love to take you to see all of the local beautiful places. I feel like I've had enough sightseeing for the time being just here on this island, so I'll let you take my place."

Jenna's mouth dropped open. "Can you take me to were that old pirate ship sank? Can we go to the zoo? How about we go to that restaurant with real mermaids swimming around!"

Brianna finally ate her dinner in peace as the two men made plans with Jenna. By the end of the night, they had a long list of fieldtrips they were going to take her on over the next few months and Jenna was absolutely gleeful.

When Nathan went to take her up to bed, she became tearful. "Daddy, I'm going to miss you. Will you call me every night?"

Nathan nodded, "Yes, Little Bird. I will call you because I'm going to miss you more than you can imagine, now let's get you up to bed."

Brianna watched Nathan's receding figure as Jackson elbowed her and walked over to pick up a few plates of dessert Debbie left for them on the counter "What's red and bad for your teeth?"

Smiling at Jackson, Brianna tried to distract herself from how much she would miss Nathan too. "I don't know, cherry pie?"

Jackson placed a small plate in front of her and said in a deadpan voice, "A brick."

Caught off guard from how corny his joke was, Brianna laughed out loud before taking a bite of her pie. After only a handful of words, she was already feeling better about Nathan leaving. Everything would be alright.

Chapter 30

Home Alone

Brianna

"Hello, ladies. Would you like me to make dinner tonight?" Jackson had come over for dinner for the third night in a row since Nathan left. Jenna gave an excited squeal and hugged her uncle.

Jackson squeezed her tight and told her, "I don't want my favorite ladies to get lonely while your daddy has to be away on his business trip."

Jenna bubbled with excitement. "Uncle Jack, can I show you the picture I made in school today?"

"Ah, a budding artist! I would love to say that I saw some of the first works of the famous artist, Jenna Riley. Yes, please show me!" Jenna took off down the hallway and he turned his attention to Brianna.

Brianna gently chastised him. "You know you don't have to come over every night that Nathan is gone. I'm sure you have your own work to do, and we're fine on our own."

I see right through his fake charm, but I have to admit, he is always thoughtful and makes me laugh. He's growing on me.

"Madame, I know that such a delightful, independent woman *could* take care of everything." He gave her a pitiful look. "But would you deny me your fine company? Would you keep me from my favorite niece? It gets very lonely in my big old house. You may not have noticed, but my father isn't exactly what we would call the best of conversationalists." Brianna rolled her eyes at Jackson, and his grin grew. "As for work, while Nathan is off being all serious and managing things for Riley Games, I'm working on a new board game series. They're escape rooms in a box. The first one takes place on a deserted island. I get all the inspiration I need just from a walk across our beautiful paradise."

Jenna came barreling down the hallway with a small canvas in her hands. "Look! It's an apple tree, but instead of apples, it grows hearts. This is the sun wearing sunglasses. These birds over here want to eat the hearts, but the dog who lives under the tree scares them away."

Jackson's mouth dropped open, and his eyebrows rose as he looked thoroughly impressed by her artwork. "Wow, you really put a lot of thought and hard work into that painting. Can I buy this masterpiece to add to my art collection?"

Jenna looked at him, astonished. "Uncle Jack! It's not for sale! Brianna said I worked really hard on it so we could hang it up in our schoolroom." She took her precious painting back from Jackson and ran it back down the hallway to her room for safekeeping.

Jackson turned to Brianna. "How does taco lime shrimp sound for dinner? Six o'clock?"

Brianna sighed and nodded her agreement. "We'll be there. Thank you for cooking for us when Debbie isn't here. Where did you learn to be such an excellent cook?"

Jackson straightened himself up like he was performing a monologue for a play. "While my dear brother was off at Cambridge University and starting a family, I was holding down the fort here on the island. I was working towards my degree online when I met the woman of my dreams." He paused for effect. "My online degree gave me a lot of freedom to travel while finishing up my classes. So, I followed her to Brazil. She owned a restaurant with the most delicious food. I helped her out in the kitchen sometimes. I stayed with her for a few months, and she taught me the basics of cooking. Alas, that relationship wasn't meant to be."

He looked at her from under his lashes with a slight puckering of his lip. "After traveling to France, I met a goddess who really helped my taste buds and culinary skills. She took my budding skills to the next level." Jackson wiggled his eyebrows suggestively to make sure Brianna caught his double meaning. "She taught me the nuance of flavor and how to mix herbs to achieve specific tastes. I still remember those meals in my dreams. Like the supper that got away..." He wistfully ended his monologue as if remembering a long-lost love.

***

After dinner, Brianna watched Jenna and Jackson laughing to-gether. *Jenna is always so excited whenever Jackson comes over to visit. He's good with her. They keep going back and forth, telling jokes and riddles.*

Jenna said, "Uncle Jack? Are you going to have dinner with us all the time now? Even when Daddy comes back, will you still come? Please! Please!"

Jackson kneeled down in front of the little girl and bopped Jenna on the nose. "I can't promise that I will be here every night, but I can promise to come more often. I think that you two ladies are quickly becoming the two I can never live with-out."

"Well, I'll be a bear at noon-time. That smells delicious!" Dugan's enormous figure loomed in the doorway. "Mind if I have a bite of the leftovers?"

"Sure thing," Jackson said. "Help yourself. Thanks for com-ing over to keep an eye on Jenna tonight."

Brianna raised an eyebrow at Jackson as he turned to her imploringly. "Brianna, darling, I asked Dugan if he would come over tonight. I was hoping... would you do me the honor of taking a walk with me tonight?"

Brianna eyed him suspiciously. "Pretty sure of yourself, aren't you? Arranging a sitter for Jenna before even checking with me?" She gave it a moment's thought. "You know what? Yes, I think we need to have a talk. Just the two of us."

Jackson and Brianna got Jenna all set up for bed. They tucked her in and left Dugan to watch over her. Brianna stopped at her room and picked up Chee Chee as a chaperone of sorts. Chee Chee sat on her shoulder, then they headed outside.

Jackson looked at her mischievously. "What would you like to do tonight? We could take a stroll down to the beach or mix up some of Nathan's riddles and see how long he takes to notice." His eyes twinkled. "My horse is nearby, so we could also go back to my place…"

Brianna needed some time to figure out how to phrase her feelings to Jackson. "I think a short walk through the jungle would be a nice way to stretch my legs after dinner and relax before bedtime. Let's head to the drawbridge, and then head back. I'm hoping to make a few glass figurines before I turn in for the night."

The two walked companionably. Jackson entertained Brianna with stories of his youthful adventures and mishaps as he traveled around the world. Brianna half-listened as she tried to think of what she would say.

At one point Brianna got a nervous feeling, like she was being watched. *It's probably nothing. I'm just nervous about how this upcoming conversation is going to go.* Too soon, they arrived at the drawbridge.

Jackson looked at Brianna suggestively. "You know, we could continue our walk across this bridge. There's a beautiful little waterfall…"

Brianna interrupted and looked at him with compassion. "Jackson, we need to talk. I think you're a really wonderful guy.

You're handsome, you have a great sense of humor, and you're amazing with Jenna."

Jackson looked down at his feet, and his shoulders slumped. "Here comes the but. There's always a but."

"But I'm not interested in a romantic relationship with you. There obviously aren't many people on this island, but I enjoy your company and I would really like to count you as my friend."

Jackson gave a dramatic sigh. "What can I say? You brought a feeling of exhilaration back into my life. A challenge to overcome. A puzzle to unravel. I guess when another man is so intensely interested in a woman, you can't help but wonder what you're missing. It makes you irresistible."

Chapter 31

Jealousy Abounds

Nathan

Nathan walked into the kitchen and stopped in shock. He'd expected to see Brianna and Jenna having a quiet dinner. In his mind's eye, they would get along well in his absence, but be lonely without him around. He'd pictured Jenna spotting him immediately, running and telling him how much he was missed. Brianna would add how glad she was to see him and how much she'd missed him too.

Instead, he came home from his two-week business trip to find Jackson in his home. Nathan watched as Jackson had Brianna and Jenna laughing so hard that neither even noticed him. There was a buffet of gourmet foods on the counter and a chocolate lava cake cooling on the stove.

Brianna placed her hand on Jackson's shoulder. "That sounds just like something Shelly would do!" *Just how chummy have the two of them gotten?*

Over the last two weeks, he'd thought a lot about his relationship with Brianna. She was his employee, and he didn't want to take advantage of her, but he thought there was something special between them and had finally decided on seeing where things went.

Nathan ground his teeth. *Looks like I was too slow on that one. Just like my brother to see something I want and beat me to it. Why does he always have to be so competitive? He better truly care about her and not be pursuing her because he noticed I was interested.*

As Nathan watched Brianna, his disappointment made his chest hurt. He understood. She was smart, beautiful, quirky, and funny. *Jackson would be crazy to let such a wonderful woman go.*

He was silly for entertaining the thought that a relationship between them would work. When it inevitably failed, he would ruin everything and Brianna would leave. He couldn't risk that happening.

At that moment, Jenna noticed him. "Daddy!" She gave an earth-shattering squeal as she barreled into his legs. "I missed you so much! I'm so glad you're home!"

At least a part of his daydreams had come true.

Brianna stood back beside Jackson. "You're back early! We weren't expecting you for another two days!"

Nathan replied, trying to keep the regret out of his voice. "We finished the game launch and everything went smoothly. I left my Vice President on site to wrap things up." He squeezed Jenna in a great big bear hug. "I missed my Little Bird too much to stay away any longer."

As he talked, Jackson put his arm around Brianna. She shot him an amused look and then stepped away to clean up the table. Jackson seemed to fall over himself in an attempt to help.

I may have to accept it, but I can't bring myself to watch it.

Nathan looked down at the little girl in his arms. "Come on, Little Bird. Let's get you into your pajamas. Why don't you tell me all about what you did while I was away? I have a funny story to tell you about my trip."

Jenna perked her head up. "We did so many fun things! Brianna and I took nature walks in the jungle, looking for insects for Chee Chee. We made mealworm cake for the chickens. We made a zoo for my stuffed animals and charged Uncle Jack twenty-five cents to get in." Her eyes lit up. "Oh, and I can't wait to show you my painting! I worked *so* hard on it!"

***

Nathan read Jenna a few stories, sang to her, and then put her to bed. *I really missed my sweet Little Bird.* Then he knocked on Brianna's door. He heard Chee Chee chatter loudly and answer first. He needed to talk to Brianna. If only to clear the air.

"Brianna, can I talk to you?"

"One minute!" Brianna yelled through the door. Nathan ran his hand through his hair and his foot tapped on the ground absentmindedly as he waited.

She opened the door and gestured for Nathan to follow her inside. She had a small table set up in the middle of her room.

It held a few sticks of unworked colored glass and a delicate multicolored glass butterfly. On the floor beside the table was a small propane blowtorch.

Nathan gestured towards the butterfly. "Wow, that looks beautiful. You really have talent."

Brianna blushed. "Thank you. Only one more month until my next fair! Hopefully, I can sell a lot of the inventory that I'm building up. Jackson offered to take me by a hot-air balloon, but I don't know. I think I'm kind of partial to traveling by sea and land."

Nathan nodded and smiled as he looked up at her shelf. "Looking at your sensational little figurines, I can guarantee you they will sell well. If you need to take an extra day or two for traveling and setup, just let me know." Nathan jumped at the opportunity to change the subject. "Speaking of Jackson, that's actually why I'm here." He couldn't look Brianna in the eye as he said what he came to say. "I've noticed that you and Jackson have gotten close. Jenna tells me he's been over for dinner every day for two weeks straight." Nathan finally looked directly at Brianna. "Jackson is a good man deep down, but I wanted to warn you. Be careful. He's a master at flirting. He's good at sweeping women off their feet and taking them on magical midnight rides through the jungle. I understand if he's charmed you. Just be cautious. Jackson isn't always the best at following through."

Brianna walked up to Nathan and looked him in the eyes. She put her hands on his arms and quietly studied his face for a few moments. Nathan could feel her closeness. She was so close and kissable. *If only she weren't my brother's.*

Calmly and quietly, Brianna finally said, "Yes, your brother has charm. Yes, your brother is handsome and funny. I really like him. The only problem is, he's not the one I'm in love with."

Chapter 32

Where is Home?

Brianna

They stood so close that she could smell his sandalwood cologne. Her hands held onto his arms and she had stared straight into his dark blue eyes that radiated love and concern. She had tried to tell Nathan how silly he was for thinking she was in love with Jackson. Nathan's eyebrows creased, and Brianna knew she had to set things straight. She was never interested in Jackson, no matter what both men had imagined.

Voice thick with emotion, Nathan looked like he couldn't tear his eyes away from her. "Brianna, I have to tell you something. I think I'm falling in love with you." Heart full of hope, Brianna smiled, but he continued talking before she got the chance to say anything.

His lips quivered as if he was saying the most difficult thing of his life. "You know how I told you my mom once worked for my dad? They never really transitioned well to being partners in a marriage. She was lonely and frustrated and things didn't work out. She left because love wasn't enough. The relationship between a boss and their employee is a power dynamic that always ends in disaster. Jenna still needs you as her governess, and I want you to stay, but I think I need to keep my distance for a while until I can get my head on straight. If you need to learn more about the island, we can plan for Dugan to take you out."

With those words, her heart felt squashed. How could she profess her love for him when he was so sure a relationship between them was doomed? She wanted to tell him he was wrong, but could things ever possibly work between them if he had broken up with her in his mind before they even started dating? This wasn't the way she thought his confession of love would go. *Will there always be obstacles keeping us apart?*

***

Brianna let the glass cool too much before she finished shaping the torso of the monkey. She was making another glass monkey for Jenna, but she just couldn't concentrate. She kept making silly little beginner mistakes and now she had to start over.

Her day had been a long one. Jenna had been cranky and not her normal jubilant self. The poor thing had some nightmares the previous night, and they both got only a little rest. Brianna understood, but that didn't mean it wasn't exhausting.

What she really needed was a break. She needed to get her mind refreshed. Usually, creating glass animals energized her and freed her mind from a hectic day. Today, she simply didn't have the focus she needed for her art.

Brianna finally put her blowtorch and tools away. She decided to go outside and take a relaxing stroll down the beach. Maybe she should try to find the place where she first landed. That would help her blow off some steam, to see where this all began. *My first home in what felt like a hostile and dangerous place. Such a foreign idea in a place that now feels so comfortable.*

Brianna dressed for the jungle and headed out the door. She easily surpassed local traps and turned down the path towards the beach. After a while, she realized she didn't pass the tree-house trap. She must have made a wrong turn. It was close to dusk now, and she was already feeling better just walking and letting off some steam.

Not knowing exactly where she was, Brianna turned around and headed back. She could still see well enough, but she got out her flashlight knowing she would need it soon. She walked along briskly, estimating that she was only about twenty minutes from the compound.

Shadows stretched from the trees, as if ready to grab her. She felt the creepy feeling of being watched again. *I really wish I had brought Chee Chee with me. Even a bit of company would make a big difference right now. If only I hadn't been in such a hurry to be alone...*

Stop freaking out! She hadn't made it to the beach, but she felt invigorated from the peaceful walk. The cacophony of jungle noises from the monkeys and parrots were calming, and the exercise had burned off her earlier frustration. Brianna whistled a cheerful tune to herself as she made her way down the pathway. It made her feel better immediately.

There was a path that went to the right. She was pretty sure that was the correct way to the beach. She should probably head back... but indecision made her stop. What a treat that would be to put her feet onto the sand and watch the cool waves lap over them like she had done with Nathan.

I have a flashlight, and it's not that far out of my way. Her head told her to go back to the compound until another day, but her heart told her that just a few minutes at the beach wouldn't hurt.

Brianna turned right down the path towards the beach. She whistled again and even skipped a bit as darkness settled. She felt mischievous. A bit like a teenager getting into trouble.

Maybe I should go skinny dipping! Who would know?

Brianna passed the treehouse and noticed that the ladder was up and something had knocked the riddle sign over. It was too dark to investigate, so she made a mental note to send Dugan this way tomorrow. She briefly wondered what malfunctioned in the trap, but promptly forgot about it as she neared her destination.

Brianna reached the beach and the big, beautiful crescent moon gave enough light that she turned off her flashlight and placed it back in her bag. A few crabs scuttled around the beach, and a group of them clustered around a jellyfish that had washed up on shore. Was that a sea turtle that pushed off from shore as she approached? Brianna took off her socks and shoes, being careful where she walked.

She stepped into the surf and shut her eyes. The moon shone over her as she listened to the small waves crashing in front of her and the soft scuttling behind her. *This is the most peaceful and beautiful place on Earth. There is nowhere I feel safer and nowhere I would rather be.*

She thought back to her time with Nathan at the waterfall. She remembered the romantic evening and epic kiss. The butterfly garden was one of the most beautiful places she had ever seen. Her lips tingled with longing.

If only I could figure out what was going through his head.

With a groan, Brianna eventually forced herself to turn away from the cold water. She put her socks and shoes back on and headed back into the jungle. Time to go back to Nathan's birdhouse. *Time to head back home.*

Her eyes adjusted to the darkness after she stepped into the jungle. She dug in her bag to get her flashlight out again, glad that she had walked down to the beach. She was feeling much more positive about her day.

Then everything went black.

Chapter 33

Taken

Brianna

Brianna woke up in the pitch dark with her face directly in the mud and debris of the forest floor. An ant crawled across her face and she tried to move her arm to knock it off. Unfortunately, it wouldn't budge. Her arms were tied behind her back and her head hurt.

What in the world happened?

Brianna listened carefully to her surroundings, trying to figure out what was going on. She could hear someone or something moving in the brush behind her. In front of her, there was no sign of anyone else.

Did I get stuck in another one of Nathan's traps, or was this one of Jackson's? She could picture their faces trying to hold back smiles as they threw little taunts back and forth and helped her out of yet another trap.

Brianna rolled over onto her back. Someone immediately placed a menacing boot above her neck. A man with black hair and scars on his face looked at her threateningly. He was wearing camouflage and wielding a large Bowie knife.

The man growled at her. "Don't try anything, missy. I'm not one to give second chances."

Brianna's voice quaked in fear and confusion. "Who are you? What's going on? Why am I tied up?"

"You are not as important as what you represent. Those two boyfriends of yours will come looking for you, and they will walk right into *my* trap." The man sneered at her. "Did they tell you what they did to my brother? My brother, Amos, is dead because of those two. They thought they could forget about him and hide on this little island of theirs, but even all of their tricks can't outsmart me."

He lifted his foot and started a small fire in front of Brianna. It was close enough to provide warmth, but Brianna soon learned that the fire wasn't for her comfort. He stepped back into the shadows, sharpening a stick into a point. "Name's Alaric," he told her before quietly settling in the darkness. He reminded her of a spider waiting for prey to walk into its web. His trap was set.

Alaric. She had heard that name before. Nathan mentioned him when he talked about a group of smugglers that came to the island when he was younger. Brianna thought back to their conversation when they went to explore Jackson's part of the island, when he told her about the incident. Nathan still felt horrible about the loss of life, but from what she heard, it sounded like he was only at fault for not calling the authorities right away and thinking he and Jackson could handle the situation by themselves.

After an hour or two, the fire was dying. Brianna tried to stay still and quiet, not sure what would provoke her captor or what he would do. Alaric stood up and shook out his legs. He restoked the fire and dug through his pack. He took out what looked like a chicken thigh. It was hard to see by firelight, but the meat looked oddly black instead of the usual light brown or white color she was used to seeing.

He took a big bite and talked with his mouth full. "Why don't you holler for them? Then the two of us won't have to wait for this to play out too long."

Brianna tried her best to keep a steady voice and not whimper back. Her head was aching. Her fingers stung with pins and needles from lack of blood flow. "Why are you doing this to me? I wasn't even on this island when you were here last. Besides, what happened to your brother was an accident."

"Don't you worry your pretty little head about it. Those two were but boys, but they couldn't mind their own business. I was working hard to make a living trading and such. My brother was just joining me for one job to get his son, my nephew, out of some betting trouble. I had a deal scheduled to go down in yonder cove when those two belligerent boys got it in their heads that they were going to take the law into their own hands."

Brianna heard a dog bark nearby. Hope fluttered in her chest. Was she going to be rescued? A trickle of fear shot through the hope. *Will they recognize the trap before it's too late?* She heard some rustling behind her. Oddly, Alaric looked totally at ease.

The enormous form of Suzie burst out of the brush. She came up to Brianna and gave her a big lick on the cheek. *I never thought I would be so excited to see that dog.* Then, to Brianna's shock and dismay, Suzie Q walked right up to Alaric and let him pet her. *Traitor.*

Alaric smiled. "Hey, girl. How are you doing this evening? How are the pups doing? Finally, they're old enough to give you a bit of a break, I see. Here, I saved you a chicken bone." He threw the bone at the dog, and she picked it up eagerly and sat down beside the fire, chewing noisily.

Alaric turned to Brianna. "She's a good girl. Just doing her job, patrolling the island every night. It's not her fault that she has to work for a bunch of murderers. When I first came back here about a month ago, this old girl had me treed all night long. I thought they would catch me for sure. Luckily, I had some snacks in my pack and I won her over after a few hours. I've kept a little extra food around for her ever since." Alaric chuckled to himself. "In fact, it's this old girl that helped me get out of a pickle or two that I got myself into while trying to navigate this forsaken place. If she had a handler with her that first night, they would have caught me immediately."

Alaric hocked a loogie inches from Brianna's face. He dug into his bag, finding some chew and a bottle of rum to wash it down. "Their trickery caused me and my mates to go on land. They ended up caught in traps and sent to the authorities. I lost a fortune in goods, but my brother wasn't as lucky. He lost his life for just trying to help his son. It wasn't too long after my nephew ended up belly-up in a swamp. Those two rich boys took my whole family, and they didn't even get a slap on the wrist in return." Alaric chewed for a while, remembering the past.

He spit and turned towards Brianna. She could see his nostrils flared and his lips were pulled back, showing his teeth as he talked. The mottled skin of his face and pulsing veins danced demonically in the firelight. "I escaped and planned my revenge. Those young men wouldn't get the best of me. While I waited for things to quiet down, I had some old Army buddies that I hid with. I told them of my miseries and they showed me some tricks. I planned up a few more of my own."

He looked Brianna straight in the eyes and gave her a half smile that sent chills down her back. Brown spittle oozed around his teeth that were rotten or missing. "I prepared to take my revenge. At first, I hid and watched. I saw how their traps worked and who they cared about. Then I tried to mess with their traps and ruin their ridiculous puzzles."

Alaric took a swig of his rum. "When they had their man fix the puzzles up brand new by the next day, I knew I had to up my game. I needed to destroy what they cared about, just like they took my brother from me. No one gets the better of Alaric." Alaric looked at Brianna in a calculating manner that made her shiver. "After all of my careful observations, I found two things that both men cared about deeply. You and that little girl. I didn't want to deal with a crying child, so I decided what I needed to destroy was... You."

Chapter 34

Don't Blink

Brianna

While Alaric recounted his story, Brianna tried to figure out where she was. *Are there any cameras in this part of the jungle? Any traps nearby that I can use to help me?*

She took in her limited view. In the darkness, one part of the jungle looked just like the next to her. *No one even knew I left the compound! Will he grow bored and kill me? How long was I unconscious?* It seemed like hours. At one point, Suzie stood up and slipped off into the darkness. *She's probably finishing her nighttime security rounds or heading back to her pups. A lot of good that does me.*

Her fingers went numb long ago, but her head had never stopped throbbing. Alaric eventually let the fire die out. Had he fallen asleep?

Brianna moved as quietly as she could in tiny, insignificant movements. She imagined Alaric as a cobra like she had seen on television, watching her, and any sudden movement would make it strike. *Please be asleep!*

Brianna made her way to her feet. It was no straightforward task with her hands tied, but she was proud that she had kept so quiet. *Come on, I can do this. My only chance is to escape.* Suddenly, she felt a flash of pain and a sharp prick on her neck. A small trickle of blood escaped the shallow wound.

Holding the Bowie to Brianna's neck, Alaric grumbled. "Where are you going? I can't have my bait walking away on me, now, can I?" He hauled her to her feet. "If the fish won't nibble on the worm, maybe I need to bring the worm to the fish."

Brianna's hope froze into fear. *What is Alaric going to do now that he realizes no one is coming for me? I don't know if I want to cry or beg for mercy.* The situation seemed hopeless.

"Seems like your fancy, pretty boys up in their castles don't care about you as much as we hoped," Alaric jeered. His eyes seemed a little unfocused, but he held his ground. "Come on. We're going to that mansion of his to surprise Nathan in his sleep. Dawn will be here in another hour. My best chance of catching him unaware is tonight."

Brianna stayed silent as they walked towards Nathan's compound. Alaric still had his Bowie knife pointed towards her back. At one point, he stumbled slightly, but he never let the knife veer. He'd drunk a bit too much, but not enough for her to catch him off guard and run away.

She frantically tried to think of an escape plan. How could she use her surroundings to help her with her arms still bound? Finally, she had an idea. She would have to time it just right to pull it off, but it was her only option.

They neared Nathan's compound, and it frustrated Brianna to realize they had been less than a ten-minute walk away the whole time. Alaric kept his eyes open and had a walking stick that he continuously popped in front of them and into the sides of the brush. He was suspicious of every step he took, but he obviously knew his way around the traps. *He must have been very observant, watching us over the last month.* A creepy chill ran down her back at the thought.

Now that she had a plan, she walked along with him passively, not making any trouble. She needed every ounce of surprise she could get to pull this off. She would only get one chance and it had to work. For her life. For Nathan's life. For Jenna's life.

They came to the entrance of Nathan's compound. Alaric shoved her forward while holding onto the neck of her shirt. "Now don't try anything courageous, pretty girl, or you won't live to regret it. Get us inside."

Brianna knew that once he was in the compound, he had no use for her anymore. In fact, she would only be a liability. *It's now or never.* Brianna's hand shook as she typed in her code and she stared straight into the eye detector, making sure not to blink.

After her code registered, the double portcullis lifted. Alaric pushed her forward like a shield as he started through the entryway. He held her close enough that the knife was no longer pointed at her back. Instead, he had it out in front of them both, as if to ward off an approaching enemy.

After they entered the first portcullis, Brianna slammed her head back into Alaric's nose and kicked backward into his knee. Alaric groaned. He fell to his knees and dropped the knife in an attempt to grab at Brianna's fleeing figure. His hand brushed against her foot, but his reflexes in his current state were too slow to nab her.

Alaric struggled to his feet as Brianna shot past the second portcullis. Just in time she shot through the gates and then the first and the second portcullis came crashing down. Between the two gates, Alaric swore.

Brianna heaved a sigh of relief and slumped to the ground. *I'm safe.*

A few minutes later, Nathan came rushing out of the house into the courtyard. His hair was disheveled, and he was only wearing boxers. She really wished she told him when she left the compound. He must have been fast asleep when the red alert alarm went off.

Nathan saw Brianna slumped on the ground in the court-yard. "Brianna! Are you all right?" He noticed her arms tied behind her in ropes and rushed towards her. "What's going on? What happened to you?" He fiddled with the ropes behind her back until she was finally free.

Brianna's chest heaved with a sob as she threw herself into Nathan's arms. Her arms still tingled as she attempted to wrap them around him. She felt cared for and secure. *My safety, in the middle of a nightmare.*

Nathan held Brianna tightly for a few moment rocking her as he took in his surroundings. He murmured to her. "Are you alright?" Brianna sniffled and nodded her head. He tilted her chin so he could look her in the eyes, "Brianna, I love you. No matter how hard I try, I can't stop. I can't believe I almost lost you tonight. Please tell me if you are really all right." He shifted and Brianna hissed in pain. Nathan gave her arms and hands a gentle massage, trying to get the blood flowing smoothly again.

Brianna looked up at Nathan and half-smiled. "I'll be fine, but you need to know I love you too, Nathan. I'm glad I got the chance to tell you. Please don't push me away again."

Alaric, frustrated at the scene, paced between the gates, drawing Nathan's attention. Nathan narrowed his eyes at the wizened old man. "Who are you and what have you done to Brianna?"

His tone was a direct contrast to the tender care he was giving Brianna. He glared at the old man as he hovered protectively over her.

Alaric's face turned purple with rage. "You don't even remember me, do you, pup?" Madness shone in his eyes. "Do you even realize what you took from me? You took what's mine, and I take what's yours. You killed my brother and took away my only family. As soon as I get out of here, I will take away everything you love."

Nathan turned to Brianna and helped her up. He may have lived a good portion of his life in fear of strangers because of this man, but he finally realized Alaric no longer mattered. He was secure for the moment and would soon be in prison. For now, he had to tend to Brianna. Brianna was the woman he loved and he was determined to be with her regardless of the cost.

Chapter 35

Home at Last

Brianna

Dugan arrived from his cottage on the outside of the compound. He heard the last of Alaric's words and spoke to Nathan through the portcullis gate. "Well, if the hog isn't all tied up. Don't worry, Nathan. The police are on their way. It will still take them a few hours to make it out here, but it looks like our intruder has already found his own sty to accommodate him until then."

Dugan looked at Nathan, shielding Brianna from Alaric's view. He ignored Alaric and asked Nathan through the gates, "Is she all right?"

Brianna responded loud enough for Dugan to hear outside of the gate, but she still couldn't bring herself to move from Nathan's embrace. "Dugan, I'm okay. Just shaken up, and a bit bruised. Nothing a day or two of resting won't fix." She shuddered and then added, "Just be careful. He knows all the island's secrets, and he has a large knife. He might have other weapons as well."

Dugan nodded, concern in his eyes. "Eh, I will keep this grizzly bear's claws at a distance." He directed his gaze to Nathan.

"Nathan, I have this under control. Why don't you take the poor lass inside? She's been a flag in a storm tonight. She looks like she could use some rest. I will be in to ask some questions after the police arrive and secure this old boar."

Nathan helped Brianna into the kitchen. His arms never strayed from Brianna's side. With one finger, he gently turned her face to look at him. "Would you like something to eat or drink? Or do you want to just head straight up to your room?"

Brianna was hungry and thirsty, but more than anything, she just wanted to be in the safety of her bedroom. She answered him shakily. "To my room for right now."

When they got to Brianna's door, Nathan didn't want to let her go. He gave her a pained stare and there was audible stress in his voice. "Brianna, I'm so sorry I wasn't there to save you. Please tell me what happened. You mean so much to me. I don't know what I would do if something happened to you!"

"Shhh." Brianna held up her finger to Nathan's mouth. "We don't want to wake Jenna." She opened her bedroom door and tugged on Nathan's sleeve for him to follow her. "Come on in. We can talk here."

Nathan quickly stoked up a fire in the fireplace as Brianna went to the bathroom and changed into a fresh outfit. She threw the old one away.

Even if it wasn't ruined, I don't think I could ever wear that again. It would always remind me of this night. Of feeling helpless and facing off with the grim reaper.

Nathan settled on the love seat in front of the fireplace. Brianna sat next to him, but it seemed that she was still too far in Nathan's opinion. He pulled her to him so her head rested on his chest and he could put his arms around her.

Nathan caressed her hair. "If you're not ready, we don't have to talk about it. I'll guard outside your door and make sure the police come back later too."

Brianna looked up at him and smiled. "No, it's okay. I should get it all out. I went out for a walk last night to the beach. Alaric dragged me off to his camp after hitting me on the head." She involuntarily shivered. "He's been staying here and watching us for a long time, over a month. He knows all about your island. Even though it was an accident, he says that he wants revenge for Jackson and you killing his brother."

Brianna moved her head off Nathan's chest and looked at him expectantly. Nathan took a deep breath and covered his face with one of his hands. "I wish I could take back that night when Jackson and I planned to catch all the smugglers. I can't believe we pictured ourselves as the heroes, presenting the bad guys to the police. In our idiotic daydream, we got our picture taken for the newspaper and a key to the city or something. We should have just called the authorities straight off." Nathan looked away. "You know, Amos' gun was pointed at Jackson, but he fell into one of our traps, landed wrong, and broke his neck. The accident caused his gun to misfire into the jungle. One wrong step saved my brother's life and caused him to lose his own."

Nathan looked at Brianna, his eyes begging for forgiveness. "I will be forever grateful that Jackson is all right, but I will never forget how Amos died. There was an extensive police investigation into it, and it was eventually ruled an accident. That's when Jackson and I swore to make sure that none of our traps or puzzles would ever harm anyone. I know Jackson stretches that promise a bit when his traps shock me, but he has stayed true to that promise too. I want Jenna to grow up in a place where she can feel safe."

Brianna reached over and hugged Nathan. She murmured into his chest, "I know it was an accident. You are a good man, Nathan. That must have been so scary for you guys, but don't worry. Jenna feels safe here. She views your traps as playground equipment."

Nathan used a finger to lift Brianna's head so their eyes met. "How about you? Do you feel safe here?"

Brianna cuddled closer. "Whatever crazy things life brings, I feel safe with you. Always. You're my safe harbor in the middle of a storm."

Nathan lowered his head and brought his lips down on Brianna's as she arched her back to meet him. He gently crushed her to him, enveloping her in his arms. His lips possessed her and soon she forgot about all the calamities of the evening. Their lips came together with growing intensity until her body hummed with the thrill of his firm embrace. The gentle caress of his hands alluded to pleasures and a promise of things to come.

All too soon, a knock came at the door. "Excuse me, sir. Sorry to interrupt, but like thunder following lightning, the police are here. They need to ask you a few questions."

Nathan moved away from her with a groan, accusatory eyes narrowed at the door.

Chapter 36

Pandora's Box

Brianna

Four weeks later, Brianna slowly meandered back to her bedroom after dinner. She still had a few hours of daylight, but tonight, she was exhausted. All she could imagine was taking a cool, refreshing shower and curling up on the couch with a cup of decaf coffee in front of the fire. Unless, of course, a special someone wanted to come cuddle with her after he put Jenna to bed.

Dinner was delicious. Debbie wasn't around today, so Nathan took it upon himself to be the chef for the night. He really outdid himself. He made a creamy mushroom chicken served over pasta. The chicken was perfectly moist and tender, and thankfully, white. When Brianna tried to compliment him, he acted oddly. In fact, all night he had barely said more than a few words to her and didn't make eye contact.

It was odd because after HR had them sign a relationship contract and they started officially dating; he was usually trying to steal a few kisses whenever he saw her. Sometimes he would whisper how beautiful he thought she was into her ear or he held her tightly and confessed how much he loved her. He was an intense man in all aspects of his life and she had fallen for him hard. *Is it possible that he's mad at me about something? I hope he isn't having cold feet about being my boss again, I thought we were over that!*

Brianna entered her room and undressed for her shower. Out of the corner of her eye, she saw something on her bed and went over to investigate. A beautifully intricate wooden box lay there. Nothing else looked out of place, so Brianna picked it up. There was no lid or apparent way to open the box. She turned it over, shook it, and started pushing on different parts of the box, but she couldn't find any kind of lock, lever, or mechanism to open it.

Interest piqued, and the shower forgotten, Brianna took the box to her desk and carefully went over it, looking for anything out of place. Finally, she noticed the bottom right corner trim on the box wiggled a little. Using only a bit of force, Brianna pushed on the trim until it slid forwards. That movement allowed for the back piece of trim to move to the right, and a small key hid in a groove under where trim had previously covered. Brianna took out the key and looked everywhere but couldn't find a keyhole. A box that didn't open? *What is Nathan playing at now?*

Brianna jiggled several more pieces of the woodwork around the box to see if anything else moved. Finally, she realized the top left end of the box twisted up, allowing a hidden lid to be lifted. Under the lid was a keyhole. Brianna used her key to open the box and found a red velvet lining with a different tiny silver key and a note.

Fireflies danced in the faerie wood, enchanting in their enticement.

I served a feast of opulence, but the allure was too compelling.

A kiss of passion was bestowed, and the entrapment did begin.

Meet me, oh beguiling one, tonight, where the water sings.

Brianna sat there, confused. What in the world? This must be from Nathan. He was the one she kissed. Unless this was some sort of joke Jackson was playing? Why would Nathan want her to meet him somewhere?

Brianna opened the door when she realized she was still partially undressed. After fixing that potentially awkward situation, she marched down the hallway to Nathan's bedroom.

Dreams of quiet reading time were long gone as she reached his door and knocked. After realizing he wasn't there, she checked his office and the kitchen. Still not finding him, she went to check Jenna's bedroom and found her and her grandfather cuddled up in the reading nook of her playroom.

Walter looked up, surprised. "Oh, I didn't think I would see you, Brianna. Nathan told me the two of you are going out tonight."

Brianna looked at him quizzically. "Do you know where I can find Nathan? He just left me an obscure note."

"Sorry, dear. I can't help you. Nathan left right after dinner, and Jenna and I have been up here the whole time since then."

Walter went back to reading, having obviously dismissed Brianna.

"Okay, thanks anyway. Goodnight, Jenna. Have sweet dreams."

"G'night! Don't let the bedbugs bite!"

Brianna went back to her room and dressed for leaving the compound. She packed her backpack of supplies and filled her water bottle while racking her brain about what the poem meant. Well, she definitely remembered where they had their first kiss. She would start there. Did he have something romantic planned?

Brianna carefully navigated her way to the hidden waterfall, trying her best to not fall and get covered in mud. *Mud-covered seems to be my natural state on this island.* For once, she wanted to keep her dignity and have her rump return home clean. Chee Chee sat patiently and quietly on her shoulder as if he knew something suspicious was going on too.

Brianna crossed the bridge and could hear the water falling not too far ahead. As she entered the clearing, she saw... nothing. Well, not nothing. There was still a beautiful waterfall and gorgeous jungle plants all around her. Regardless, her heart dropped in disappointment. *Nathan isn't here. I had half expected the area to be decorated, and a table set out with dessert or something.*

Brianna looked around and finally spotted a bright pink pet rock with eyeballs that Jenna had made sitting beside the waterfall. She picked it up. The underside had a crude picture drawn on it with a marker. It looked a bit like the treehouse where they had first met. *Is he sending me on a wild goose chase?*

Brianna stuck the rock in her backpack and made her way back to the main path of the island and then towards the treehouse. She missed a turn and had to backtrack for a while, but eventually, she could see it. *If Nathan thinks I'm going to climb up there, he'd better think again. I remember being trapped up there too vividly to do that again.*

Brianna neared the treehouse and saw no sign of Nathan, so she called out, "Nathan! Are you up there? I really don't want to climb up into your booby-trapped treehouse and get stuck in a net again. Can you come down here?" She didn't get an answer.

She neared the treehouse and looked around at the brush to see if there were any signs that someone had been there. She scared a small rodent about the size of a mouse out from behind a log, but didn't see any obvious signs of broken branches or footprints. Brianna went to the board that held the treehouse riddle. She chuckled to herself. *I remember being so happy thinking I found the owner of this island when I first came here. Imagine Nathan living in that small treehouse.*

The back of the board had something duct-taped to it. Brianna unpeeled the tape to reveal a small recording device. She pushed play and heard Nathan's voice. "By now, I'm sure you're wondering why I'm having you traipse all over the island. Don't give up yet. Please. I promise it will be worth it if you see this to the end." Nathan's voice paused. "Two more steps will bring an end, only if you can catch a hen."

Brianna listened for a few more moments, but nothing else seemed to be on the recording. *He's playing a trick on me. He wants to see me make a fool of myself again by chasing down the chickens. Two more steps, though… that means I must be near the end. He must have some reason for going to all of this trouble, and his voice sounded very sincere in the recording.* Finally, convincing herself to continue with the scavenger hunt, Brianna headed to the secret garden.

When she got there, the small stone door within the large door was closed but unlatched. Cautiously, she pushed it open, but there was still no sign of Nathan. Bingo the llama came over to investigate, but after a few sniffs, he went on his way. Instead of being spread across the garden like before, most of the animals were clustered around their sleeping areas as if awaiting the sun to set soon.

Brianna walked towards the chickens and they seemed a lot more sluggish than when she saw them last. She realized there was a cooling mechanism near the coop and the chickens all seemed clustered in the cool air. It must have activated when it was particularly hot and muggy. Brianna stood there for a few minutes, enjoying the cool air herself, but unfortunately, it wasn't enough to dry the sweat that continued to accumulate on her brow.

Brianna looked over the chickens and noticed that one had a small barrel around its throat. *She looks familiar. Probably the one I eventually caught last time.* Brianna reached and caught the chicken and held it still for a few minutes until it calmed down. Then she carefully removed the barrel from the chicken and set the bird down.

The barrel had a keyhole, so Brianna fished the tiny silver key out of her pocket that she had originally found in the decorative box with her first note. The key wouldn't open the barrel, so she studied it. It was green and had a picture of a tree, a bird, and a butterfly on it. Carrying the small barrel carefully, she made her way to the greenhouse and opened the double doors.

Nathan sat on the bench under the tree. When he spotted her, a grin spread across his face. The sweet scent of flowers filled the air. The birds trilled and butterflies swarmed in every size and color imaginable as Brianna walked towards Nathan.

"Did I pass your test? I figured out all the riddles. Is my reward a kiss?" Brianna asked softly.

Nathan smiled at her, got down on one knee, and asked, "Did you get the barrel open?"

Brianna shook her head and handed him the barrel. He twisted it, inserting the tiny key, and it popped open. Inside was a ring. A large diamond ring with two smaller diamonds nestled beside it on a white gold band.

"Brianna, you mean so much to me and to Jenna. You make me laugh and feel like I'm alive again. I love you and I can't imagine my life without you. I want to wake up next to you every morning and I want you to be my wife. Brianna... would you marry me?"

Brianna, surprised, replied with the first thing that came to her mind. "You let a chicken carry around a diamond ring?"

Nathan laughed. "See, I never know what you'll say or do when I'm with you. You've trapped me in a way that I never want to be free. Besides, the chicken didn't lose it." Nathan looked at her hopefully.

"Oh, Nathan!" Brianna threw her arms around him and knocked him off balance. "Yes! I will marry you. I can't wait to puzzle through this crazy life with you." Nathan placed the ring on Brianna's finger, and she kissed him.

When they finally broke for air, Nathan looked down at Brianna with a twinkle in his eye. "What do you think about a treasure hunt honeymoon?"

Will they lose their paradise?

Brianna and Nathan overcame a litany of lethal obstacles together. The trials and tribulations they faced only brought them closer together, but how much is too much to handle?

As the newlyweds leave their island paradise accompanied by Nathan's daughter, they were hoping for a blissful, family-oriented, honeymoon treasure hunt.

But when the map they're following leads them to a tangle of myths and mysteries, can the couple work together to locate the hidden treasure? Or will this adventure be what tears the new family apart?

Chapter 1- All Dressed in... Flames

Brianna

"The bride is on fire!"

Brianna stopped walking down the aisle, mortified.

I'm the bride!

The guest nearest to her jumped up from their chair, causing it to go flying backwards into the guest behind. Chaos erupted on the beach around her, and Brianna smelled smoke. Panicking, she started running back down the aisle, trying to get the flames as far away from the guests as possible.

Should I stop, drop, and roll in the sand... in my wedding dress?

She was a few feet away from the ceremony but veered toward the ocean.

"Brianna!" She heard her name being yelled as someone grabbed the veil off her head, sending bobby pins flying. She spun around, eyes searching wildly to see Nathan, her future husband. He threw the veil onto the sandy ground and stomped on it until all the flames were out.

Brianna looked around at her dress and saw no other signs of fire. Nathan bent down, picked up the blackened lacy white veil, and held it out. His eyes watched her carefully, as if waiting to see if she would laugh or cry. A crowd was gathering around them, her mother the first among them. Nathan gave Brianna a small smile and whispered so only the two of them could hear, "You ran away from our wedding."

Taking a deep breath, Brianna looked up at him and gave a soft chuckle before smiling shakily. "What can I say? When I saw who I was about to marry, I decided to swim for it!"

They both laughed together, and Nathan pulled her into a hug and rested his chin on the top of her head. Soon, Brianna felt small arms wrap around her legs and heard the high-pitched voice of her soon-to-be step-daughter, Jenna. "I'm glad you're okay. Do you want me to get you a bucket of water to keep you safe while you marry my daddy?"

Brianna patted Jenna on the shoulder as a photographer snapped photos of the future family holding the burned veil. "I think I'll be all right now, honey. I'm just going to give those tiki torches a bit more space."

Nathan moved her to the side and checked her over. "Would you like to try again or reschedule?"

Brianna looked around at the crowd murmuring amongst themselves and gave them a smile to let everyone know she was unharmed and feeling fine. She hugged Jenna to her side and looked back at Nathan. "I know we pulled this wedding together quickly, but I can't wait to marry you, Nathan. Let's try again. I didn't let any of the puzzles and traps on your island deter me. I'm not about to let a little thing like being a blazing bride impede our happy family."

Nathan turned to the crowd. "If everyone could make their way back to their seats, we are going to try to get married again."

The crowd moved in a very unorganized fashion. Brianna's mother blew her a kiss. "Good luck, honey!" She heard faceless voices from the crowd say, "Someone keep an eye on the aisle. That girl can run!" and "Blow out all the torches or she'll catch her hair on fire next." She wasn't nervous before, but now her stomach was filled with butterflies.

Nathan headed back to a small platform that overlooked the sea and stood beside the pastor. Brianna led Jenna back to the beginning of the aisle. She eyed the tiki torches that were stuck in the sand and lined the edges of the aisle. Small wisps of smoke trailed out of the tops where they extinguished them.

Take two of getting married. Hopefully, this time, she wouldn't have to run away. *Just watch. I'll probably trip and fall on my face during this go around.* She was lucky that a handsome, wealthy man like Nathan wanted to marry her, but how many times would he have the patience to try again?

Brianna's best friend came back with them and messed with Brianna's long brown hair while the violin trio played again. She whispered in Brianna's ear, "Just keep your eyes on the rich guy in the suit and you will be fine."

After rolling her eyes, Brianna smoothed her dress out and tried to calm her nerves. She looked down the aisle to see her good-looking groom, Nathan, standing there with his dark hair slightly mussed from running his hand through it, and his cummerbund made the pooch around his middle stand out slightly. He stood with a wide grin, patiently waiting for her. It was all she could wish for.

Jenna looked up at her, and her short brown hair, all curled and pinned to the top of her head, hardly moved. With wide, doe-like eyes, she whispered, "I'm all out of flowers."

Taking a handful of flowers out of her own bouquet, Brianna quickly took the petals off and dropped them into the little girl's basket. With a big smile and a quick hug, Jenna started down the aisle. Happily, the six-year-old girl sang *Happy Birthday* while walking down the aisle. It melted her heart, and Brianna heard the guests muttering, "Aw."

Looking around, Brianna saw the breathtaking beauty of her paradise island wedding. Everything was perfect. The sun shined brightly, but not too hot. The turquoise ocean was smooth, with small waves lapping the beach. Her mother and best friend came out for the occasion, and best of all, she was no longer on fire.

The music changed to the *Wedding March*, and Brianna walked down the aisle towards her bright future where she would live happily ever after. Luckily, she didn't believe in superstitions or bad luck at weddings. Her life was now going to be like a dream come true.

The ceremony was short but beautiful. The reception was full of delicious food, dancing, and laughter. After things were winding down, Brianna sat on the cool, slightly quieter edge of the party, watching her guests drink and dance the night away. Today was fun, yet exhausting. She'd met so many new people from Nathan's family and work that her head spun.

Tomorrow, they would visit with family and friends and say their goodbyes. After spending so much time planning the wedding, she hadn't had time to pack for the honeymoon. She would have a few whirlwind days to pack up their belongings for the next three months. They were taking Jenna and going to Scotland to follow the treasure map Brianna found on this very island. She was so excited; she couldn't believe she had to wait days to leave.

Before long, Nathan found her and joined her on the outskirts of the party. He softly murmured, "If you want, we can sneak away. My brother offered to put Jenna to bed for us tonight."

Looking at him out of the corner of her eye, Brianna smiled. It felt like a long road to get here. She fake yawned and stretched her arms. "Yeah, I am getting mighty tired. I'm sure I will fall asleep as soon as my head hits the pillow."

Leaning down, Nathan gave her a slow kiss that made every nerve in her body fire. She kissed him back eagerly, gripping his strong biceps, letting her lips do more of the talking than her words.

Brianna heard someone clear their throat, causing her to break her focus on her new husband and look up. She didn't recognize the man, but there were so many business associates and friends that she had barely met.

"Excuse me. I hate to interrupt, but I thought you would want to know that your daughter got sick all over the dance floor. She's asking for you two."

Nathan ran his hand through his hair, and Brianna gave him a small smile. "I'm sorry. I think someone had too much cake when she knew I was otherwise occupied watching you."

Brianna pulled his arm as they started heading towards the dance floor hand-in-hand. "It's okay. If Jenna needs us, then we'll be there. There will be time for us later." The adoption paperwork was all filled out and ready to be sent in tomorrow morning. Soon, Jenna would be her daughter too.

With so many people blocking their way, Nathan led by moving to the right, and Brianna led by moving to the left. They looked at each other and chuckled as neither of them could make progress before letting go of each other's hands and making their own way to find Jenna.

FREE Reads! Blundering Through Paradise

Download free novellas at www.mirandaherald.com

Their thirst for adventure has turned into a fight to survive...

Brothers Jackson and Nathan wanted to reconnect for the summer on their island home. What better way than trying to impress the women they are pining for by catching a crew of smugglers raiding their tropical paradise?

It seemed simple enough. Set traps and let the island do the rest. Unfortunately, unforeseen obstacles sprung up, and Jackson and Nathan find themselves fighting for their lives. Uncovering riddles. Deciphering clues. As Nathan and Jackson blunder through their life-or-death adventure, they learn a little something about the greatest mystery of all... love.

Embark on adventure in this prequel novella featuring beloved characters from ***Puzzling Through Paradise Series***.

10 Prequel Scenes from the Loves Cats Series
Excerpt from Willa's Blooper
Reel

Katrina sorted all the fresh flowers into piles around her living room. *This smells wonderful. I hope they keep this powerful scent for the shower tomorrow.* She sat down in the only open space left on the floor and looked around her.

She had twenty-three flower centerpieces to finish by tomorrow. They were going to meet at eight in the morning to set up the hall for her sister, Susan's bridal shower. *I wish I had an easier time at work today. I was hoping to be fresher before tackling this.*

I'm just swamped at work right now. We had a lot of new cats come in recently. Last week, one of my volunteers told me they got a new job, and she doesn't have the time to help anymore. Another told me today that they were moving. It looks like I will be recruiting new volunteers next week.

Katrina picked up one of the glass vases and groaned. *This is going to take me all night, but what choice do I have? I guess I will have to stay up as late as it takes to finish this project.* She turned on the television in the background and filled the bottom of the vases with glass beads.

Willa sat napping behind her on the couch while she fiddled around with the flowers. Katrina tried a few different arrangements until she got the perfect look. She fiddled around with tying a perfect bow from the coordinating ribbon and then snapped a picture to send to her sister.

Good. One arrangement done, twenty-two to go. At my current rate of one flower arrangement per every half hour, that's only eleven more hours to go. Katrina put her head in her hands. *What have I gotten myself into?*

Katrina got to work. At one point, Willa came over and sat on top of a pile of flowers. "No, no, Willa. Come on. You can't sit there. You'll smash them. Here, it's almost dinnertime. Why don't I get you some food?" Katrina got up and poured cat food into Willa's dish. Willa munched happily as Katrina went back to work.

Luckily, now that she got the design down, she pumped out eight more arrangements over the next two hours. Katrina was midway through the next one when she decided that she really needed a break. She stood up, stretched her legs, and made some tea.

When she got back into the living room, she sat back down in front of her partially finished arrangement. *I thought I already put a purple one in there.* She picked up a new purple one. *I guess I didn't. The flowers are already running together.*

Katrina had twelve arrangements complete when she noticed that there were half as many of the yellow flowers as the pink and purple ones. *Oh no. The florist must have miscounted. I don't have enough yellow. What can I do? Maybe if we use the ones with yellow flowers on every other table, it won't be a big deal that some have yellow and some don't.*

She tried out arranging a centerpiece with no yellow flowers and added extra baby's breath so that they still looked full and put it beside the completed arrangements that had yellow. *I like it. Instead of being overwhelmed with yellow, it gives more of a hint of yellow.* Convinced it solved the problem, Katrina continued on.

Around two in the morning, Katrina was down to her last two arrangements. She was growing cross-eyed and developed a weird aversion to pink, purple, and yellow flowers. She reached for a flower to her side, when she realized that there were none of the pink flowers left.

Katrina became suspicious and looked around. *It's one thing if the florist miscounted the yellow flowers, but I recounted the pink and purple ones only a few hours ago. The only one other living thing in the house was... Willa.*

Katrina turned around to see Willa innocently sitting on the couch behind her. Unfortunately, the thief made a mistake. Upon closer inspection, she saw a yellow flower petal in her fur. Exhausted, she sternly asked, "Willa, what have you been doing with my flowers?"

Willa continued to look on, completely innocent. Katrina pretended like she was back at work, making another flower arrangement, while carefully watching the remaining purple flowers.

Out of the corner of her eye, she watched Willa silently pad over to the flower pile. She picked a flower up in her jaws and traveled behind the couch to sneak it out of the room, unseen. Katrina stood up slowly to see where she was taking the flower.

Willa turned the corner into her bedroom and climbed under the bed. There she laid her latest acquisition on-top of a nest of flowers she made. Immediately, she rolled all over them, crumpling the new flower to match the other ruined flowers.

Katrina felt like she could cry. *I worked so hard on these arrangements all night. I'm so close to finishing. Where am I going to get more fresh flowers at this time of night?* She gently scolded Willa for taking things that weren't hers. Willa lowered her head and slunk further under the bed, knowing she was caught.

Katrina picked up the scattered pieces of flowers. *There's no salvaging these. I simply don't have time to go pick up new flowers tomorrow morning. These last two centerpieces were for the head table. I can't just set them up there with a few purple flowers and some leftover baby's breath flowers.*

Willa looked out under the bed and softly meowed. A cranky Katrina scowled. "Maybe I should put you in one of the centerpieces. At least then it would look full. Then Susan could bring her cat, Biscuit, to put in the second one. It would look perfectly full and balanced." The offhanded comment sparked an idea in Katrina's mind.

***

The next morning, Susan gushed over the flower arrangements. "I can't believe you finished these all yourself! They turned out beautiful and smell great too."

A bit about Miranda Herald

Typing by moonlight and powered by tea, I love reading and writing whenever I can fit it in. I find a good mind boggling puzzle or escape room exhilarating and was excited to include them in my latest works. I hope you enjoy my puzzling twist on romance and join my characters for many more adventures!

I love to hear from my readers and want you to join my community on Facebook, Tiktok, and Instagram. Check out my website to find all of my freebies, novels, and social links. You can find everything at my website **www.mirandaherald.com.**

Join my subscription community for pre-release books and exclusive exclusive content!

https://reamstories.com/page/ldxyuocbpf